—THE—
SALINGER
SISTERS

A Match
Made In Heaven

—The—
Salinger Sisters

A Match Made In Heaven

Shari MacDonald

WATERBROOK
PRESS

A MATCH MADE IN HEAVEN
PUBLISHED BY WATERBROOK PRESS
5446 North Academy Boulevard, Suite 200
Colorado Springs, Colorado 80918
A division of Random House, Inc.

The characters and events in this book are fictional,
and any resemblance to actual persons or events is coincidental.

ISBN 1-57856-137-X

Printed in the United States of America

To my beloved niece, Naomi Ann MacDonald—
one of the most beautiful people, inside and out,
I have ever known.
What an honor it is to know and love you!

The Salinger Sisters Series

One

"You want me to find your brother a wife?" Lucy Salinger stared at the earnest-looking blonde perched on the seat across from her desk, then down at the outdated photograph in her hand. Taken more than ten years earlier, the photo had captured the image of a skinny teenage boy with braces; longish, sun-bleached surfer hair; and an engaging, toothy grin that suggested he did not know the true extent of his own geekiness.

"Campbell won't sit still long enough for a real sitting," the woman complained bitterly.

"Within a month, you want *this* guy to be married?" In four years of professional matchmaking, Lucy had thought she'd heard everything. Until now.

"That's right." The woman nodded eagerly, causing her crown of expensive-looking platinum curls to bounce. "It's a wedding emergency."

"A…'wedding emergency.' I see." Lucy pasted a convincingly sympathetic smile on her face and flashed a look at her raven-haired assistant, Gabrielle Palermo, who stood in the office doorway, her mouth puckered in ill-concealed amusement. *Mama said there'd be days like this.*

At that moment, it was hard not to wonder if she'd made a mistake in choosing her career—despite her surprising

1

success so far. As far back as Lucy could remember, she'd had the gift of recognizing which people belonged together. When she was ten, she single-handedly orchestrated the courtship of her very single—and decidedly nerdy—fifth-grade teacher, Mr. Harmon, and the lovely, shy, and equally single school librarian, Miss Lee. A coup by anyone's standards.

During high school, and into her early twenties, Lucy had continued to use her gift, happily pairing off friends and potential boyfriends like animals destined for the ark. After college, with four engagements already to her credit—and with no idea of what she wanted to do to earn a living—she had laughingly threatened to start her own matchmaking agency. When dared by her sister Daphne to go through with it, Lucy decided to take a risk and borrowed money from her advertising mogul father to lease office space in downtown Los Angeles. It was a complete turnaround for her, career-wise. Four months after earning her bachelor's degree in art history, Lucy Salinger entered the corporate world, opening her doors to what turned out to be an immediately adoring public.

She had fully expected to be out of business in less than a month. But to her surprise, Lucy quickly signed up a handful of clients and enjoyed a few early successes—one of which involved a popular local blues musician, reported in a flattering article in the *L.A. Times*. The rest was history. Four years later, Lucy Salinger was the president and facilitator of Rent-a-Yenta, named after the Yiddish word for "one who meddles," usually referring to wrinkled old Russian women. Perhaps attracted by the irony—though Lucy was a matchmaker, at twenty-six years old she was far from elderly—the papers had dubbed her "the single woman's, and man's, best friend." As a result, she now owned and operated one of the most prosperous dating services in the city.

It wasn't just her natural instincts that made the business so successful. Lucy worked hard too—interviewing clients, distributing marketing collateral pieces, spending long hours finding, as her assistant Gabby liked to say, "a Fred for every Wilma" who came through her doors. It was a passion with Lucy…a dream that no one in the world should have to live life alone, unless he or she chose to. She'd seen how her father suffered from loneliness after her mother passed away, had experienced the pain of rejection firsthand, and would do anything to help others avoid a similar fate. Because of that, she worked long hours that kept her very busy and almost made her forget that she sometimes felt lonely too.

Most of the time her work brought her much fulfillment and satisfaction. But then, there were other days…days like today, when she wondered what kind of wacko would willingly become a modern-day Yenta, when she wished that she had settled for being something nice and stable and normal. Like an underwear inspector—she envisioned a peaceful existence as alternate identity "No. 9"—or a professional bungee jumper.

"And what, exactly, constitutes a 'wedding emergency' in your opinion?" Lucy asked diplomatically, trying her best to keep her tone devoid of any judgment. It was clear from the determined look on Alexandra Canfield's face that she meant what she was saying, regardless of how crazy it might be.

"Maybe her brother's pregnant," Gabby suggested helpfully.

"I—no, I'm sure he's not." The tiny woman turned in her seat and gave Gabrielle a look of confusion. Her powder-white features turned a pale pink as she slowly realized what Gabby had implied.

"Don't mind Gabrielle, Ms. Canfield," Lucy said soothingly, throwing her smart-alecky assistant a look of warning. "She's kidding, of course."

"Of course," Gabby said, nodding seriously. With one hand, she pushed her long, dark curls back over one shoulder, a look of innocence on her lean, tanned features. In her crisp, white cotton shirt and black velvet jeans, she looked more temperate than she often behaved. It was hard for some people to believe that inside she was not a demure, well-mannered young woman, but a firecracker: ready, willing, and able to detonate at a moment's notice—hard to believe, that is, until she opened her mouth to speak.

Gabby batted her eyelashes innocently at Alexandra, her smile all sweetness and light. Lucy tried not to laugh. She'd hired Gabby nearly a year ago, as a favor to Daphne, Lucy's younger sister and a college friend of Gabby's. As it turned out, Gabrielle was a bit of a wild card. But Lucy did find her highly entertaining and fully capable of handling the basic filing, message taking, and bookkeeping for which she was paid a modest salary. Occasionally she got on Lucy's nerves, particularly when she begged, as she did at least once a day, for Lucy to let her help with the matchmaking itself—or at least to let her date what she called "some of the good ones."

Lucy had more than one reason for resisting. First, and perhaps most important of all, was her policy of not dating clients. She didn't do it, and she certainly wasn't about to let Gabby. It was unprofessional; it was as simple as that. Besides, Gabby only liked the idea because it was a lark. She liked meeting men and being wined and dined by them, but she wasn't ready to settle down. And settling down, of course, was the whole point to Lucy's matchmaking service.

Lucy knew what her mission was. She wasn't there to help men and women find dates; anyone could do that. No, her purpose in life was to help people find their lifetime mates. And she was willing to do anything to make that happen. Day after day, she went to baseball games, to the symphony, on whitewater rafting trips, to bookstores—any place men and women congregated—so that she could strike up conversations, make friends, and get to know people who had the same interests as her clients, hoping to find each one a match.

No, as wonderful as Gabby was, she had her own agenda. And Lucy wasn't willing to trust her male clients' well-being to a woman who still considered blind dates "a fun evening." Still, Lucy could hardly blame her for her behavior this morning. Even she was forced to admit that this particular client was a little strange.

Dressed in an elegant, nut-brown silk shirt and tailored skirt the color of rye, Alexandra Canfield made Lucy feel positively frumpy in her own slim-fit trousers and tangerine dress shirt, tied casually over a white tee. Despite the woman's upscale attire, however, she managed to appear anything but "together." Her small, black eyes darted around the room, giving the impression of a small bird scanning its surroundings for potential predators. Nervously she fingered the slim handle of her black leather handbag and looked from Lucy to Gabby, then back again.

"I'm afraid there's been a bit of a misunderstanding," Lucy said smoothly, wondering how she might quickly extricate herself from the situation in which she found herself. "You see, I thought this appointment was for you, Ms. Canfield. I don't usually find matches for people who aren't my clients. If your brother doesn't come in, himself, I'm afraid I can't do anything for him."

"Oh, of course. Of course," Alexandra Canfield broke in nervously. "I understand completely. And he'll be here, I assure you. I told him I had made the appointment. I'm surprised he's not here already. He does tend to forget things, I'm afraid. He starts studying and loses all sense of time—you know how it is. But he knows this is important to me. I'm sure he'll be here any moment."

If he even exists, Lucy thought cynically. A quick glance at Gabby convinced her she was thinking the same thing. Quickly she looked away before Gabby's wry expression caused her to laugh.

"All right, then." Lucy took a deep breath and absently began to run her fingers through a small pile of multicolored paper clips on her desk. "Why don't you tell me a little bit about this 'wedding emergency,' and I'll tell you whether I can do anything to help you. But let me begin by saying I never make time guarantees. I'm not here to find the first person available for my clients. I'm here to find the right person. There's a big difference, and I can't make something happen that isn't meant to be. Do you understand what I'm saying?"

"Of course," the woman repeated brightly. But Lucy couldn't help but think Alexandra hadn't heard a word she'd said. "This is, however, a rather special set of circumstances. I'm sure you'll be intrigued."

"Intrigued. As you say." *Not quite the word I would have used, but it'll do for now.*

"I'm all ears," Gabby said brightly. Moving in from the doorway, she grabbed a stiff, plastic office chair that stood against the far wall and planted it next to Lucy's desk.

Lucy eyed her wearily. True to her character, Gabby was trying to insinuate herself into the middle of the situation. Usually Lucy found Gabby's behavior amusing. But this morning she was feeling a bit too tired to play games. The night before, she had suffered through nightmare after nightmare in which she was trying to find her mother. Such nightmares were not unusual; Lucy had experienced them periodically since her mother died when Lucy was a small child. But though the nightmares were commonplace, they were still disturbing—and exhausting. When her alarm had buzzed obnoxiously at 7:00 A.M., Lucy had grumpily crawled out from under the covers, feeling as if she'd had no sleep at all. So here she was: facing not one, but two crazy women. It was more than one person should have to deal with, she thought, allowing herself the luxury of one private moment of self-pity.

"Tell me, Ms. Canfield," Lucy said in a friendly tone. "What does your brother do for a living?"

"He's a psychologist," the petite woman said proudly.

"Hmm." Lucy tried to avoid eye contact with her secretary. "How nice for you...I mean, him." The general fuzziness in her head gave way to a slow, rhythmic pounding as Gabby let out a brief, rude snort. She wondered if this psychologist— or was it psychiatrist?— of Alexandra's knew that she thought he was her brother.

"Gabrielle, could you please get me some aspirin from the first-aid kit in the bathroom? I feel a migraine coming on." Lucy smiled at her client apologetically. "I'm sorry. Please excuse me. You were saying...?"

Alexandra Canfield needed no further coaxing to spill her tale. She inched forward even further in her seat, something that Lucy would have considered impossible if she hadn't seen it with her own eyes, since the woman had already seemed to have a rather precarious perch. "I was just explaining that my brother, Campbell, is a psychologist. Which is a rather large part of the problem."

"Problem? Oh, I see. The, uh, 'wedding emergency' you spoke of earlier?" Lucy struggled to keep derision from her tone.

"Exactly!" Alexandra beamed at her as if she were a kindergartner who had just received a perfect score on her first spelling test. Lucy felt as though the woman might dig into her purse at any moment, pull out a gold star, and slap it on Lucy's forehead. "You see, Campbell has been in college for...oh, I don't know how many years. First he had to get his bachelor's degree, of course. And then his master's. Then his doctorate. All he cared about was school. And now it's his clients. He doesn't take any time to date. He hasn't even tried to find a wife!"

"How terrible," Lucy said dryly. "And this is a problem for you because...?" *Careful Lucy; you're getting testy. Be nice. This woman is still a client. Sort of.*

"It's a problem for me because I care about my brother!" Alexandra said, sounding clearly defensive. Her lower lip extended slightly in what Lucy guessed was her version of an adorable, feminine pout. *Save it, sister.* Lucy resisted the urge to roll her eyes. *It's women like you who give our gender a bad name.*

"Here, Luce." Gabby was back, two tiny, pink pills in hand. Lucy grabbed them thankfully, tossed them into her mouth without thinking twice, and downed them with the bottle of water she kept on the corner of her desk. Alexandra eyed her reproachfully as if watching a drug addict getting her latest fix.

"Again, please forgive me." Lucy sat back in her chair and willed the headache away. She waved one hand briskly in the air. "Do go on."

"Well. You see, our father was one of the most successful real-estate developers of this century. Early in the seventies, he made a great deal of money in land deals. He died ten years ago, leaving Campbell and me each a substantial sum of money, which we were to inherit on our thirtieth birthdays. The only problem is, our father was..." She paused and looked around the room furtively.

Automatically Lucy glanced around the room as well. Nothing seemed out of the ordinary to her. Except, of course, for the odd little woman seated across from her and her dark-haired, lunatic assistant, now standing next to her, hanging on her every word.

"Well, our daddy was a bit, er, eccentric," Alexandra confided discreetly.

"No!" Gabby looked terribly shocked. One hand flew to her chest, as if to still the fluttering of her heart.

"You don't say." Lucy sighed. If anything, the pounding in her head was worse than before. She tried to force back a yawn that threatened to hijack her face.

"Yes!" Alexandra seemed pleased to have finally made an impression. "He insisted that if we were to receive our inheritance, each of us had to be married. If we weren't, the money would go to some charity or another."

That, at last, caught Lucy's attention. She sat up and tried to focus. "You've got to be kidding. Is that even legal?"

"Well, I can assure you I have my lawyers looking into it," Alexandra said, sounding much put-upon. She smoothed the fabric of her dress demurely. "They're still examining the legal language that was used in the will. Mind you, I'm fine. Believe it or not, I already turned thirty."

"Get out of town!" The look of disbelief on Gabby's face reached unnatural proportions. She pointed one bony, tanned finger in the woman's direction. "You?"

Alexandra threw her an uncomfortable sidelong glance. "And..." She turned back to Lucy, apparently recognizing that Lucy was safer than Gabby. "I made sure I married before then."

"Um...congratulations," Lucy said, searching for words. *I think.*

"Thank you." Alexandra inclined her head graciously. "But my brother, Campbell, bless his heart, isn't married yet, and he turns thirty in one month." Lucy wondered if she was really seeing things correctly: Were those actual tears in the woman's eyes? "He'd rather the money didn't become an issue here, though. With the marriage, I mean," Alexandra said. "He doesn't want the women he meets even to know about it, though that just sounds absurd to me. Why, I don't think he even cares about his inheritance."

"And why do you?" Lucy asked.

"I beg your pardon?"

"I said, why do you? Care about your brother's inheritance, I mean?"

"Well…because I care about him, of course," the woman said coolly. "About his welfare. His future."

"I see." Lucy pondered this for a moment. Across the desk from her, Alexandra opened her mouth to speak once more, thought better of it, then finally snapped her lips shut and shrank back in her seat. Whether because she had been challenged or simply because she had nothing further to say, her posture of temporary confidence was gone, making her seem like a small child trapped in a woman's body.

Seeing this, Lucy felt her heart soften—just a bit. Spontaneously she reached across the desk and, to her own surprise, found herself patting the woman's hand. "Alexandra, I can see that you feel strongly about this," she said gently. "I don't pretend to understand all the family dynamics involved, but this seems to be very personal to you, so of course you're feeling very emotional about it. But I assure you, this is not the sort of thing I would be good at. Your brother needs to find his own wife, at his own pace. Love can't be rushed."

Alexandra seized on this last phrase. "If it's a matter of a rush charge…"

Lucy gave a short, sharp laugh. "No, no. That's not it at all! I'm sorry, I just don't know how to explain this better. This isn't a video dating service. I'm a matchmaker. I put people together who I believe in my heart really should be together. It can't be about the money." She slid the photograph of the unfortunate teenager across the table, back to its owner.

"But it's not about money," Alexandra protested faintly as she accepted the picture. "I really do want to see him happy!"

"I know you do," Lucy responded kindly, and for an instant she believed it. "But I just don't feel right about this, about the reasons that have brought you here. You've heard the clichés, I'm sure: Love has its own reasons; the heart finds its own path... They're all true. Matches can't be forced. I'm afraid I just can't help you, Alexandra." She stood and extended her hand, a gesture that she hoped would signal a strong but compassionate end to their meeting.

Obediently Alexandra stood. "But...you were my only chance," she tried one last time, enlisting shame to help her in her plea. "Campbell wouldn't agree to go to one of those regular dating services," she said imploringly. "He wanted something personal...someone who would understand him and what he was looking for."

Despite the absurdity of the situation and the distraction of her headache, Lucy felt a twinge of sympathy for the woman who seemed so desperate. Her resolve began to weaken. "I'm sorry," she said as firmly as she could. *Don't cave in, Lucy. You're doing the right thing,* she told herself. *Please leave, lady. Leeeeeaaavve.*

"Well..." Alexandra gave her a precarious smile. "You'll call if you change your mind?"

"That won't happen, I'm afraid," Lucy said gently. "But I do wish you and your brother all the best."

"Yes. I see. Well, thank you." Alexandra turned abruptly. And then, at last, she was gone.

Gabby went to the doorway and watched her go, hands on her slim hips. "Whew!" she said, once the outer office door had closed. She whistled loud and long. Lucy hoped Alexandra hadn't heard.

Gabrielle turned to look at her, and the expression on her face was one of admiration. "That was beautiful. Poetry, even."

Lucy laid her head down on her desk and allowed her forehead to hit the top with a tiny thump. That little interaction was harder on her than she'd thought. She was actually feeling a bit woozy. "What was beautiful?"

"The way you handled that little oddball. Where do you think she was from? The Planet of Overbearing, Controlling Sisters? Or maybe some local halfway house for delusional heir wannabes?" She dropped into the chair Alexandra had vacated.

"Oh, stop." To Lucy's surprise, the words came out shrill and whiny. With her forehead resting against her forearms, she stared at the polished wood grain under her chin. The ache in her head hadn't subsided. In fact, it was actually a bit worse. But, strangely, she felt herself beginning to care less about the pain, as feelings of apathy and detachment set in. "Gabby, am I depressed?" she mumbled, her lips touching the desktop as she spoke.

"Are you what?"

Lucy raised her head dramatically and fixed Gabby with a glassy-eyed stare. "Do you think I'm depressed? You know...bummed out. Despondent. Blue."

Gabby shrugged. "How would I know?"

"I thought you knew everything." Lucy's head hit the table again with a muted thump.

"All I know is, you look terrible."

"Thanks loads. It's my headache, you know. Maybe I should take more of those pills. The first two don't seem to be working. What brand were they, anyway?"

Gabby blinked at her. "How should I know? It's your aspirin."

Lucy thought about that for a moment. "Uh…our aspirin's not pink. I thought you'd given me something out of your purse."

"I gave you whatever was in the bottle under the sink, like you said." Gabby, sounded irritated by the interrogation. She continued to focus on a troublesome hangnail that commanded her entire attention.

Lucy sat up straight. "Which bottle?"

"Whatever. The bottle bottle."

"Gabby…?" Lucy's voice held a faint warning.

Gabrielle looked up with a sigh. "I don't know. Whatever bottle you have under there."

"I have two bottles under the sink, Gabs. One's aspirin; the other's a bottle of antihistamines I picked up for Daphne."

"Well…maybe I gave you Daphne's antihistamines." Gabby shrugged. "Oops."

Antihistamines. Something in the back of Lucy's mind registered a hint of alarm. "Oops…whoops. Hey, that rhymes." She giggled, put her mouth back on the desk, and began to do facial push-ups with her lips. Up and down her head went. "Hey! Wook at me!" David Letterman, eat your heart out. That had to be a Stupid Human Trick.

Antihistamines…Lucy tried to think. What had the doctor in college said about her and antihistamines not mixing well? She'd had a similar reaction during her junior year at UCLA, the one and only time she'd taken them before today. If she remembered right, she'd been fine after ten or fifteen minutes. The reaction would end soon enough. Anyway, it wasn't an unpleasant feeling. She just felt…goofy. At least she wasn't breaking out in a rash all over her face—that had been another possibility the doctor had told her to expect if she ever took the pills again. At least she *thought* she wasn't breaking out in a rash. Deciding maybe she ought to check, Lucy tried to touch one cheek with her index finger and accidentally poked herself in the eye. "Ow!" she said with feeling.

"Oh, good grief." Gabby eyed her incredulously.

"What?"

"You're reacting to those pills."

"I'm not overreacting." It took great effort, but Lucy managed to glare at her with at least one eye.

"I didn't say 'overreacting.' I said 'reacting.' You're acting drunk. You're drunk on antihistamines!" The tall brunette looked half-amused, half-horrified.

"'m not drunk," Lucy protested, though she was feeling rather strange suddenly. "Just feeling kinda sleepy"

"And silly, if I'm not mistaken." Gabby folded her arms and rested her head on them so she could look Lucy in the eye. "Get your tongue off the desk, Luce. It's not sanitary. Or, for that matter, normal. Are you okay?"

"Did you know," Lucy said dramatically, feeling the room begin to pleasantly recede, "that fake wood tastes just like fake cheese?"

"Ugh." Gabby rolled her eyes. "I don't even want to know. Come on. You'd better let me take you home." She walked around the side of the desk and grabbed her by the arm, but Lucy's body had assumed the form of cooked spaghetti. "Lucy," she grunted, trying unsuccessfully to pull her to a standing position. "For goodness' sake, help me, you little wacko."

"'m not a wacko," Lucy protested. "A lil' nap might be nice, though," she mumbled and slumped back against the desk.

"Hmm." Gabby looked at her critically. "I don't know if that's a good idea. I'd better call the doctor. Better yet, there's a new one with an office down the hall. You wait here. I'll go get her. Stay awake if you can. And try not to drool too much."

"*Har*-har-har," Lucy threw after her huffily. But further argument was beyond her. Torturing Gabby would have to wait. For now, all she wanted to do was lay her cheek against the smooth surface of her desk and close her eyes for a minute.

"Excuse me? Miss? Hello?"

"Gr...unh?" Lucy raised her head slightly, feeling something wet on the side of her cheek. What was that noise? She jumped slightly, as a strong hand gripped her forearm and shook it.

"Are you all right?" A voice, strong and rich and utterly masculine, reached into her semiconscious state, causing her heart to skip a beat.

"Wha—?" The scent of aftershave and deodorant—and man—tickled her nostrils. Where was she? What happened? Sensing that she would regret opening her eyes, Lucy tried it anyway. She was rewarded with a glimpse of thick, wavy blond hair; a strong, clean-shaven jaw; and penetrating, bespectacled gray eyes that peered at her intently.

"I take it you had a rough night?" The words were not spoken unkindly.

"Mm. Yes," Lucy mumbled sleepily, her previous night's nightmares coming to mind. "How did you know? I—" A feeling of dread came over her as she realized the meaning of the stranger's words. "*No!* It's not what you're thinking at all! This is not a hangover. I mean, I never—" That sobered her up slightly.

"Shh...hush now." The man in the eyeglasses gave her a compassionate, if somewhat owlish, look.

Feeling like a lab rat about to lose its life at the hands of a genuinely remorseful scientist, Lucy forced herself to sit up straight and survey her surroundings. No little green men...no spaceship...no other helpless victims...Nope, she hadn't been abducted by aliens. So what had happened? She was still in her office, which was odd since she vaguely remembered Gabby saying something about taking her home.

Lucy forced herself to look at the man square-on and wondered if perhaps she was actually hallucinating. She saw a lot of attractive men in her line of work, but this one—this one was exceptionally appealing. In addition to his wonderfully thick—she guessed very touchable—blond hair and soft gray eyes, the man had a fine sense of style. Dressed in chinos, a white T-shirt, and a soft twill shirt the color of bark, he looked both comfortable and stylish.

Without meaning to, she smiled. Normally, Lucy didn't allow herself to react emotionally to men's physical appearances, fearing that it would somehow affect the outcome of her matchmaking process. But because she was feeling so relaxed already, with all her defenses down—or perhaps because there was just something special about this man—Lucy found herself totally captivated.

"Are you sure you're all right?" The man looked unconvinced, but he released his grip on her arm.

"Mm. What?" Lucy said dreamily, then realizing she must look foolish, lifted her chin from her hand, where it rested. "Don't be silly. Of course I'm fine." She narrowed her eyes at the expression on his face. "What?"

"Nothing." The man smiled but kept his eyes trained on her face. "Nothing at all. It's just that you have a little…" He waved one finger in her direction and gave a little grimace of distaste.

"What?" Lucy put one hand to her cheek…and met something wet.

How lovely. Slobber.

"Oh…uh, sorry." She pretended to shrug it off but was certain her burning cheeks betrayed her humiliation. "How rude of me. You must think I'm a nut case, Mr.…?"

"Howard," he supplied.

"All right…Howard, then." Lucy's mind was reeling. *I didn't ask your first name. But, then, I don't remember asking you to my office at all.* "How can I help you…Howard?" Lucy shook her head, hoping desperately to clear it. Things still seemed fuzzy, though her feelings of embarrassment were somewhat sobering and served like a splash of cold water to her earlier silliness.

The man looked at her strangely.

"Howard?" she prompted.

"Well," he began uncertainly. "I'm here to sign up for your…uh…services." His face flushed bright red at the word "services," and he looked around him as if to see if anyone had seen him come in.

Even in her state of semistupor Lucy managed a glare. "Well, you needn't make it sound like this is some sort of prostitution ring. What 'services,' exactly, do you think we provide?" Her voice was smooth and even, but cool.

"What? Oh no…" He laughed then, completely unoffended by her tone, but thoroughly amused by the implication. "Whoops! That was a major faux pas, wasn't it? Sorry. It's just that I've never done this sort of thing—tried a dating service, that is," he clarified. "Not that there's anything wrong with that. But I feel sort of embarrassed, I guess. Like you'll make a judgment or look down on me because I'm here. Like maybe you'll think I can't get dates or something."

"Don't be silly," Lucy said, allowing herself to make a brief assessment of the man, as she commonly did in her job. At six-foot-two, with a slim build and finely drawn features, he was, in fact, one of the most attractive men she had ever seen. She doubted he'd ever had trouble getting a date in his life. She certainly would be interested if he weren't a client. In fact, Lucy found him to be very attractive indeed. The mental acknowledgment caused her cheeks to burn even hotter. No doubt he would be hard pressed to make such a charitable statement about her...considering the slobber and all.

The thought surprised her. Every day she met attractive, interesting, thoroughly eligible bachelors, but Lucy rarely gave a second thought to what one of them would think of her. When people asked her why she didn't date the men she represented, she simply explained that it would be unethical. But if truth be told, Lucy would be forced to admit that she'd never been overly tempted to break her own rule. She suspected it had something to do with her past record in the romance department—left at the altar years before, she still felt burned. It was important to her to keep at her work, to know that love worked for some people even if it hadn't worked for her. Someday maybe she'd give it another try. But not yet.

She was happy enough with the way things were now. Maybe she wasn't thrilled, but certainly she was comfortable being single. Just because she was able to help fix people up, did that mean she had to have a man herself? She knew plenty of couples in bad marriages—including her sister Felicia. And she knew women with incredible ones—like her sister Catherine. And if there was one thing she'd decided over the years, it was that she wouldn't settle for less than the best.

Howard now sat in the chair opposite Lucy, apparently having accepted that she was, at least for the time being, "fine" as she claimed. A strange little smile played about his lips as she smoothed back her hair and wiped away the remaining trail of saliva on her cheek.

Mercifully, Howard directed the conversation to a less humiliating subject. "That's a great picture," he said, nodding at a photo sitting on the edge of her desk, just beyond the path of drool. "Big Bear, am I right?" he asked, referring to the popular resort area in the San Bernardino mountain range outside of Los Angeles.

"You're right." Lucy felt a flush of pleasure at his recognition. "It's my favorite vacation spot." In fact, it had been ever since she was a child. Though her family had traveled extensively and had visited many vacation destinations locally and abroad, Lucy had always enjoyed the warm familiarity of Big Bear and tried to visit there once a year with all three of her sisters. The photo Howard had pointed out was taken less than one year earlier and showed the women standing on the porch at one of their favorite rental cabins in the woods—a place owned by Gabby's parents.

"Who are these people?" Howard asked amiably.

Lucy momentarily forgot her unease and simply answered. "See the honey-colored blonde at the back of the group? That's my oldest sister, Catherine Salinger-Riley. She's president of the Salinger/Riley Advertising Agency here in town, which she owns and operates with her husband, Jonas."

"She certainly looks happy," the man observed.

Lucy nodded. "She's a newlywed. Can you tell?"

Howard let out a brief laugh, its rich, full sound filling the room. "I can, absolutely. Look at that glow; it's unmistakable. And the woman beside her, the one Catherine— it's Catherine, right?—the one Catherine has her arm around?"

"That's Fee," Lucy told him.

Discreetly he refrained from mentioning the melancholy look on the woman's face, though Lucy knew it was there for him and all the world to see. Looking much older than her twenty-eight years, dark-haired Felicia resembled a rather sweet, sad-eyed Madonna. Perhaps in part because with two children—Dinah, age eight, and Clifford, five—Fee was the only mother in the group. But the unhappiness in her eyes, Lucy knew, had nothing to do with Fee's children and everything to do with her husband, Robert, who had emotionally abandoned Felicia years before and was suspected by his wife of cheating on her as well.

In contrast to Fee's sadness, bright-eyed baby sister Daphne—two years younger than Lucy at age twenty-four—stood in the foreground, grinning from ear to ear. "This one looks like trouble," Howard remarked, causing Lucy to marvel at his discernment.

"That's true. How did you know?" she asked incredulously, stifling a yawn. Clearly, the effects of the drugs had not worn off, but her curious companion was managing to distract her.

"Mm..." Howard studied the photograph carefully. "Something about the look in her eyes, the strength of her stance, the two fingers she's holding over your head, like antennae."

"Oh, *that.*" Lucy laughed and looked at the picture more closely. "The bunny ears. I had forgotten." Standing next to Daphne in the photo, she looked like the younger woman's twin. The resemblance was uncanny: Both had dark chestnut curls and bright blue eyes, though Daphne looked more childlike with her petite build—five feet four inches compared to Lucy's five feet six—button nose, and funky, semi-hippie-ish style of dress. The more professional of the youngest sisters, Lucy had a style of her own, a slightly rounder face— "angelic," a former boyfriend had called it, perhaps before encountering Lucy's somewhat less-than-heavenly stubbornness—and a much more disciplined work ethic. But the two women were extremely close—not only sisters, but close friends—and even lived together at a rented beach house in Malibu.

All this she managed to keep from blabbing, despite the effects of the drugs, although she did explain to Howard that Daphne was her youngest sister and worked at Salinger/Riley with Cat, as an account executive.

"She looks happy too," Howard observed. "Another newly-wed?"

"Almost," Lucy laughed, "but not quite. She tried to elope, but Cat stopped her. And then Cat got married instead."

Howard shook his head. "I'm not sure I follow."

"I'm not sure I did, either," she admitted. "But let's just say they're happy. Daphne's still with her boyfriend, Elliott, and I suppose they'll get married someday too. As long as everyone's happy, I'm happy."

Howard narrowed his eyes at her, sharpening his gaze. "Is everyone happy?"

Under his scrutiny, Lucy felt the delicate hairs on the nape of her neck rise, like goose bumps. "Not exactly. Felicia's had a hard time of it." *Why am I telling a stranger all this? Fee would kill me.*

"And what about you? Are you happy?"

Lucy gave him a startled glance. "That's a rather personal question," she managed to get out.

"It is, isn't it?" Howard sounded unconcerned. He threw her a smile that was full of confidence and humor. "I suppose, then, we ought to get to the personal, serious questions you have for me."

Rarely at a loss for words, Lucy was speechless. "The...'serious questions'?" she finally managed after several moments.

"That's right." Howard grinned wickedly. "The ones you're going to use to help get me a wife."

"Right...wife." Why did he look as though he was joking with her? Normally clever and quick-witted, Lucy found herself mumbling half-phrases, like a cave woman, in this strange man's presence. "Questions. Serious." Maybe the drugs had an even greater effect on her than she'd thought. "Well," she tried again, "maybe we should start at the beginning. Where did you hear about our, er, services?"

Howard's lips twitched as he struggled to keep from laughing again. "Your company is rather famous, you know, here in the city. Everyone talks about it. It's the 'in' thing to go to a matchmaker these days, rather than a video service. At least, that's what I hear. I'm not real big on fads, myself. I was simply drawn to the concept of getting more personal attention. Not being a number, so to speak."

Oh, you have my personal attention all right. Lucy looked away nervously, bewildered by the direction of her thoughts. All right, so the guy was cute. No. Beyond cute—he was *gorgeous*. And, if her admittedly rusty antennae still worked, it was even possible that he was flirting with her. But that didn't change the rules: Clients were hands-off. Besides, since when was she even in the market? She was perfectly content with the way things were. There was no need to go messing up her life by getting personally involved, especially since she didn't feel a great need to have a man in her life in the first place.

"That's perfectly understandable." She pushed the wayward thoughts from her mind and flashed what she hoped was her most professional smile. The man stared back at her, not looking impressed as she had hoped, but for all the world as though he might laugh out loud. Feeling inexplicably hurt, Lucy focused on her small hands for a moment and tried to regain her composure. What was with this guy, anyway? Didn't his parents ever teach him not to be rude? Her pride stung from the obvious lack of respect he felt for her.

Feeling only slightly more poised, Lucy glanced back up at the attractive stranger, fully intending to give him a look of detachment. Yet in that brief instant when their eyes met, she felt caught…oddly drawn in by his penetrating gaze. For just a moment Lucy returned the thoughtful look of a man she'd never seen before in her life, yet who seemed to truly see her…not as one sees the gas station attendant, or mailman, or grocery store clerk—as nameless, faceless providers of a necessary service. Nor did she feel that he saw her strictly as a man regarding a woman—as one with the potential for a romantic alliance…although at some level a part of her sensed that interest was there too.

No, what Lucy felt in those brief moments was a simple recognition of who she was as a person. As his eyes—soft and gentle, yet oddly piercing—searched hers, Lucy felt vulnerable…yet somehow accepted and understood. And it struck her that her earlier assessment must have been wrong; regardless of his laughter, the man did respect her, not based on her accomplishments—he had no way to know those—but simply as a fellow member of the human race.

Lucy turned away abruptly. Where did all that come from? That did it. Absolutely no more drugs of any kind for her…for the rest of her life.

"I suppose we should start by reviewing what I—er, what we have to offer," she said, escaping gratefully into the familiarity of her well-practiced marketing spiel. "Rent-a-Yenta is a funny name, of course. A gimmick, I suppose you could say. But it also explains what I do: I get to know people and then I match them up, sort of the way older women in the community used to do. Most dating agencies have you fill out a bunch of paperwork, which they feed into the system to come up with computer-generated matches. Or they may put all the info into notebooks and have each client complete a video interview, which other members can view. I don't do that. I'll ask you to fill out some forms, just like the other companies would. But they're just for my personal use. I'll use them to learn about you, and then I'll try to find you the woman God has picked out for you."

The man's eyebrows raised. "The one God has picked for me?"

Lucy met his gaze evenly. "That's right. I won't force my faith on you, Howard. But I do pray about each client; I make Jesus and prayer a part of the process on my end."

He nodded soberly, appreciatively. "So how, exactly, do you know who will be right together?"

Lucy shrugged. "Sometimes it's just completely obvious to me, I feel it so strongly. I couldn't be more sure if there were big neon letters written on their foreheads: '*I belong with Jack*' or '*Fix me up with Heather.*'" Howard grinned. Lucy smiled back. "Other times," she said, "I just have a good feeling about it, and I use my best judgment. Once in a while, I feel nothing...for a really long time. Maybe more than a couple of years. When I first sense that happening, I give people the option of waiting, keeping in mind that it might take awhile, or I give them their money back. Very rarely—I've only had to do this once or twice, mind you—I'll know in my heart that I can't help someone, and I'll refund his or her money right away. I usually try to weed those people out during the screening process though. It's much easier that way. Much less offensive." She grimaced. "It's hard to explain to people that 'I don't think you're supposed to meet anyone right now.'"

Howard nodded. "And what if God does want them to meet someone and that someone isn't here right now in this city? Do you ever feel like you're interfering with his plan?"

Lucy felt pleased. The man wasn't treating her like she was a wacko, as some clients did. This one actually got it. "If I ever do feel that way, I just tell the person and let the chips fall where they may. A couple of times my clients have met their future mates while at my service, though in other cities and through other means. One of them insisted on paying me anyway, saying that I helped prepare her to recognize her future husband once she met him. I don't know if that's true or not, but I thought it was nice of her."

"That's great." Howard nodded appreciatively. "I admire your process. My Christian faith's important to me too. I'll admit, it makes me feel a lot more, uh," he gave her another curious look, "confident in trusting you with my love life, or should I say, lack of it." He hung his head shyly, like a nine-year-old who has just asked for his very first kiss. "I'm afraid I haven't dated much," he admitted. "I was a shy kid. But even as an adult, I've been hesitant to get involved until I feel it's right. Guess I don't want my heart to get trampled on or something."

Lucy stared. *Good grief, did this guy actually blush? I didn't know men even did that!* "Well, don't worry," she said in a rush of warm feelings. Suddenly she wanted to put her arms around the nine-year-old and comfort him. "I promise, your heart is safe with me." As soon as the words were out of her mouth, she realized how intimate it sounded. "Oh! I mean, uh…"

Howard gave her a mischievous wink, a maneuver that made him look, maddeningly, more devastatingly handsome than ever. "I was hoping you'd say that," he said, sounding charming. "So…what do we do now?"

"What do we do?" Lucy's head was still swimming. *Coffee? Dinner? Maybe a night at the theater…?*

"Right. Where do we start?"

"Oh, right." Lucy giggled, then stopped and swallowed hard. She was not a giggler. "Well, I generally like to block out at least an hour for the initial interview," she explained carefully, trying to get her thoughts in order. "I need to find out all about you: what you're looking for, what your life is like, what's important to you, et cetera, et cetera."

"Sounds fairly painless."

"Mm. I'll try to be merciful," Lucy said playfully. Inside, she felt a warm feeling coursing through her veins. At last she had the meeting back under control. She didn't look like a nitwit any longer. She was the one doing the majority of the flirting…just the way she liked things to be. Perhaps if he was very kind to her, she would allow Howard to take her out for coffee after all. Coffee wasn't technically a date, anyway…was it?

Feeling somewhat smug, Lucy led Howard through her fee schedule, as well as the list of questions she would be discussing with him at their next meeting.

"And now, there's just one more thing we need to go over," she said briskly, reaching into her desk to pull out an information card. "I need to get your name, phone number, address…you know, the basics. Then I can get a file started for you, and we can set your first appointment. How does next week look for you?"

"I think I can fit you in." The man reached into an inside jacket pocket and pulled out a small day planner. "My schedule's fairly packed during the day, but I'm sure we can work something out. Or maybe push it back to the next week." He flipped through the pages of his planner.

"I sometimes meet with clients in the evening if it's necessary. I mean…if you want to." Lucy's face flushed with warmth. That wasn't true at all. She took great pains, in fact, to keep her personal and professional lives separate. She opened her own day planner and stared into it, unable to meet Howard's eyes. Could he tell she was lying? How horrible! She was appalled at her behavior. But for some strange reason, she was looking forward to seeing him again and hated the idea of letting a week or more go by.

He did not respond at first, and Lucy felt her ears begin to burn. Finally she raised her eyes timidly, expecting to find that he had recoiled in dismay at her forwardness. Instead, he looked thoughtful, bemused. "That's a very kind offer," he said at last. "I'd love to meet with you next week. Tuesday night maybe?"

"Great." Lucy's heart flooded with relief. She flashed him a bright smile. "Why don't we pencil it in for an hour and a half. That way, we can eat as well. Do you like Mexican? Or Chinese? I know a great little place called Wu's over on Wilshire. We could meet at seven if that's not too late for you."

"Seven is perfect. And Chinese is my favorite." Howard patted his left shirt pocket. "I even carry my own set of chopsticks."

Lucy laughed. "Please. I'll bet you can't even play 'Chopsticks.'"

Howard raised his thick, dark eyebrows at her. "Do I hear a challenge?"

Lucy glanced around her office helplessly. "I'm afraid I'll have to take your word for it. There's no piano here; I can't make you prove it."

"Oh well. I have a piano at my apartment. I'll show you there one day," Howard said casually and sat back in his chair.

At your apartment...? Lucy gave him a searching gaze, but his expression gave nothing away. He appeared to have made the comment with no more thought of romance than if he had just offered her a piece of smelly cheese.

"Maybe," she said noncommittally and made a great show of examining his card. "What is your occupation, by the way? What makes it so hard for you to get away during the day?"

"I'm a doctor," Howard answered simply. A doctor...In her mind's eye Lucy could picture Gabby salivating, delighted that Lucy had signed up another of the good ones. And Howard, it appeared, was a very good catch, indeed. At least that's what Lucy would have said if she were one to compare men to fish...which she was not.

"What kind of fish—er, doctor—are you?" She blinked hard. Howard blinked back, apparently speechless.

Good grief, she must still be suffering from her antihistamine overdose. At least she hoped she was still suffering from an antihistamine overdose. If not, she had a much more serious problem.

"Uh...a psychologist, actually," Howard said finally, giving her a long, slow smile.

This time Lucy could feel herself blush clear to the roots of her hair. *No wonder he's grinning. He sees me as his next client and figures I'm so crazy I'm bound to make him a millionaire.* She resisted the urge to suggest they trade services.

"Great. You're my second psychologist today...sort of." Lucy suspected, however, that she'd have much more difficulty finding Alexandra Canfield's nerdy brother a match than she would finding one for a dreamboat like Howard. "Your address and phone number?" She scribbled the information down in her crazy chicken scrawl under Howard's watchful eye. "That's it," she said at last. "Except...I guess I need your last name."

He cocked his head to one side, like a curious cocker spaniel. "I'm sorry. It's Howard."

"What? But—" Understanding dawned on her. "Pardon me. I'm afraid I jumped to conclusions. I thought Howard was your first name." How embarrassing. "All right, then." Lucy rubbed out her last entry on the card. "So, Howard is your last name." She filled the letters in as she spoke. "And your first name is...?"

"Campbell," he supplied obligingly. "Dr. Campbell Howard. I had an appointment at one, which I just missed."

Lucy stared at him with a look of alarm that Howard—or was it Campbell?—didn't immediately recognize.

Whatever his name, the gorgeous stranger scribbled something in his day planner, slipped the pen back into his pocket, and smiled at her amiably. "Again, I apologize for being late.

I've certainly enjoyed talking to you. And I have to admit, I'm beginning to think that Alexandra was right," he said thoughtfully. "This may be interesting after all."

And as Lucy gaped at him, her eyes and mouth both open wide, it occurred to her that might be the understatement of the year.

Two

"Campbell Howard?" Lucy nearly dropped her pencil. "You mean, *the* Campbell Howard?"

"Well! It's not often that I hear a response like that when I introduce myself," the man chuckled. "But, yes, it's me, the infamous Campbell Howard. In the flesh." He beamed, clearly taking it all as one big joke. "I take it you've seen my 'Wanted' poster in the post office?"

"You're Campbell Howard?" Lucy repeated dully. "You are? As in Alexandra Canfield's brother, Campbell Howard? The guy-who-stands-to-inherit-a-lot-of-money-if-he-gets-a-wife-in-a-month, Campbell Howard?" He blinked at her, clearly uncertain how he should respond.

Suddenly she wished the man had left her alone in her earlier tongue-to-desk stupor. This was the guy with the crazy sister? The one who agreed to a romantic match just so he could get his inheritance? The man who had sold out for money? Surely this was some sort of cruel joke. "But...but Campbell Howard is a geek!" she burst out, remembering the photograph of him as a teen. How could this impressive specimen of a man possibly be the same person?

Once again she was appalled at the words that were coming out of her mouth—even though she meant them. Her guest appeared unfazed. "This is some sort of test, isn't it?" he asked

31

in a dry tone. "This is to protect your female clients, right? You want to see how I respond to unexpected situations? See if I turn violent when pushed too far?" He looked around the room inquisitively. "Fess up. Am I on *Candid Camera?*"

"No, you are not on *Candid Camera,*" Lucy answered testily. All feelings of affinity were gone. "But I did meet your sister this morning, and I'm afraid I can't help you...Dr. Howard."

"I see," Campbell said, though his furrowed brow expressed clearly that he didn't. "Of course, that's your prerogative. Might I ask why, though?" Lucy felt herself becoming grumpier by the minute. Didn't he get it? And why did he have to sound so infuriatingly polite?

She gazed at him levelly. "Why can't I help you?" *Because you're a user, a fake, a danger to women everywhere...including me.* "As I explained earlier, Dr. Campbell—"

"Dr. Howard," he corrected cheerfully.

Lucy sighed. Of course. Campbell was his first name. "Excuse me. Dr. Howard—"

"Please. Call me Campbell." His tone was friendly, easy.

Lucy hesitated. "Fine. Campbell. As I was saying—"

"My friends call me Cam," he suggested cheerfully.

"Dr. Howard, please!" Lucy glared at him. "As I said earlier, my goal is to help facilitate the matches that I believe are, well...preordained. I told your sister earlier, and I will tell you now as well: I don't force or manipulate matches that aren't meant to be. Certainly, in the past I've helped people find each other within a month. But I couldn't promise the same would happen for you. I couldn't go into this with that as my goal. And even if I found you the 'right one' within thirty days, I couldn't in good conscience support a decision to marry that quickly. It's...it's..."

"Insane?" Cam suggested.

Lucy sighed again. "Well, now, you would know that, wouldn't you?" she said, remembering that he worked in the mental-health field. She eyed him uneasily, unsure of how he would respond to her outburst. Anger, defensiveness, frustration, blame…all were possibilities. She was prepared for any reaction…except the one she got.

Laughter. It began as a chuckle and soon spread to a full-out bellow that filled the room.

"Touché," Cam grinned.

Lucy stared. "That's all you can say? Touché? I'm serious, you know. This isn't a game to me. I take my work very seriously." Even as she spoke, she heard the tone of her voice and envisioned herself as a little girl playing grownup, stomping her foot to emphasize her point. As ridiculous as she sounded, however, she wasn't about to back down. "People sometimes think it's strange that I'm a matchmaker," she told him testily. "Like I should get a 'real' job. They don't take me seriously. But I assure you, this is my real job. I wouldn't be doing it if it wasn't important to me. And I'm not going to let you or anyone else take advantage of my clients. I can tell the difference between someone who's serious about finding a person to give love to and someone who's out to get his selfish needs met. I assure you, Doctor, I'm no fool."

Campbell's eyes flickered automatically to her forehead, and he appeared to force back a grin. "Of course you're not," he said kindly.

"What?" Responding to the look, Lucy quickly threw one hand to her head. To her horror, her fingers met something stuck to the skin just above her left eyebrow. With a heart full of dread, she grabbed the offending item, lowered her hand to eye level, and slowly opened her fist one finger at a time. There on her palm lay a neon-green, plastic-coated paper clip.

Her mind raced as she searched for an explanation. How could a paper clip have gotten stuck to her forehead? Unless... She'd been absentmindedly playing with a pile of paper clips when Alexandra was in the office. A stray must have dropped to the desktop just in front of her, then stuck to her skin when she pressed her forehead to the desk. Had it been there the entire time she'd been talking to Campbell? Her heart sank. No wonder he'd been so amused when she'd been trying hard to appear the calm, composed professional.

He grinned, causing her anger to rise even further. "Uh—you have a little thing on your—" he began innocently, waving a finger at her forehead.

"Ha, ha. Very funny." Lucy threw him a murderous look. "You know, you could have told me."

"You're right." Cam's smile softened, and he gave her a look of kindness. "I should have spoken up. At first I was worried because you seemed sick. Then, once you came to, I didn't want to offend you by saying something rude right off the bat. And after we'd been talking for a while, it seemed too late to say anything." The smile faltered. He appeared genuinely uncomfortable now. "I figured that sometime after I left, it would drop off and you wouldn't even notice. But you're right; there was no excuse for me not saying anything. I'd be pretty hacked off if I were in your shoes. How did it make you feel when you found that clip stuck to your head?"

"Well, I—" Lucy felt herself being pulled in by his warmth and charm. "Hey! I'm not one of your patients, you know," she grumbled. "I accept your apology. Now, let's just forget about it. There's really nothing else to say." There was no point in dragging this out any further. In a moment Campbell would get up and walk out of her office, and she'd never have to see the infuriating man again.

So why did she feel so awful?

She stood, expecting Cam to do the same.

Apparently he wasn't as good as his sister at taking cues. "Ms. Salinger," he said softly, keeping his seat. "Er, Lucy, right?" She nodded unhappily. "Maybe you have nothing else to say, but I do. I'd like you to hear me out. Please...sit."

Against her better judgment, Lucy sat. She looked at him expectantly. *Well...?*

Cam remained seated for a moment, looking at her thoughtfully. Then, exhibiting an uneasiness she hadn't seen from him before, he rose to his feet and began to pace the room. For several minutes there was no sound but the soft squeak-squeak of rubber soles against the cream-colored linoleum flooring. Back and forth he walked as Lucy watched, feeling strangely downhearted. She thought about breaking the silence but decided against it. He wasn't going to get off that easily. Whatever the guy had to say he'd have to find a way to do it all on his own. And then he'd have to leave. So there.

At last Cam stopped his nervous pacing. Folding his arms across his chest, he regarded her with a look of genuine respect. "I have to admit, Ms. Lucy Salinger," he began, "that I'm quite impressed with you. With your business and your principles. There aren't many people who would do what you do, the way that you do it. You have character. And whether or not I see you again after today isn't the point. Regardless of what happens next, I want you to know that character shows."

Lucy watched him, unblinking, unable to tear her eyes away. And as he spoke, her heart swelled. *You like me.* She heard in her mind the voice of Sally Field, crying out her Academy Award acceptance speech: *You really, really like me.*

"But enough about you," Cam said more lightheartedly, as if reading her thoughts, and threw her an irreverent grin. "What I really want to do is explain myself. It's clear from your response that you've formed a few opinions about me, my sister, and this whole big mess I'm in."

A look of disapproval settled onto her features. She'd almost forgotten why she disliked him so much. "Obviously," she quipped.

"And who could blame you?" Cam seemed undisturbed by her blatant displeasure. "Let me guess: You think I'm a scheming, exploitative, money-hungry user who believes women exist solely to make themselves available for my vast and evil purposes."

"You forgot 'lying, conniving, heartless, and shallow,'" she said calmly.

"Excuse me," Cam said, sounding genuinely remorseful. "Please add 'lying, conniving, heartless, and shallow' to the aforementioned list," he said, giving a little half-bow.

Lucy's lips twitched. She said nothing.

"However," he continued, "I'd like the opportunity to clear my name. Believe it or not, I'm really not the monster you take me to be." He planted himself once more in the chair across from Lucy, but she could see that at this point his light-hearted attitude was slowly shifting to something a bit more somber. She leaned back in her black leather chair—needing the distance between them—drawing comfort from the chair's soft, familiar folds.

"Seriously," Cam said, looking genuinely distressed now, "I'm so sorry for the way this situation has been communicated to you. I wish I'd been here earlier when Alexandra came in." He leaned forward as if making a great confession and spoke in hushed tones. "Between you and me, I'm sure it wasn't a coincidence that I missed the appointment. Subconsciously I probably was trying to sabotage the whole visit to Rent-a-Yenta." His mouth twitched as he uttered the words.

Ouch. Lucy blinked at him. That stung. "You make it sound

like you didn't even want to come," she said a bit angrily. "What's wrong with Rent-a-Yenta?"

"I didn't mean it like that," Cam said quickly. Wisely he refrained from laughing, despite the childish sound of the question. "My attitude has nothing to do with you and everything to do with me. As I said earlier, I do feel a little embarrassed about being here—mostly because you're a beautiful woman, and I can't help but wonder what you think about me coming to you for help."

Beautiful woman, huh? Lucy sized him up carefully as he spoke. He appeared to be sincere, but who knew what the man was really up to? He was a psychologist—a master at reading and understanding people, after all, wasn't he? No doubt, he knew that calling her beautiful would make her stomach turn tiny flips and cause her temperature to rise half a degree. Surely he knew what made people tick. Perhaps that just made him even better at carrying out his manipulation. She continued to scowl at him, even as she felt herself being drawn in by his charms.

"You see, my sister, Alexandra, has spent nearly her whole life watching out for me," Cam explained. "My mother died when I was only thirteen, so Alex became sort of a surrogate parent." Lucy stared at him, incredulous. She didn't know which shocked her more—the revelation that Cam called his snooty, thoroughly un-tomboyish, high-society sister "Alex," or the fact that he, too, had tragically lost his mother at a tender, vulnerable age.

"Our father died several years later, when I was nineteen. I was already in my freshman year at Harvard when it happened. Father's money was tied up for a while in probate. I almost had to drop out of school. As you already know, I'm not supposed to inherit the bulk of my inheritance until my thirtieth birthday."

He shook his head. "My father was a brilliant man, but he didn't really think things through when he planned his will. He approached it as though the money wouldn't be needed for many years. He wanted to make sure we were mature enough to handle the financial responsibility when the time came. Father wouldn't even consider the possibility that Alex or I might need the money sooner. He was certain he'd be around to provide for us both until long after I'd graduated. Of course, it didn't turn out that way, and I had to rely on Alex and her husband, Wallace, to help me get through school. Wallace is a stockbroker on Wall Street and was doing very well at the time. Unfortunately, the last few years weren't quite as successful. He made a few bad choices that really cost him and Alex a great deal of money—including a fair amount of her inheritance. They're pretty deeply in debt now, and the loss has taken its toll. I feel for them. They're good people."

They're weird people, Lucy couldn't help thinking to herself.

The thought must have leaked out onto her features—Cam gave Lucy a knowing look. "Don't worry. I do realize that my sister can come across as a bit of a nut bar."

She frowned. "Are therapists really supposed to call people 'nut bars'?"

"Sorry." He shrugged. "It's a technical term."

"I see." She smiled gently, despite her resolve to remain detached.

"But despite being a nut bar—pardon the technical jargon—Alex really is a sweetheart."

"I'm confused," Lucy said, feeling rather perplexed. "I'm a pretty good judge of character. I have to be, in my line of work. And I could have sworn your sister was after the money. She came across as a, uh…"

"A real control freak? Which, by the way, she is."

Lucy made a face. "Is that another technical term?"

"As you say. But control freak or not, my sister does love me."

"And the money?"

Cam appeared unconcerned. "Who knows? She just might love it too. In any case, she cares about it a lot more than I do. Frankly, I'm doing well enough financially. I wouldn't say I'm filthy rich, but I have a very comfortable life…no complaints. Still, there's the matter of the money I borrowed from her and Wallace. Alex wants it back now, understandably. And though I'm paying her back as quickly as I can, let's face it: Tuition isn't exactly cheap, especially at Harvard. And I was there for a lot of years."

"I'll have to take your word about the cost," Lucy told him, having gone to UCLA. "And I've enjoyed this little jaunt back into your family history, I truly have. You may even have convinced me of your sister's pure-as-snow motives regarding your inheritance—though the jury's still out, my friend, on what I believe your motives to be," she said cynically. "All this is beside the point, though, since I fail to see what it has to do with me."

"That's what I like about you, Lucy." Cam beamed. "You get right to the point."

That's what bugs me about you, Dr. Campbell Howard, she thought wryly. *You don't.* She had to admit, though, she was intrigued—just as Alexandra had predicted she would be.

"—what this has to do with you," he was saying, "is simply this: Alexandra has been trying for over a year to get me to find a woman. Admittedly, she'd be happy with any woman. Her frustration comes from the fact that I haven't even tried. Like you, I don't see the point in manipulating or forcing a relationship to happen. I figure I'll just let nature take its course. Or rather, to be more accurate, I'm trying to do what you talked about: let God have control of the situation. I haven't been overly concerned about it, anyway. I mean, I want to get married someday. But I haven't met the right person yet. Until I do, I figure, why worry about it? You know what I mean?"

Do I ever. Has this guy been reading my mail? "Maybe," Lucy said noncommittally.

"Things have gotten a little difficult though in the past month," Cam confided. "Alex has been pressuring me a lot, and I've been trying to maintain healthy personal boundaries. Finally I realized that Alex couldn't make me do anything but that my taking a step in her direction would go a long way toward healing the rift between us. So I agreed to try your matchmaking service. She'd tried several times to sell it to me, and it seemed like less of a meat market than the other places."

"Less of a meat market?" Lucy sniffed. "It's not a meat market at all, thank you very much."

"Like I said," Cam said calmly, "not a meat market at all. So I let Alex make an appointment, which she did for today. Even though I had resolved to come with an open attitude, I was still mad about the situation—until I got here, that is. Until I saw you lying on your desk like a stuffed rag doll...without the stuffing."

"Please, don't remind me," Lucy moaned. "I wouldn't be surprised if I needed therapy after this."

Cam smirked. "If you do, I know a good psychologist. But I hope you're not too embarrassed. I thought it was highly amusing...once I realized I wasn't going to have to call 9-1-1, that is," he laughed.

Or perform mouth-to-mouth resuscitation, Lucy thought ruefully. *That must have been a relief for you.*

"At first, I was intrigued...then entertained. But I'll tell you one thing, Lucy," he said convincingly. "I knew right away that

I liked you...that working with you would be fun. So all that said, Yes, I know the chances are slim that I'll find the right person within a month. And you're right—moving ahead, even if I did, might not be such a good idea. Still, I'm willing to enter into the process and see what God does...if you are."

"Do I hear a challenge?" Lucy said in a low voice, repeating his earlier question.

"If that's what it takes to get you to take me as a client," he said simply.

Lucy gave him a dubious look. She didn't know what to make of this Campbell Howard. Tall, well-built, and apparently always ready to laugh, he was more outgoing, confident, and lighthearted than she would have imagined Alexandra's unfortunate younger brother could be.

And what was the deal with all that flirting? One minute he was acting as though he was attracted to her, for goodness' sake, and the next, he was telling her he wanted her to find him a wife! Something stirred inside Lucy, a feeling that was strong, undefinable, and clearly primitive. She'd show him a thing or two! *All right, fine. I'll find you a wife, then, if that's what you really want.*

"You've made your case, Counselor," she said at last, standing once more in a gesture of dismissal. This time, Cam rose to his feet as well, ready to let her wrap up their discussion. "If you're sure this is what you want, of course I'll be happy to help you."

Cam looked pleased. "That's wonderful."

"Hmph," Lucy said noncommittally. *We'll see how wonderful you think it is when I'm done with you.* "So we're meeting Tuesday night then? At Wu's? Seven o'clock?"

He reached out and grabbed her hand, a gesture that first startled, then disturbed her as his warm fingers pressed against her own.

41

"Seven o'clock at Wu's," he agreed. "I'll be the one with a rose in my teeth. Or should I make it an olive branch?"

Lucy sighed. "Make it those famous chopsticks you were bragging about, and you've got a deal."

"How could you leave me like that?" Lucy wailed. She gave her assistant an accusatory stare. "Anything could have happened to me in the state I was in. I could've been robbed, beaten, kidnapped."

"I know," Gabby said soberly, looking properly repentant. "Or enormous paper clips could have stuck themselves to your forehead."

"It isn't funny," Lucy moaned.

"Aughh! It's The Attack of the Giant Paper Clips!" Gabby jumped up and waved her arms in the air, her face a distorted mask of terror. "Hide your letterhead! Hide your résumé! No report is safe!"

"Ohhhhhhh." Lucy let her head fall to her desk in defeat.

"Careful now," Gabby chided, dropping her arms and abandoning her dramatics. "You know, that's how you got yourself into this mess in the first place."

"You're heartless," Lucy grumbled. "Go away."

"Un-unh." Gabby shook her head and settled herself into the chair Cam had sat in earlier. "I want to hear more about this guy."

"No." Lucy set her mouth in a grim line. "You left me to my fate. I don't think I'm talking to you anymore."

"Stop pouting," Gabby ordered. "I told you, I was talking with Dr. Evans down the hall. You're lucky I didn't call an ambulance. Fortunately, your reaction was just a mild one. You were perfectly fine by the time I dragged her back to the office."

"'Fine' being a relative term, of course..."

"Too bad there weren't any cute male doctors on hand,"

Gabby mused. "Maybe I could slip you some antihistamines tomorrow, and we can try this again?"

"You're heartless, do you know it? After all I went through, all you can think about is your love life."

"All right then, spill it. Tell me about your ordeal. What's this guy's story?"

Lucy turned away from Gabby's interrogation. She hadn't really wanted to go into it. Her point was simply that Gabby was being insensitive, that's all. "There's no story—" she began, but to no avail.

"Wait a minute. Isn't this guy some kind of doctor?" Gabby waggled her eyebrows suggestively. "Hey, that's right! That's what his sister said."

"Down, girl," Lucy said warningly. "Now you're the one drooling."

"Is he cute?"

"Um…do you remember the picture Alexandra showed us?" Lucy hedged. The last thing she needed was for Gabby to set her sights on the man. Not that she'd set them up, but it was a complication she didn't want to have to deal with. Besides, she was feeling strangely private about Cam and didn't feel like sharing the intimate details of their conversation, as if that would spoil it somehow.

"That geek? Eew. Say no more. He may be worth a lot of money, but even I have my standards." Gabby shuddered. Lucy didn't have the heart to correct her. "You decided to take him as a client after all? I was sure you wouldn't after what you said to his sister."

"I know." She grabbed a pencil from a cup on her desk and began to chew on the eraser. "Let's just say he convinced me."

"Whatever." Clearly tired of the conversation, Gabby began to prowl around the office. "Have you got anything to eat in here?"

Lucy dug into a side drawer and rummaged around until she came up with a small plastic package. "Just a granola bar that looks like it's been around since 1989."

"Perfect." Gabby reached across the desk and snatched it up. "These things are like Twinkies—indestructible."

"Ugh. I hope your stomach's indestructible," Lucy said dryly.

"I'm healthy as a horse," Gabby quipped.

"Keep eating everything in sight, and you'll be half as big as one too," Lucy warned.

"Probably," the tall brunette mumbled around a mouthful of oats. "Speaking of eating, what are you doing next Tuesday? Daphne and I were thinking about catching dinner and then hitting a couple of art openings. Wanna join us?"

"Oh...I, uh...can't. Sorry." Lucy felt her ears burn, just as they had when she'd lied to Cam. Gabby, however, was twice as observant—but only a fraction as gracious—as he had been.

"What's the matter? You look guilty," she accused. "What are you up to, anyway?"

"Nothing." Lucy tried to sound convincing, but she could feel herself break into a sweat. She'd always been a terrible liar. "I'm just meeting with a client, that's all."

"A client? Right. You never meet with clients at night."

"Well, there's a first time for everything." Lucy kept her tone light. There was nothing unusual about going out of her way for a client, she told herself. If she just pretended everything was normal, maybe Gabrielle would give up and leave her alone.

"I suppose." Gabby still looked unconvinced but apparently decided the topic wasn't worth pursuing. "Well then, Daph and I will pick up something for you, if you like, and swing it by the office. How late are you going to be here?"

Lucy tried to keep a straight face. "You don't have to do that."

"It's no bother. What do you want us to bring?"

She swallowed hard. This was why lying was such a big mistake. It always got out of hand. One fib led to another, then to another...until she finally had to come clean and suffer the consequences. Might as well confess now.

"If you must know," she said a bit huffily, "it's a dinner meeting." Surely Gabby would get the hint and let the subject drop.

Unfortunately, Gabby wasn't the hint-taking type.

"A dinner meeting?" she snorted. "Since when do you *do* dinner meetings? It's completely against every policy you have. Not that you have that many policies." She looked at Lucy incredulously. After a moment her eyes narrowed. "Wait a minute. Who's this meeting with?"

"Um..."

"Out with it, Paper Clip Head."

"Oh, all right," Lucy sighed. "I don't know why you're making such a big deal out of this. I'm meeting with Campbell Howard to find out what he's looking for in a woman." Lucy swallowed hard, hating the way that had come out. "For my research, I mean. You know, just the usual, basic info gathering. There. Are you happy?"

"You and Campbell Howard?" Gabby waved one slim, tanned forefinger at her. "You and the geek? Are you pulling one over on me?"

"Well...," Lucy said haltingly. "For one thing, it's just a meeting. There's no 'me and the geek,' as you so elegantly put it. No romance involved. Nada. Nyet. The guy wants me to find him a wife, for goodness' sake."

"Maybe he'd like to find you," Gabby suggested with a leer.

"Stop it, Gabs," Lucy said. It was normal for her to feel a bit protective of her clients, but this time the feeling was especially strong. "I wish you wouldn't talk about him like that.

He's a nice guy, really, though a bit irritating. Besides…" *Go on. Out with it, she ordered herself.* "I have to admit, Cam's not really such a nerd. In fact, he's really rather attractive."

"Now it's Cam, is it? I see." Gabby folded her arms. "How attractive, exactly, are we talking here?"

"I'd say…somewhere between Robert Redford and Barney Rubble," Lucy said evasively.

"Oh really?" Gabby pondered this. "As cute as that? You know how I looove Barney."

"Watch yourself. Barney's married," Lucy chastised.

"Indeed. And it looks as though Dr. Campbell Howard will be married soon, too, if my boss has anything to say about it," Gabby teased, then jumped to her feet and began a childish dance around the room. "Lu-cy li-ikes Camp-bell. Lu-cy li-ikes Caaaaaamp-bell," she sang in her best little-girl voice.

"Gab-by needs a ref-erence," Lucy countered.

"You can't fire me," Gabby said confidently, knowing full well the emptiness of Lucy's threat. "I know the truth. Plus, I can help you in your scheme. Pretty generous of me, I must say, considering that you tried to hide this one from me in the first place. But I'm a forgiving sort. I'll help you get your man."

"*You'll* help *me* get *my* man?" Lucy stared at her. "And just who do you think is the matchmaker here?"

"Save it, sister. It's about time someone stepped in and rescued you from yourself."

"And just what is that supposed to mean?"

"It means that for years you've been letting all the gorgeous, eligible single men in this city slip through your fingers," Gabby said matter-of-factly, "and I'm not going to let it happen again."

"Maybe I didn't want any of those men to stick to my fingers," Lucy grumbled.

"Maybe."

"And maybe I don't want this one, either. Did you ever think of that?"

"Think what you want. But De-nile ain't just a river in Egypt, Luce."

Lucy rolled her eyes. "Spare me your two-cent analysis. I don't need you to tell me I'm in denial."

"True." Gabby grinned and gave her a look of smug satisfaction. "I'm an amateur therapist, anyway. We'll leave the in-depth analysis to your future husband." She smirked. "Dr. Campbell Howard!"

Lucy settled her chin into the palms of her hands and gave a heavy sigh. *Lord, spare us,* she prayed, *from nosy friends, from amateurs at love…*

…and from well-meaning matchmakers.

Cam Howard sat in the driver's seat of his Toyota RAV 4 sport-utility truck, staring blankly at the instrument panel. Beneath his hand the key hung in the ignition, waiting to be turned. He was already running late for an appointment at the research lab, but strangely Cam felt no motivation to go anywhere— except right back up to the office of the bright-eyed, fiery-tempered yenta who had taken his predictable day and turned it completely upside down. Cam's hand dropped.

What he'd said to Lucy was true. He'd been dreading the meeting all week. No doubt he'd shown up a half-hour late in a passive aggressive attempt to botch the entire deal. Alex had been nagging him to go for so long he had figured he'd finally do it just to please her. But showing up was as far as he had been willing to extend the olive branch. He had no intention of being married off, especially for the sake of money. He wasn't even interested, really, in going on any dates. He didn't want anyone to get hurt—least of all himself. Why even head down that path when he hadn't any plans to go where it led?

It wasn't that Cam considered marriage a bad thing; he was actually quite a fan of the institution. His parents had been happily married as far as he could recall. And he planned—or at least hoped—to make wedded bliss a part of his life one day in the future. But for now he was focused only on his work. It kept him too busy to be lonely for long.

Lucy was right about one thing: He was a bad risk for her clients. He wasn't serious about finding someone right now. Certainly not just for the sake of getting his inheritance. But actual love—love that happened of its own accord—well, that was something else, something he might actually consider if the circumstances were right. He wouldn't mind finding someone to care for, someone who cared about him. Someone smart and funny and beautiful and strong-willed...someone a bit like Lucy.

Cam blinked. The thought caught him off guard. Lucy. If there ever had been an unlikely candidate for a girlfriend, it was she. When he first walked into her office, he'd been certain that she was nursing the king of all hangovers. Even now, he didn't know what the problem had been, but he'd been close enough to see that her eyes weren't bloodshot, and there was no trace of alcohol on her breath. She'd sounded sincere when assuring him of her sobriety and had quickly roused from her semistupor. No, whatever it had been, it wasn't from drinking. He was convinced.

Once she raised her head from the desk, Cam completely forgot about her problem. His attention immediately was captured by the vulnerable look in her sapphire blue eyes. Her dark, tousled curls had fallen over one eye, and he'd struggled to keep from reaching out and sweeping them to one side. Under his hand, the skin of her forearm felt warm, and he'd released her as soon as he was sure she was in no physical danger.

It was her smile, though—her innocent, wide-eyed smile—that completely disarmed him. When she first peeked up at him, Lucy had given Cam a look that seemed almost one of recognition. She appeared delighted to see him, filled with trust. That look had melted his heart. So much so, in fact, that when she finally learned who he was—and then abruptly turned on him—he had been at a complete loss as to how to respond.

She'd addressed him as Howard, not Campbell, at first. He'd liked it so much he figured he would have changed his name if that's what Lucy wanted to call him. "Howard Howard." Now wouldn't that be nice? Cam shook his head. The woman had gotten to him, that was for sure.

"I'm not going to let you—or anyone else—take advantage of my clients," Lucy had told him angrily. She was a tigress, all right. A fighter. He'd have to be careful not to get on her bad side. And it would be hard not to if he stayed on as a client—Lucy would know soon enough if he was sincere about finding a wife. *"I can tell the difference between someone who's serious about finding another person to give love to and someone who's out to get his own selfish needs met,"* she'd told him forcefully. Cam wasn't sure he wanted her—or even himself—to find out what the truth might be. He wasn't terribly comfortable staying on as a client. But if he quit now, surely Lucy would be convinced that she'd been right about him all along—that this was nothing more to him than a game. The only other option was to express his intentions toward Lucy herself. But that seemed like the worst idea of all—especially since even Cam didn't yet know what those intentions might be.

An insistent ringing interrupted his thoughts, and Cam reluctantly grabbed his cell phone from the seat beside him and flipped it open.

"Cam Howard here," he said gruffly. "Oh. Hi, Alex." His face flushed, and he looked around as if his older sister might be right outside the vehicle watching him, reading his mind. "Yeah, I just left her office. What?" Cam took a deep breath. "Yeah. I decided I'll do it," he said quietly but firmly. He pulled the phone away from him as Alexandra's joyful screech pierced his ear. "But on one condition," he said, moving the phone back to his lips. "We're doing things my way. No more meddling from this point on, okay? Why?" Cam hesitated. "Let's just say I want to be very careful about this. Because—and even I can't believe I'm saying this, Alex—I think this whole little plot of yours may lead to something good after all."

Three

"Whatcha doin'?" Gabby pushed her way, unannounced, through Lucy's office door—an enormous chocolate-and-marshmallow Moon Pie clutched in one hand. She stared incredulously at the pale green and orange objects on the corner of Lucy's desk. "Good grief, are those carrots? And celery?"

Lucy did not move, keeping her feet in position on top of her desk and her eyes trained on the file in her hand. "Very good, Gabs. How'd you know? I was certain you'd never seen a vegetable in your life." She glanced up at her friend and gave her a look of disgust. "And look at you! Stick thin. You make me sick. What's your secret?"

Gabby flashed her a million-dollar grin. "Just good, clean living I guess."

"Ha, ha. Good one," Lucy quipped. "If you didn't want to tell me, all you had to do was say so." She turned back to the papers she'd been perusing.

"At the risk of repeating myself, whatcha doin'?" Gabby leaned her lanky body over the desk, trying to sneak a peek at the contents of the manila folder held by her boss.

Lucy cast her a derisive look. "If you must know, little Miss Nosy, I'm trying to find some potential matches for Dr. Campbell Howard."

"Oh, really? For Dr. Howard, eh?" Gabby clapped her hands together in mock delight. "This should be good." She snatched up two folders Lucy had already deposited on the desk. "Monica Valentine…Donna Dillard." The files fell to the desktop with a slap. "Reject pile," she noted.

"What?" Lucy opened her eyes wide. "Don't be silly. Those are the keepers."

"Excuse me?" Gabrielle grunted. Lucy looked up to see her cramming one slim finger into her ear and wiggling it vigorously. "Sorry, I thought you said these were the keepers," she said.

"Oh, for crying out loud," Lucy grumbled. She closed the file she held. "Okay, I'll bite, since you're going to tell me what you think whether I want you to or not. What's wrong with Monica and Donna?"

"Are you kidding?" Gabby dropped into a chair dramatically, as if her explanation might take awhile. "Where do I even start?"

"I don't know. Why don't—"

"How about with Monica?" Gabby rubbed her hands together like a mad scientist, relishing her role.

"All right."

"All right, then. Monica Valentine." Gabby looked at Lucy grimly. "In a word? Brr."

Lucy tilted her head to one side and raised an eyebrow. "Brr?"

"Yes." Gabby nodded vehemently. "Brr. I've always said it would take years to find a man who could thaw her out."

Lucy shook her head. "Oh, come on. She's not that bad. Is she?"

Gabby stared her down. "Ever hear of Frosty the Snowman?"

"Yes."

"Mr. Freeze?"

"Mm-hm."

"The Abominable Snowman?"

"Uh-huh."

Gabby closed her eyes solemnly. "Amateurs," she said, then took another gooey bite of Moon Pie.

Lucy grimaced. "Oh, stop it. You're exaggerating."

"I'm serious," Gabby mumbled. "I'm catching a cold just thinking about her."

Lucy considered her assistant's words. Granted, Monica was a bit on the cool side, but she also had many other qualifications men desired: looks, brains, poise.

"And let's not forget," Gabby said in her know-it-all tone of voice, "that she hates men."

That was pushing the issue too far. "Don't be ridiculous!" Lucy argued. "She came here to find a match, didn't she? Does that sound like the actions of a woman who hates men?" The slim brunette gave her an incredulous look. "What? Okay, I'll admit, she's a bit of a feminist."

"Lucy," Gabby said patiently. "*I* am a feminist. I believe in social, political, and economic rights for women equal to those of men. I've even been known to speak on behalf of, and fight for, those rights. But I am not a militant feminist, which our friend Monica is. Trust me; I've heard her talk. She hates men."

Lucy still was not convinced, but she didn't want to argue any further.

"Whatever," she grumbled. "What about Donna? You cer tainly can't say she hates men."

"Are you kidding?" Gabby chortled. She coughed, sputtered, and nearly choked on her Moon Pie. "She loves men. She loves them so much, she'd do anything to get one! Face it, Luce. Donna would take any match you sent her way, as long as he was male."

"Then she and Cam will be perfect for each other," Lucy said irritably, tired of being second-guessed. "Since he wants a wife just for the purpose of getting his inheritance, I suppose any woman will do."

"You don't really believe that's true." Gabby shook her head. "If you did, you wouldn't have taken him as a client in the first place. I know you better than that."

Lucy kicked her feet off the desk and dropped them to the floor, leaned forward, and rested her chin in her hands. "To tell you the truth, I don't know what I think, Gabby. He may be sincere enough, but I can't really be sure." She'd been thinking about her newest client all weekend. Never before had she felt so curious and confused about someone who had come to her for help. She'd hoped that she would be able to come into the office on Monday morning, scan through a few files, find the right woman, and be done with it. Back to business as usual. Why did this all have to be so hard?

"You were sure enough about Cam to sign him up as a client," Gabby pointed out. "That counts for something."

"I guess it does." Lucy nodded. "I guess I am jumping the gun a little bit—I haven't even interviewed him yet. I'm sure when the time is right, I'll find him a lovely woman." She was starting to have her doubts though. Usually she had strong feelings right away about who a client should be paired with— or at least what sort of person would be right for him or her. With Cam, however, she was coming up with no strong feelings one way or another. "You worry too much, Gabby," she said, wanting to get back to the task at hand. "Donna is a perfectly nice person."

Gabby nodded. "And according to you, Cam is too. I'm sure they'll be quite happy together."

Lucy's face clouded over at the thought.

54

"Aha!" Gabby sat up straight and jabbed one crumb-covered finger in Lucy's direction. "I knew it! You do like him!"

"I do not!" Lucy protested.

"Oh, yeah?" Gabrielle challenged. "Then why are you trying to sabotage his dates?"

Lucy was appalled. "I can't believe you'd even suggest such a thing! Sabotage? Why don't you just call the Better Business Bureau and turn me in? Get it all over with?"

"Very dramatic," Gabby said smoothly. "But I don't think it's as serious as all that. Maybe you're just having an off day—or week. Why don't you let me pitch in? I can think of at least one woman who would be perfect for our fine doctor," she said helpfully.

Lucy's eyes narrowed to slits. "Don't even think about it." She wasn't about to let Gabby play matchmaker with her.

Gabrielle sighed. "Relax. You're not the only woman in the world, you know."

"Oh." Lucy considered this for a moment. Her cheeks flushed as she realized her mistake. Almost immediately, however, her embarrassment gave way to feelings of protection toward Cam. "Gabby—" Lucy didn't like where this line of conversation was leading. "I'm not setting him up with you," she warned.

"Thanks for the compliment." Her friend rolled her eyes. "But actually, I was thinking that maybe Janie McCallister would be a good match for Cam."

Lucy squirmed in her seat. She didn't like the sound of that at all. "No. I'm sure that wouldn't be a good idea."

"Why not?" Gabby looked confused. "She's gorgeous, smart...has a great personality. You've said all along that you wanted to find Janie someone really wonderful. You like Janie."

It was true. Janie McCallister was one of the most likable women ever to have utilized Lucy's service. She was also breathtakingly beautiful, with classic features and a mane of gold—and she was a brilliant, well-educated lawyer, with a fantastic win record. The woman had high morals and was reported to win her cases with completely honest tactics. Best of all, she had a strong faith in God and wanted nothing more than to live within his will. On the surface, she seemed perfect for Cam.

But in Lucy's heart, the pairing felt all wrong.

It had occurred to her earlier in the morning that Cam and Janie might be well-suited for each other, but she had quickly dismissed the thought. The truth was, she did have strong feelings about Cam's potential match, and every instinct argued against fixing him up with Janie McCallister. The woman was wrong for him. She had to be. It was as simple as that.

"Liking Janie isn't the point," Lucy said casually. "The point is she and Cam would never work out."

"Do tell." Gabby gave her a look of great interest. "And why, exactly, is that?"

Lucy licked her dry lips. "Because he's so..." She tried again, "Janie just has this way about her that I think he'd..." Feeling suddenly like a trapped animal, she averted her gaze. "I don't know. It just wouldn't be right. I feel it."

"You feel it, huh? If you want to know what I think—"

"I don't," Lucy said dully.

"—I think you like Cam," Gabby said, ignoring her protest.

"Gabrielle, I—"

"And furthermore, I think you want to save him for yourself!"

Lucy stood abruptly and slapped one hand on her desk. "Do you mind?"

"I'm just making a simple observation," Gabby said calmly, unfazed by her reaction. "If you want to deny it, that's your business."

"Yes. It is my business," Lucy said huffily. She planted both fists on the desk, assuming a posture of control. "And so is Rent-a-Yenta. So if you don't mind, I think I'll make the decisions about matching people up."

"Fine, fine. I can take a hint." Gabby tossed her long, dark hair over her shoulder with one hand, popped the last gooey bit of pie in her mouth with the other, and rose regally from her chair. Most people would have been offended by the tone Lucy had taken, but it didn't seem to have ruffled Gabrielle's feathers in the slightest. "Do what you want. Set the guy up with whomever you choose." She turned on her heel and threw one last warning over her shoulder. "But don't come to me all upset when things don't turn out the way you'd planned."

When Gabby had finally stepped out the door, Lucy took a deep breath and sat back in her soft black leather chair.

She'd thought Gabby would never leave. But even though her physical presence was gone, the memory of her words lingered.

And Lucy couldn't help wondering if, for once, her outspoken assistant wasn't right after all.

"More tea?"

"Mmm? Oh yes. Please." Nudged from her reverie, Lucy gratefully relinquished the small teapot to her efficient young waitress: barely more than fifteen, Lucy guessed, but already more gracious and gifted at serving than she ever hoped to become. She watched closely as the young Chinese woman swept the pot away with a polite half-bow and a fleeting smile on her ruby red lips.

Lucy peered at her carefully as she made her retreat. Thankfully, there was no sign that the girl thought her odd for drinking the entire contents of the teapot by herself. It was bad enough that Lucy had been sitting there alone for more than half an hour, worrying. She didn't need anyone to think she had been stood up. Whatever had possessed her to come to the restaurant so early? When she'd arrived, her black suit was pressed, her makeup fresh, and her hair fluffed, puffed, and well sprayed. Now she felt generally lumpy, wrinkled, sweaty, and limp. So much for being prepared. That Boy Scout motto was highly overrated.

She'd been inexplicably nervous about this meeting all day. Normally she was completely composed with her clients, but this one made her nervous. She'd tried to figure a way to regain her sense of control. Naively she had thought it would make her feel more relaxed to arrive before Cam did. That way she could spread her things out on the table, make it "her" territory, giving her the home-court advantage. She had pictured the scene clearly in her mind's eye: Cam would arrive a couple of minutes late and slightly out of breath. Embarrassed by his tardiness, he would fall all over himself with apologies. She, in turn, would laugh confidently—unconcerned—and explain that she hadn't even noticed, she'd been so immersed in her book—one of the classics: *The Brothers Karamazov* or *Don Quixote* perhaps.

Fearing that she'd look too studious, however—too much like a coed—she considered sitting at the table and poring over client profiles—ever the devoted professional. But that was no good, either, she finally decided. It would simply make her look like she had no life outside of work—somewhat true but hardly appealing.

Not that being found appealing by Cam was the point, Lucy reminded herself. He was a client, nothing more. Why had Gabby filled her mind with such thoughts? Before she'd left the office that day, her assistant had attempted one last time to make Lucy see things her way.

"Make sure you take complete notes on everything this guy says," she instructed, "so we can use all this information to your advantage."

"And what is that supposed to mean?" Lucy asked, managing to sound quietly offended, although it was perfectly clear what Gabby was saying.

"It means you're going to snag this one, of course! And you call yourself a matchmaker?" Gabby snorted.

"Uh...I call myself ethical. And I call *you* deluded."

"Well, I call myself a realist. And if you are realistically going to catch this fish, my friend, you're going to have to use the right bait. Find out what he likes, what he wants, what makes this guy sit up and say, 'Hubba-hubba.'"

"Gabby," Lucy grumbled in frustration. "Forget it. For the last time, I am not going to 'catch this fish.'"

"I'd think twice if I were you. Remember: Men want to be caught," Gabby said stubbornly. "Especially this one. He's paying you to find him a mate, for crying out loud. And he stands to gain mega-dollars if you do."

Lucy's heart sank. "That's a horrible thing to say—even if it's true." She lifted her upper lip in distaste, like a horse whinnying. Inside, she felt her stomach muscles tighten. Gabby was trying her best to encourage her to pursue Cam, but she was really just reminding Lucy of all the reasons she never could.

"Come on, tell me the truth," Gabby said, giving her one last pleading smile. "You like him, at least a little bit." She held out one thumb and forefinger to indicate how much Lucy was supposed to care.

"Oh, all right," Lucy said, relenting at last. "I will admit one thing, and only one, but only to make you feel better. I'm not saying I like him, but…I do think Cam is a nice guy," she said softly, then continued with a rush, "assuming he's telling the truth and his motives are clean regarding this money thing, of course."

"I thought so." Gabby grinned. "Tell me what you like about him."

"Gabby—" Lucy looked away.

"Come on. Humor me. My life is so empty. I take all the perks I can get."

"I…" She paused. "I can't explain it. I tried to turn him down…tried to get him to leave. But he actually stood up to me. And the way he did it was just so…so…"

"Attractive?" Gabby suggested.

"Has anyone ever told you that you have a one-track mind?" Lucy glowered at her but gave in. "Actually, it was more endearing than attractive, I'd say. And, well, sweet in a way. But yes, he is quite gorgeous too—which only makes this whole situation more difficult!" The statement was the closest she'd come to confessing her feelings outright, and Gabby seized it.

"What's so hard about it? I mean, you like the guy. Maybe he likes you."

"Oh, I don't know about that." Lucy felt a twinge of something that felt like delight. What if Gabby was right? "And even if it was true, so what?" She tried to sound as if she didn't care. She didn't, did she? She couldn't.

"So?" Gabby gave her a look of exasperation. "So…go in for the kill!"

"Delicately put," Lucy said dryly. "But you're missing the point. I do know a lot about this guy already, and I'm going to know more very soon. He's trusting me with the most private details of his life, and I have to honor that trust. Besides, he doesn't want a woman to date him because of his money—Alexandra made that perfectly clear. Face it, Gabby. I know too much about him for him to ever feel comfortable seeing me on a personal basis. He'd only think I was after his inheritance.

"And that's another thing—this business about his inheritance. I don't like it. The whole situation makes him sound like a moneygrubber, no matter what his excuse. He seems nice enough, but you just never know." She shook her head. "I'm just not sure about him."

"Lucy, how can he be a moneygrubber? It's *his* money."

"Not yet it's not. And I'm not going to let him use anyone—me or one of my clients—to get what he wants."

The conversation had taken place just two hours earlier, and still it haunted Lucy. Glancing at her watch, then the door, for perhaps the fortieth time that evening, she tried to brace herself for Cam's imminent arrival. The waitress had not yet returned with her tea, and with nothing to drink, she felt unsure of what to do with her hands. Unfortunately, her plan of reading or studying files had fallen flat. In her rush to get to the restaurant early, she had inconveniently forgotten both *The Brothers Karamazov* and her briefcase. She gripped the small, round, nearly empty teacup with one hand and swished it around in the air, making kaleidoscope-type patterns in the chopped-up tea leaves still at the bottom. She stared at them, and it struck her that they looked like a Rorschach ink blot— perhaps whatever she saw in them would reveal something about the hidden depths of her psyche.

Vigorously she spun the cup, intrigued by the thought. The chopped-up leaves settled in the remaining golden drops of tea, making two distinct pools of black specks, distributed, she thought, in the shape of heads—one slightly larger than the other. *That's the man,* Lucy thought, considering the larger blob. *And that's the woman.* She wondered absently what would happen if she turned the cup to one side and made one blob bump up next to the other. It was certainly worth a try.

"Hello, Lucy." Cam's rich, warm baritone broke into her thoughts. Immediately embarrassed at being caught causing "tea faces" to kiss, Lucy jumped up and smashed her head into the hanging light directly above the table.

"Ouch!" she cried. Both hands flew to her head, causing her to drop the cup she held in her hands.

"Ouch!" Cam echoed as the pottery fell five and a half feet before landing hard on his foot.

Lucy's face distorted with horror, her eyes open in an expression of disbelief. Mortified, she stared at him. But in that brief second, despite her pain, she couldn't help but notice that Cam actually was more attractive than she remembered—even with a scowl on his face. Dressed in olive green corduroy pants and a beige button-down shirt over a white T-shirt, with his eyeglasses perched precariously on his nose, he looked both masculine and scholarly. It was a good look for him. Perhaps reading a book would have been the right choice after all.

"Oh! I'm so sorry!" Ignoring her own throbbing head, Lucy bent over halfway and held her hands helplessly over Cam's foot while the copper lamp swung wildly above them. Within seconds the tiny young waitress was beside them, her own hands flapping like birds in the air. All around them, customers gaped.

"It's all right." Cam laughed as he spoke to Lucy and the waitress, who had bent over to pick up the cup. "Just a bump, I promise." He glanced around at the watching crowd. "Show's over, folks," he said good-naturedly. "Nothing to see here. You can go back to your dinners." Several people grinned; others simply turned away, not getting the joke. But all seemed to lose interest after seeing there was no bloodshed.

After muttering something in Chinese that Lucy could not understand, the waitress, too, scurried away, leaving her to face Cam alone.

"Uh...whoops," she said sheepishly, trying not to show how humiliated she felt. "Sorry about that. You, uh, startled me."

"Don't worry. It happens all the time," Cam assured her soothingly. "I have that effect on women. They see me, jump up in shock, try to run away..."

"I wasn't running away," Lucy said defensively. "I was just surprised, that's all."

"I see." Campbell nodded seriously. "Except...wait, I could have sworn we had an appointment—"

Lucy glared at him. "Stop it!" She playfully slapped him on the arm, then immediately regretted it when his eyes lit up. *Oops. That was definitely flirting. Better stop it, Luce, before this gets out of your control.* "If you insist on teasing me," she sniffed, turning away, "I'll have to charge hazard pay."

"Well, we wouldn't want that." Keeping his eyes on her, Cam motioned to the booth. Obligingly, Lucy took her seat, and he followed suit. Overhead, the lamp still swung gently.

Within seconds the waitress was back at their table with fresh tea and a pair of menus. Grateful for the distraction, Lucy clutched hers in one hand and read through all five pages, considering each menu item, while using the time to regain her composure.

"I hear their Mu-Shu pork is excellent," she said, feeling suddenly thankful for the shelter of small talk. For several minutes she carried the conversation on in that vein, feigning great interest in the restaurant's famed General Tso's chicken and crisp spring rolls.

Quietly Cam listened as she prattled on, asking a polite question now and then regarding her favorite menu items.

"Did you bring your famous chopsticks?" she asked at last. Cam patted his pocket proudly. "You'd better believe it." "I don't. Prove it," she ordered.

Obediently he pulled out two wooden sticks wrapped in a paper sheath and laid them on the smooth Formica tabletop.

"That's it?" Lucy didn't even try to hide her disappointment. "They look like regular old chopsticks to me."

"What did you expect?" Cam threw her a look that made it clear he considered her a novice. "Excalibur?"

Lucy shrugged. "Whatever. I don't get it. Must be a guy thing."

He grinned. "Actually, I snagged these when I came in," he admitted. "Mine are, uh...at the repair shop."

She raised one eyebrow. "What's wrong with them?"

He nodded soberly. "Splinters. It's pretty serious."

Lucy managed to look grim. "I'm so sorry."

"Thanks."

When the waitress came back, they placed their order. Since the portions were huge, they decided to split an order of sweet and sour chicken with extra steamed rice. After the waitress left, Lucy decided to take the meeting in hand.

"I'm afraid I forgot my briefcase, so this interview won't be as formal as I might like. I can still ask you several questions, however, just to find out the basics: you know, your background, what you're looking for in a mate."—*Your vital statistics, what you do to make your hair look so soft and touchable...Stop it, Luce!*—"your emotional availability." She blushed. "Although I'd imagine that as a therapist, you have any major issues worked out already."

"You'd imagine," Cam said mischievously.

Lucy gave him a sidelong glance but decided he was kidding and let the comment pass. Drawing a deep breath, she prepared for what was usually an enjoyable part of the process for her—getting to know her clients on a deeper, more personal basis. Enjoyment wasn't what she was feeling this time though. Fear, confusion, and self-consciousness all hit closer to the mark. What was it about this man that disturbed her so?

"Ahem." She cleared her throat loudly, nervously. "All right then, we might as well get started," she suggested. "Why don't you begin by telling me exactly what you do?" She longed for a notebook and pen to hide behind. In their absence, she was forced to focus solely on Cam's face, its lean lines painting a compelling picture of character and humor and tremendous depth. She fought the urge to look away.

"I'm a behavioral psychologist, actually," he stated simply. Lucy liked how he said it: plainly, without bragging, yet without embarrassment. He might as well have been telling her that he had blond hair, as, indeed, he did. Sun-lightened and thick, it swept across his brow, giving him a rather jaunty look that matched his carefree attitude. *Aren't psychologists supposed to be serious?* Lucy thought defensively.

"A behavioral psychologist," she prompted. "Which means...?"

"In my case it means I look at the reasons why people behave the way they do. I work over at the university with a team currently studying the onset of sudden behavioral quirks. For example, if someone who's very organized becomes forgetful, or a person who's usually very graceful suddenly becomes accident-prone."

Instinctively, Lucy remembered hitting her head on the lamp when Cam arrived. She hated to think what that little episode had revealed about her deepest desires.

"Do you like what you do?" she asked. "Working with 'nut bars,' I mean?"

Cam grinned. "Actually, I love it. But patients don't get

called 'nut bars.' That's an endearment reserved exclusively for family."

"Ah. I see. I'm sure Alexandra feels honored."

"She might, if she knew I'd said it. However, I'd rather we just kept it our little secret." As he spoke, Cam leaned over the table and lowered his voice to a whisper. From that proximity, Lucy could see every line of his features. For a fraction of a second, she imagined herself reaching out and smoothing the tiny wrinkles around his eyes with her fingers.

Swallowing hard, she lowered her hands from the table to the booth's bench seat and tucked them underneath her legs, just to be safe. It wouldn't do for her to lose her composure all at once, like one of Cam's patients.

"My lips are sealed." Instantly regretting the reference to her lips, Lucy noticed Cam's eyes flicker to her mouth, then quickly away.

Was it a trick of the light, or was he the one blushing now?

"What about your family?" she asked. It was an abrupt change of subjects, but she was desperate. "You said you lost your mom when you were just a little boy." Lucy still felt a tightness in her chest as she thought about the loss of her own mother when she was five. Few memories remained, except the impression of a powerful, loving presence; the soft smell of lilac water, which her mother used as perfume; and the remembrance of a warm lap where she was always welcome. Her heart still ached for her mom at times, even twenty-one years later. She envied Cam having known his mother but couldn't help but wonder if it was worse for him to have lost someone he'd known more deeply.

Cam nodded. His expression was serious, but his eyes did not appear haunted as Lucy felt her own must.

"How did it happen?"

"A car accident," he said, meeting her gaze evenly. "There

wasn't any warning. It hit me hard at the time. I spent a long time searching for answers, railing at God. I suppose it was that search for answers that led me, in part, to study psychology."

"But answers come from God, not from man, don't you think?" Lucy felt uncomfortable. Perhaps she didn't have the strongest faith in the world, but at least she knew what she believed. After what he'd said last week about admiring her faith, she'd assumed that Cam came from a similar place.

"I believe everything that is good and true comes from God," Cam agreed. "Psychology isn't my religion; it's my work. I know the difference. If I look to psychology for fulfillment, I'm going to come away empty. But if I use it to understand myself better, to help me know what drives me, motivates me…makes me who I am, then I can use it as a tool to help me relate better to God, to understand what's real and true. That's what I believe."

Lucy thought about this for a minute. She'd never been especially comfortable straying outside the lines in life. She knew what her boundaries were—social, religious, moral—and she did her best to stay within them. Yet at the same time, she generally didn't feel judgmental toward others. She'd represented clients of every religion she could imagine and had shared with them as much as she could about her faith. But in the end, she knew the decision was their own, and there was nothing more she could do for them but pray. It's wasn't her job to save them; it was her job to love them, and she did that the very best she could.

But for some reason, Cam's beliefs mattered a great deal more to her than any other client's had. It wasn't that she didn't believe in psychology; she actually knew it to be very helpful and had known dozens of people whose lives were transformed by short-term and long-term therapy. But she knew psychology could be not only a help, but a trap or a crutch; and it seemed inexplicably important to her to know that Cam understood the difference.

"So the ultimate goal is...what? Making people healthy again?"

He thought about this. "It depends on what you mean by healthy. A lot of times people bury feelings like fear, guilt, anger, and anxiety. When they don't deal with these emotions in a productive way, they find another way to express them through psychological neuroses or physical manifestations like stomachaches, headaches, or even worse: disease. It's actually good when people start showing signs that there's some inner trouble because then we can help them deal with it. Hopefully, before it permanently affects their physical health.

"The point isn't to make those feelings go away, but to help that client accept and face that emotion and to discover the situation that caused it as well as the gifts it brings."

"Even horrible situations, like divorce...or death?" It sounded absurd. What were the gifts in those?

"Even horrible situations." Cam nodded. "Once people know what they feel—no matter what it is—then they can start to understand their emotions...and share them with God. And once we're honest with God, then we can truly be healthy and truly find peace."

Feeling satisfied that Cam had his priorities in order, Lucy began to relax. Before she had an opportunity to ask any further questions, however, their food arrived.

Giving Lucy a look that communicated concern about whatever disaster might be coming next, the waitress lowered two steaming plates piled high with tender chicken and bright, glistening vegetables. Bowls heaped with white rice followed, along with yet another pot of golden Chinese tea.

"So...tell me a little bit about yourself," Lucy said, nervously pouring the tea. "I know a bit about your family, and I know what you do now. But what are you like as a person? If I talked to close friends who had known you five, ten years, what would they say about you?" Feeling pleasantly in control at last, she dug into her mound of food with her fork—having decided she wasn't proficient enough with chopsticks to use them without embarrassing herself. The first bite was incredible, sweet and tangy and something else she couldn't quite identify.

"Well, you're really putting me on the spot. I wasn't prepared for that question."

Lucy swallowed. "That's the point," she told him honestly. "I don't want people to tell me what they think I want to hear. I want to know the truth—the good, the bad, and the ugly. That's the only way I can help." Hungrily she took another bite, followed by another.

"I'll try to oblige," Cam said wryly. "Let's see...what my closest friends would say? Hmm. That's tough. I suppose they'd say I am loyal, almost to a fault. I'm playful. I like the outdoors. I'm friendly. I like to go for walks—"

"Add 'drink out of the toilet,'" Lucy mumbled around a mouthful of rice, "and you'll make a fine golden retriever."

"No fair," Cam complained. "You try describing yourself sometime. It's not as easy as it sounds."

"I could do it...if I wanted to." As soon as the first few words were out of her mouth, Lucy knew she had made a mistake.

"All right, then. Go ahead."

"Uh..." She reached for her glass of water and took a long sip, buying time.

"Go on. I'm fascinated. Really." Cam settled back, arms folded. He was obviously enjoying this.

"Well...I'm fun, I guess," she began nervously, wiping her hands on the pink paper napkin in front of her.

"That's true." He reached for his own napkin and pretended to write on it with an imaginary pencil. "I'll vouch for that."

She giggled. "Uh...I'm a go-getter."

"Obviously." Cam continued to take notes.

Lucy was beginning to feel a bit more confident now. "And I've been told that I'm just a little bit wacko."

"Conceded," Cam said with a nod.

"Conceited?" Lucy's mouth flew open. Did he actually add *conceited* to the list? Suddenly she didn't feel relaxed anymore. She felt downright furious. Of all the nerve! She sat up straight and gave him a look as black as death. "Why, you! I can't believe you actually said that to me! And you want me to fix you up with one of my clients? You wish!" Ungracefully she started to crawl her way out of her seat. "I knew this was a mistake! Why, you're even worse than I thought! Of all the rude—"

"No, no!" Cam protested, waving his arms in the air. "I said *conceded,* as in, 'I concede your point.'"

"—sophomoric, egotistical—what?" Lucy froze in place as his words finally sank in. "Oh. Conceded. Well." She swallowed hard. "Of course, that makes more sense. Given the context of the conversation."

"Let's see. *Par...a...noid,*" Cam spoke slowly, pretending to add to his list on the napkin.

"All right, all right." Lucy was beginning to wonder if maybe he had a point. Reluctantly she crawled back into the booth.

"Now what was all that about?" Cam spoke in a reasonable tone, but Lucy had difficulty meeting his eyes.

"I'm so embarrassed."

"You keep saying that," Cam observed. "What's that feeling about?"

The question made her feel like she was his own personal lab rat. "Are you taking notes for your study?" Lucy said glumly.

"Only if you want me to." She couldn't tell if he was serious or not.

"Nah. I'll take a rain check." Lucy stared at her hands. What was the matter with her? Why was she reacting so strongly to this man? It couldn't be those wayward thoughts about dating him, could it? She knew better than to entertain fantasies like that.

"I'm not sure what the problem is, exactly," she explained at last. "It's just that you…you make me nervous." It was true. Even her skin felt prickly. She resisted the urge to scratch.

"Nervous. How?"

"Like I'm afraid to trust you, even though I want to. It's not normal for me to feel this way," she assured him. He must have thought she was an idiot. "Usually I know right away whether I think someone is trustworthy or not. I have very good instincts." She jutted her chin in the direction of his napkin. "You can add that to your list of notes if you want."

But Cam was through playing their little game. "Why are you afraid you can't trust me?" he said, his voice soft and low.

"Because of this whole stupid money thing." Lucy breathed a sigh of relief. It felt good to finally just say what she had been thinking all week. "I know you say you don't care about the inheritance and that you don't even care, really, whether or not you find a wife. In fact," she eyed him curiously, "you don't seem overly interested in finding a mate at all. If I'm not mistaken, you said this whole thing was pretty much for Alexandra's benefit."

Cam nodded.

"And even though it probably sounds strange coming from me—a matchmaker who is supposed to be finding you a

71

wife—I'd like to believe you're not serious about finding some-one because it means there's no chance of your using her. But I'm not sure what to think—and there's so much at stake, you know? But even if I can believe you, that means you're just going through the motions and that I probably shouldn't be working with you at all. If I introduce you to someone, she's going to get emotionally involved. She could easily start to care about you. What if this is just a game to you? What if you turn out to be a jerk? What happens then?" Lucy felt as if she might cry.

Cam looked at her gently. "It sounds like you feel very strongly about this."

"I do," she said, wondering why she sounded—and felt—so forlorn.

"Why is this so personal for you?"

"Personal?" Lucy looked up sharply. "I never said it was personal."

"It sure sounds like it is."

With her words still echoing in her ears, Lucy had to admit he was right. She wasn't about to tell him the complete truth, though: that she had been left at the altar years before and was now determined to make sure none of her clients was ever burned that badly. "Well, I care because this company, this service, represents me, I guess. I don't want anyone to get hurt." The explanation sounded flat.

Cam didn't push the issue. "All right, then. You've explained why you're not sure you can trust me. But you said too—twice, in fact—that you want to be able to. I'm curious. Why?"

Lucy felt her throat constrict slightly. She still felt nervous, itchy. She gave in to the urge to scratch her arm. Why did she want to trust Cam? It was a good question and one that had no ready answer. For four years now she'd been interview-ing potential clients. Some she felt good about; others, she did not. She just felt what she felt and made her decisions accordingly.

This time, things were different. Everything inside her called for her to trust this man—this adorable, infuriating man—who sat before her. Why couldn't she? And what did it matter if she didn't?

"I'm afraid I can't answer that," she said helplessly. The constriction in her throat was getting worse. So was the itchiness that made her want to scratch. Reaching for any distraction, she took another forkful of chicken and rice, but could just barely choke it down.

It wasn't really an answer, but Cam seemed satisfied.

"What about you?" he asked, deftly steering the conversation to other subjects. "I know you have three sisters. Any brothers?"

"Nope," she said, grateful for the change in topic. She scratched her neck now. Her throat still felt tight. "Everyone in the family was in that picture. Except for Fee's and Cat's husbands, of course, and Felicia's children, Clifford and Dinah. That's all of us. I'm an orphan, too, like you." She said it lightly, but Cam wasn't fooled.

"Oh, Lucy. I'm so sorry," he said, and she could tell by the tone of his voice that he really was.

"Don't be silly," she told him, shrugging. "I'm fine. I didn't go through anything you didn't, and I don't see you crying. You dealt with it, and you went on. Am I right?" She flashed him her trademark smile, but Cam wasn't buying it.

"I'm still dealing with it," he said simply. "Are you?"

Lucy poked at a bit of chicken with the tip of her fork. Was she dealing with it still? Certainly the loss of her mother impacted every day of her life. Did she think about it? Not often. But no doubt she felt it in some way every day of her life.

"I think that question is a bit personal," she said finally.

"I know it is. Don't worry. You don't have to answer if you don't want to." Cam paused, then said, "Why don't you go back to asking me personal questions?" he said brightly. "You haven't asked whether I squeeze the toothpaste from the end or the middle, or whether I prefer boxers or briefs."

Normally Lucy would have laughed, but she was too busy trying to clear her throat. What was this, some sort of twenty-four-hour, sore-throat germ that had hit all of a sudden? It was getting harder and harder to swallow; she had abandoned her meal completely by now. And the itchiness was almost more than she could take.

"I'm sorry," she said, wrinkling her brow. Even talking was beginning to hurt. "But I'm not feeling well."

"Look, I'm sorry," Cam began. "I shouldn't have pushed. Please stay—"

"No, I'm serious," Lucy said, waving one hand in front of her face. "I really do feel sick. It's so strange—almost like an allergic reaction. I get this way—only much worse—when I eat nuts."

Cam turned pale. "Cashews?"

"Uh-huh." Lucy's breathing was starting to get uneven. "Peanuts and walnuts too. But nobody puts nuts in sweet and sour chicken."

"Um...apparently Mr. Wu did." Nervously Cam held up his fork, which he had used to spear something brown and crunchy.

"But—" Lucy's eyes grew wide as Cam sprang into action. She'd been so busy talking to him, she hadn't noticed what she was putting into her mouth.

"Excuse me!" Cam cried, grabbing their battle-weary waitress by the arm as she passed. "I'm a doctor, and I need you to call 9-1-1 and get an ambulance. This woman is going into

hypophylactic shock." Without a word—but with a reproach-
ful look in Lucy's general direction—the woman ran out of
the room to comply.

Hypo-what? She was pretty sure there was no such thing.
What a bluffer! Lucy raised an arm to reassure Cam, but it
was too late. He was on a roll, and by that time she could no
longer even speak.

Cam grabbed Lucy's arm and pulled her unceremoniously
from the booth. "This is an emergency!" he shouted to no
one in particular as he dragged her to her feet.

And with that, he reached down, swept her up into his
strong arms, and stormed toward the front door.

Four

"Stop it. You're killing me!" Catherine giggled, gripping her side. Peals of laughter rang through the living room like music as Lucy's sisters listened in delight and disbelief to the sorry tale of her night at Mr. Wu's—and at the local emergency room.

As they did every week, the four women had gathered for their traditional Wednesday night "sisters' dinner." This week it was Lucy's turn to serve as hostess—and despite the trauma of the previous night, she had managed to throw together a decent meal of green bean casserole and Shepherd's pie, followed by hot apple crisp smothered in ice cream.

Their hunger more than satiated, the women now were settled in various corners of the living room, scraping up the remaining bits of dessert left in their bowls, determined not to let a single granola crumb or drop of melted vanilla go to waste. Near the window, Cat sat in a tomato red chair with her legs tucked beneath her, looking out over the ocean— something she often did at the beach house to help her unwind from a hectic day at the office.

At one end of the green-and-white striped couch, Daphne lay lazily outstretched, while Lucy hunched uncomfortably into the opposite corner. Several feet away in a battered, green velvet thrift-store chair sat Felicia, looking even more forlorn than usual. Her dark hair hung limp about her ears. Though she wasn't the most fashion conscious of the sisters, she generally looked presentable. Today, however, Lucy wondered if she'd even bothered to drag a comb through her lifeless locks. As Lucy confessed to her sisters what had happened the night before, though, even Fee looked interested.

Ever the entertaining youngest child, Daphne jumped to her feet, stuck her thumbs in the belt loops of her jeans, and strutted across the living room—her short mane of chestnut curls bouncing as she walked. "I'm a doctor!" she announced in an exaggerated attempt at a baritone. She halted abruptly and threw one arm up in the air, as if stopping traffic. "This is an emergency!" she cried. "Get me an ambulance! Call 9-1-1!"

From her position in Lucy's favorite overstuffed chair, beneath a woven afghan, Felicia smiled tremulously, the first positive expression that had appeared on her face all evening. A feeling of relief flooded over Lucy. Seeing Fee smile made Lucy's whole miserable experience worthwhile.

"I'm glad you're all having fun at my expense," she grumbled anyway. "That's the whole reason I exist, you know—to bring you girls enjoyment."

"And you do such a good job of it," Daphne quipped. She flopped back down onto the sofa, dropping her feet unceremoniously into Lucy's lap. Lucy drew one finger delicately along her baby sister's right foot, and Daphne yelped, throwing her a look of mock irritation, and pulled her dogs back into a less offensive location.

"You're teasing, though. Right?" Cat broke in. She twisted in her seat, turning her body fully toward Lucy, her interest piqued. "They didn't really call an ambulance?"

"Oh, you better believe they did!" Lucy would be having flashbacks for the rest of her life. She could still see the customers at the Chinese restaurant, their noses flattened against the steamy windows, watching as the paramedics loaded her into the care car, with Cam hovering over her like a protective mother hen. "They gave me an epinephrine injection, and I was fine by the time I got to the hospital. But I'll never be able to go into Wu's again, that's for sure!" *I won't ever be able to face Cam again, either,* she thought morosely.

"Now, now, that's just pride talking," Cat chided her.

"Well, it's about time my pride made an appearance," Lucy grumbled. "I swear, it's been on vacation for the last week and a half."

"Oo-oo!" Daphne raised her hand in the air like a kinder-gartner. "Tell us again about how Cam carried you out of the restaurant." She giggled.

Lucy gave her a withering gaze.

"Carried you, huh? Hmm. That sounds interesting." Cat lifted one eyebrow. "Was it fun?"

"You two hens are worse than Gabby," Lucy grumbled.

"What does that mean?" Felicia said in a halfhearted attempt to join the conversation.

"Gabby thinks Lucy likes this guy," Daphne explained, sounding thoroughly important.

"Really?" Catherine perked up at this. Abandoning her position at the window, she strode across the room and planted herself on the sisal rug at Lucy's feet.

Lucy tried again, unsuccessfully, to wither Daphne with a look. She'd sensed all along that hiring a friend of the family was a bad idea. Now she knew why: Information leaks. As if Daphne needed more ammunition than she already had.

"Thanks a lot, sprout," she grumbled.

"You're welcome."

"This is exciting," Cat said, sounding quite pleased indeed. "It's been a long time since you've liked a guy, Luce. There hasn't been anyone since Rick, has there? And that was your junior year of college."

Lucy gave her a heavy-lidded glare, trying hard to communicate how little she appreciated the comment. "Well, for goodness' sake, call Chuck Woollery and get me on *The Dating Game*. This is a crisis." Her stomach lurched slightly as she remembered Alexandra's wedding emergency. Alex was determined to get Cam married off. And Lucy still had mixed feelings about her involvement.

"I didn't mean it like that," Cat said reproachfully. "I was just pointing out that it's been awhile since you've had a boyfriend." She spoke gently, careful only to hint at the subject that was still a sore one for her younger sister.

"Thanks so much for reminding me," Lucy said a bit sharply. "It's not a big deal, though. I go out on plenty of dates, thank you very much." It was true. She had met many men over the years—at the gym, at church events, at parties—and had gone out with a good number of them, although never more than a couple of times.

"I know you do, sweetie. I didn't mean to judge. It's just that all your dates are so...so..."

"Temporary," Daphne provided.

"Exactly." Cat nodded.

"Technically," Daphne went on, "you have been dating. But I believe the spirit of the law calls for going out more than twice with a given person."

Lucy glared at her.

"I'm just saying how nice it is that there's someone with potential," Cat inserted diplomatically. "Finally." The last word was spoken in hushed tones, almost under her breath.

"'Potential' is all it is," Lucy sighed. Clearly she would have to nip this thing in the bud, or she'd never hear the end of it from her sisters. "I'll admit: He's got some impressive qualifications. He's a nice guy, cute..."

"A doctor," Daphne added mischievously.

"A doctor!" Cat sat up straight.

Lucy rolled her eyes. Daph and her big mouth. "He's also a client, I might add," she said coolly.

"So?" Cat said.

"So?" Daphne echoed.

"So? *So?*" Lucy stared at them incredulously. "Am I the only one in this family with ethics? With scruples? I can't date a man who hired me to find him a match!"

"Why not?" Cat looked confused. "He didn't say anything about who that match had to be, did he?"

"Yeah." Daphne fixed her gaze on Lucy. "Did he?" Lucy resisted the urge to poke her youngest sister with one toe.

"You two are incorrigible. I won't even dignify that with a response. You know, just because you all have men, that doesn't mean I have to have one too. Right, Fee?"

Lucy turned to her sister; Fee could always be counted on to provide backup. Surprisingly, however, Felicia didn't say anything. It was several moments before she spoke, and when she finally did, it was barely audible.

"I don't think you can say we all have men," she said at last. Lucy shook her head. She didn't get it. Both Fee and Cat were married, and Daphne was still quite serious with her boyfriend, Elliott, whom she had been seeing for the past year. Daphne was her roommate there at the beach house; she saw her every day. If anything bad had happened on the Elliott front, surely she would have been the first to hear.

She glanced back at Felicia, and the look she saw there quickly provided the explanation she'd been looking for. "Oh, Fee!" Lucy jumped up and went to kneel beside her, followed closely by Cat and Daphne. How could she have been so self-centered? Lucy had thought Felicia was just in a mood; but once she finally looked—really looked—she could see all the signs. Fee's eyes were puffy and bloodshot, and her face bore the faintest trace of mascara streaks from what must have been an earlier crying jag. "What happened, honey?"

"Robert says…he's leaving me." Felicia reached into her pocket and pulled out a shredded tissue. "He says there's…someone else."

Cat gave Lucy a speaking glance. This was what the sisters had dreaded for months. It was common knowledge that Robert didn't give Felicia the love and respect she deserved. In the last year, however, he'd traveled more and more frequently, supposedly for business reasons. Felicia hadn't voiced any suspicions, but the other three sisters had begun to believe that Robert was cheating on her. Now it seemed their fears were well-founded.

Lucy settled herself on the arm of Felicia's chair and wrapped her arms around her sister. "I'm so sorry. Robert's a fool, and you know it," she said roughly. "We all know it. This stinks." She stretched one arm around her sister's shoulders and pulled her close. "You deserve better than this, Fee," she said, stroking her soft, dark hair with her free hand, allowing her to let out the tears that begged for release.

Everyone deserves better than this, she thought, visions of past and present clients flickering through her mind. None of her matches had ever ended in divorce that she knew of. Now more than ever, she realized the incredible responsibility she undertook every day when she went to work. It was her job, in part, to make sure these men and women didn't get hurt. No matter what, she had to protect them— and herself—using all the strength and wisdom she could muster.

And if that meant turning away potential heartbreakers like Campbell Howard, then so be it.

It was clear to her now what she had to do.

Lucy arrived at work the next morning feeling irritable, anxious, and thoroughly exhausted from lack of sleep. During the fleeting moments of unconsciousness, she had rested fitfully. She had awakened every hour, haunted by competing memories of the cheery get-well flowers Cam had sent to her office—a detail she had wisely chosen not to share with her sisters—and her resolve of the night before to cut Cam loose from her matchmaking service.

The morning passed slowly and uneventfully. Unable to concentrate on her work, Lucy had focused instead on personal business: making doctor's appointments, paying her office rent, straightening out her files. Still, the hands of the clock crawled like snails. By the time ten o'clock rolled around, she was completely stir-crazy and desperate to get outside for a breath of fresh air.

Reaching under her desk for the athletic shoes she kept there for late afternoon workouts, Lucy slipped off her sleek, leather, stacked-heel mules and exchanged them for the more comfortable footwear.

"I'm going for a walk," she announced to Gabby as she marched through the outer office.

"Dressed like that?"

Lucy looked down at her odd ensemble: a classic-fit wool skirt, matching black jacket, lilac blouse…and a pair of worse-for-the-wear athletic shoes with sports socks.

"You're right." She frowned. "The lilac doesn't really go, does it?"

"Ha, ha. Suit yourself, if you want to be seen in public like that." Gabby turned back to her own books without another word. In black stretch-knit pants, loafers, and an ivory velour blouse, Gabby looked far more professional than she behaved.

Once outside, Lucy's disposition improved greatly. Contentedly she breathed in the spring air—fresh smelling, even in the city. All around her, people were walking, purposely making their way from one appointment to the next. Feeling grateful that she didn't have to be anywhere that morning, that she could take the time to simply think, Lucy decided to stroll around and people-watch for a while.

Just down the block she saw a couple walking hand in hand. She couldn't see their faces from the back. Lucy watched as the man bent down, his light curls touching the young woman's darker ones, and whispered something in her ear. The tiny brunette threw back her head and laughed, the sound dispersing immediately into the city air.

Feeling slightly comforted, Lucy turned and let her eyes settle on a figure walking briskly toward her on the same side of the street. Dressed in a black coat, the man communicated a sense of urgency with his strides. Curious, she looked more closely, then drew in her breath as recognition hit her.

No! It couldn't be. But as the man drew closer, she knew that it was—Cam. Headed directly for her building apparently, although he would run into her before he reached it. She'd planned on talking with him sometime this week, but she wasn't prepared yet. She hadn't figured out exactly what to say. And frankly, she didn't feel ready to say good-bye.

Helplessly she looked to the left then the right, hoping for someplace to hide. Far from any doorway, she had few options to consider: keep walking forward and hope that Cam would simply pass without noticing her; turn around and head in the opposite direction, praying that she would outrun him or that he would pass; or cross the busy street mid-traffic and trust that she wouldn't get hit.

Though the third option was somewhat appealing, Lucy didn't really feel lucky today. And the prospect of facing Cam head-on was more than she could handle. Running into him on the street—especially while looking like this—was hardly the way she'd pictured their final meeting.

That left her with only one choice: turn and head quickly in the opposite direction. One quick glance convinced her that he hadn't recognized her: His eyes were trained directly on the office building she had just vacated.

Lucy spun on her rubber-soled heel and pointed herself in the direction of the nearest coffee shop. She could hide out there for fifteen minutes or so, grab a window seat, and watch until she saw him exit the building again.

Still, there was the chance that before he got to the office complex he would catch up with her and recognize her. With one last, desperate glance at her cross trainers, Lucy stepped up her pace and began to jog in the direction of Starbucks.

She had taken no more than ten steps when she heard a voice call out from behind her.

"Lucy! Lucy, is that you? Wait up!"

As her heart raced, Lucy considered pretending that she hadn't heard him. He was too close for that, though. All she could do was claim she was on her morning run and hope that he would leave her alone to finish.

She turned to face him. He was less than twenty feet away.

"Well, hi, Cam!" she said, making a great show of gasping for breath. "Whew! Sorry, I was just, uh…running."

Cam stopped and looked at her, unlikely athletic outfit and all.

"I can…um, see that." He looked perplexed.

Please don't ask…oh, please don't ask.

"Uh…do you normally wear your work clothes when you go running?"

"Why, yes! Yes, I do," Lucy chirped, her face burning.

"And that's because…?" Cam fished.

"It, uh, saves me time. Don't have to change. Just hop into

the ol' cross trainers, and I'm out the door." For a moment Lucy panicked. Had she remembered to keep gasping for breath? She took in an extra deep gulp of air, for effect, and managed to choke on it.

Cam reached out and pounded her sympathetically on the back.

"But don't you...you know...uh...?" From the look on his face, she could tell what he was asking.

"Nope. I don't sweat," she lied. "I'm not a sweat-er. Ha, ha!" she laughed nervously. "I'm actually more of a vest." She felt herself turning a deep red as Cam blinked in the face of her pathetic attempt at humor. Well, good. Maybe he'd think she was experiencing heat stroke and excuse her ridiculous behavior. Although, chances were he'd probably just call 9-1-1 again.

"I was just coming up to your office to talk to you," he said, wisely recognizing that he wasn't getting anywhere with his line of questioning.

Lucy turned her body in the direction she'd been headed, pretending to interpret that as a regretful dismissal on his part. "Oh, that's too bad. I'm sorry I missed you." In her attempt to sound remorseful, she realized she was pouring it on a bit thick. She brightened immediately to compensate. "Maybe later this week?" She jumped up and down and pumped her arms, running in place, hoping she might soon make a hasty exit.

"That's okay," Cam said. He seemed in no hurry to let her go. "I'd rather tell you now. It'll only take a minute. Why don't I run along with you?"

Lucy let her eyes run down his moss-colored turtleneck, khaki pants, and oxfords. "But you're not dressed for—" she began. Cam just looked at her, effectively silencing her argument. "Oh, all right," she grumbled, then began to breathe quickly again. Unfortunately, her running act was a bit inconsistent. She hoped he hadn't noticed.

She turned and began to jog down the sidewalk with Cam at her side.

"Like I said, this won't take long," Cam began. He sounded dejected. Lucy tried not to look at him, keeping her eyes on the sidewalk ahead of her. She felt like a fool.

"Okay," she puffed.

"I just wanted to thank you for everything," Cam said as he trotted alongside her. "But you see, I've been thinking about it, and I really don't think this is a good idea."

Lucy jammed her right foot hard against the sidewalk, bringing herself to an abrupt halt. "Excuse me?" She had been planning on cutting Cam loose from her program, and now he was firing her?

He came to a rest beside her. "Please don't take this personally. It has nothing to do with you." His voice was calm and reassuring, smooth as silk.

Lucy bristled. Of course it had something to do with her! Whenever someone said, "It has nothing to do with you," you could be sure it had everything to do with you. "Right. This is about what happened the other night, isn't it?" She faced off with Cam, hands on hips.

"What do you mean?" He looked clueless. "What happened?"

"Hello? The ambulance? The nuts? The little trip to the hospital? Admit it: You think I'm a loon. A wacko. A nut bar. You think I'm incompetent."

"Lucy." He smiled. She glared, trying to keep her heart from melting. Why did he have to keep doing that? "I do not think you're a nut bar. Nor do I think you're incompetent." What was with the sweet talk? If he thought he was going to weasel his way out of this one, he was crazy. No guy was ever going to dump her again!

"I don't believe you," she said stubbornly. "You're quitting."

"I'm not quitting," Cam assured her. "I'm reassessing."

"Same thing," Lucy grunted. She turned away and started to run again. Cam caught up and jogged alongside her once more. "I refuse to accept your resignation. I've...I've—" Lucy thought quickly. "Why, I already have someone I want you to meet. It would be irresponsible—unethical, even—for you to back out now."

"You found someone you want me to date? To...be with?"

"I have," Lucy fibbed. "She's perfect for you." For a fleeting moment, she remembered that she had been poised to tell Cam to get lost. But things had changed. He had lost faith in her. His decision wasn't based on not wanting a match; if it was, he shouldn't have signed up in the first place. He just didn't think she could do it. Well, she'd show him! "As a matter of fact, I was just going to call you. Why don't you come up to my office, and I'll give you her number."

"Really?" Cam sounded unconvinced. "Are you sure that's a good idea?"

"Would you start trusting me, for goodness' sake?" Lucy wasn't going to let Cam walk away now. She picked up the pace, making further conversation impossible. They were already on the opposite side of the block. By the time they had returned to the front doors of her office building, both she and Cam were gasping for breath—and she had her plan completely fleshed out in her mind.

As they entered the tiny, two-room Rent-a-Yenta office, Gabby gave Lucy a look of open-mouthed amazement. Lucy was sure she knew what Gabrielle was thinking. *And I thought you looked bad when you left.* She hoped Cam didn't replay their earlier conversation in his mind; it was now abundantly clear that she did, in fact, perspire.

"Please come into my office," she said, trying to sound more competent than she felt. Looking like a prisoner about to be sentenced, Cam obediently dropped into the chair opposite her desk and tried to catch his breath while Lucy pawed through a stack of client information cards.

"Here it is," she cried triumphantly at last. Monica Valentine. Smart, confident, attractive Monica Valentine. Cam needed a strong woman, that was clear. And women just did not come any stronger than Monica.

Lucy handed him the receiver and began to dial.

"Hold on just a second," Cam said nervously. He took a deep breath of air. "I'm still a bit winded." He reached for the water bottle on the edge of her desk and without asking, raised it to his lips and began to gulp.

But it was too late; the phone was already ringing.

"Hello? Hello? Is anyone there?" a female voice asked, sounding both irritated anxious when there was no immediate reply. "Hello?"

Impatiently Lucy waved the phone at Cam. Spewing water as she pulled the bottle from his mouth with her free hand, he took the receiver from her and held it to his lips while gulping in several breaths of air. Loudly.

"Ai-eeeeeeeeeeeee!" The screech from the phone sounded loud enough to be coming from the next room. "I don't appreciate obscene phone calls, you creep!" Monica yelled so loudly Lucy could hear her from across the desk. Horrified, she thought about what Gabby had said. Man-hater, indeed. "Keep your heavy breathing to yourself," Monica was yelling. "If you ever call here again, I'm calling the police, you...you reprobate!"

Cam stared at the receiver as the dial tone buzzed angrily in his general direction.

"Yes, I can see that this is an excellent idea," he said at last, then gave Lucy the thumbs-up sign and a phony grin that stretched from ear to ear.

"This is turning out just as I'd pictured it in my night-mare—er, dreams."

Lucy had been seated at her desk for not more than ten min-utes when Gabby patched through an urgent call the next morning.

"Take a message, would you, Gabs?" she begged into the speaker phone. "It's too early. I need a minute to run through my schedule and catch my breath." *And collect my thoughts.* It was a miracle that she was even at work this early. She'd tossed and turned all night long again, only to drop off at around three-thirty that morning. Lucy didn't know why she was so restless. Confusingly, irritatingly, Campbell Howard kept coming into her mind. She felt both anxious and amused when she remembered the expression of shock that had been on his face after he got off the phone with Monica.

Lucy had quickly taken the situation in hand, calling Monica back and explaining what had happened. The woman proclaimed the circumstances "a bit bizarre" but graciously accepted Lucy's apology and agreed to meet her would-be suitor. Cam, on the other hand, was somewhat harder to convince. At first he'd resisted calling Monica himself, say-ing that he thought it was a rather inauspicious beginning for a relationship. But Lucy encouraged him to give it a chance—and after a much more civilized, if brief, phone conversation, he made a date with Monica for that very evening. Things had come together nicely, just as Lucy had planned.

For the rest of the night, however, she'd obsessed about the two. She felt strangely guilty, knowing in her heart that Gabby was right: Cam and Monica really weren't a good match. Even though she had denied it, she knew it was true. She didn't know why she'd insisted on setting them up. Perhaps it was because she had thought of no one else more appropriate for Cam and was afraid he would see her as a failure. Certainly it had something to do with feeling backed into a corner; she'd felt compelled to make an instant decision. With Cam threatening to leave the service, she'd had to do something to make him stay. She felt horrible, however, having made such a poor choice. But perhaps things weren't as bad as all that. Maybe she was overreacting. The two probably had a very nice time. She was still mulling the situation over when her first call came through.

"Um, I think you'll want to take this one," Gabby told her. "It's the Ice Queen's date."

"Oh." There was no mistaking who Gabrielle meant by "the Ice Queen." She stared at the phone. "Put him through." Her heart skipped a beat. The phone's ringer sounded, jangling her nerves. Lucy picked up the receiver—unwilling to take this call by speaker phone with Gabby just in the next room. "Hey, Cam!" she said, keeping her tone bright. "What a nice surprise." *I hope.*

"Hey yourself." His voice was rich and rumbled pleasantly in her ear. "I just wanted to call and say a very special thank you for sending me out on what I would have to say was the most interesting date of my life."

Lucy's face fell. *Thank you?* "Of course. That's what I do." She tried to read his tone of voice but couldn't decipher exactly what Cam meant. Had the date gone that well after all? The thought, maddeningly, discouraged her.

For a moment neither one spoke. "Is that all?" she said at last, surprised at the snappishness of her response. She took a deep breath and tried to sound more enthusiastic. "You just wanted to say thank you? Because you're certainly welcome, but I've got to get back to—"

"Don't you even want to know how it went?"

Lucy bit her lip…and took the bait. "Of course. Did things go well?"

"I suppose that all depends on your definition of 'well.'" Nervously Lucy tapped one finger on the telephone handset, willing him to get to the point. "I suppose if you consider a shouting match about chivalry versus chauvinism," Cam said evenly, "a woman assaulting her date, and a man paying for two dinners that never got eaten a success, then I'd have to say we had one of the best evenings in dating history."

"Oh no," Lucy moaned, sympathizing with him now. "What happened?" But she could already deduce the facts for herself.

"It started out well enough," Cam said in a casual tone. "I picked her up at her office—she didn't want me to go to her house. But when we left her building, I opened the door for her and—"

"Don't tell me she got mad?" Gabby had been right. Monica *was* a bit extreme.

"Mad? *Mad?* I thought she was going to slug me, right there in front of everyone on Hill Street."

"I'm so sorry—"

"But wait!" Cam said through what sounded like gritted teeth. "There's more. When we got to the restaurant, which I let her choose, she turned away slightly to remove her coat. I went to help her, put one hand on her shoulder, and—*wham!*"

Lucy closed her eyes and shuddered. "'Wham'?"

"She spun around on one foot and kicked me in the chest! After I explained that I was only trying to help her and not hurt her, she mumbled something about learning to react quickly during a kick boxing self-defense class, then calmly let the maître d' lead her to our table."

Lucy decided that maybe now was not the time to tell Cam she took kick boxing too.

"I'm so sorry," she repeated.

"But later," he told her, his voice rising, "after we had ordered our meals and endured many long, awkward minutes of small talk, I committed the truly unpardonable sin!"

By now, Lucy's face was completely buried in her hands. "Uh, I'm afraid to ask."

"She was talking about one of her clients, a woman who was suing her fertility doctor for a million dollars because he hadn't been able to facilitate her getting pregnant. Monica went on and on about how kids were so important to this woman and how she had suffered. So of course I asked what she thought about having children someday. It was a simple question—I was just making conversation." Cam sounded embarrassed.

"She didn't see it that way?"

"She," Cam said hotly, "thought I was assessing her as a potential baby-making machine. After lambasting me in front of at least thirty other diners, she stormed out of the restaurant—leaving me with the bill."

Lucy struggled for words. "Cam, I…I just don't know what to—" This was terrible. The worst dating disaster of her entire career. She was horrified. And yet, before she could stop it, a snicker escaped her lips. Lucy clamped one hand over her mouth.

"What was that?" Cam jumped on the sound. "Did you just laugh?"

"No," she lied. Another snort escaped.

"You did! You *did* laugh! Why I ought to—" But before he could verbalize an offended response, Cam began chortling as well.

For several minutes the two of them snickered, giggled, then belly laughed as the humor of the situation fully struck them. At last Lucy wiped the tears from her eyes and said more seriously, "Oh, Cam! You do know, don't you, that I really am sorry?"

"I know," he said with feeling. "And you do know, don't you, that I wasn't ever mad at you? Not really." He said it as though he meant it. The comment warmed her heart.

Lucy smiled. "If you say so."

"Well, then—" Cam paused awkwardly, then cleared his throat. "I don't really know what else to say. I guess it's pretty clear that this was a bad idea for me to try this. So I suppose there's nothing else to do but—"

Lucy sat up straight in her chair. He was quitting? Just like that? How could he? She glanced around her desktop in a panic. Cam couldn't just disappear like that! She grabbed the nearest file that was at hand.

"Nothing else to do but call...Donna Dillard!" she said brightly.

For a moment Cam didn't even respond. Finally he said in a quiet voice, "You can't be serious."

"Of course I'm serious. You'll like her." Lucy tried to sound confident. Who cared what Gabby thought? Donna was a very sweet woman. Perfect for Cam. A licensed social worker, she, too, was trained in the field of psychology. Not only that, she was socially skilled, very attractive, and made a mean chocolate chip cookie. He would have nothing to complain about. The argument wasn't really convincing, though, even to her. "Donna's not like Monica at all," she finished. At least that part was true.

"Lucy, I—"

She knew she had to get off the phone fast or he'd wiggle his way out of her life for sure. "Here's her number," she said and gave it to him, making him repeat it back to her. "Give her a call. Have lunch. See what you think." Even as she spoke the words, she was ashamed of herself. Donna wasn't any better suited for Cam than Monica had been. Gabby was right. And since when had *she* become the most discerning matchmaker in the office? But Lucy could not back out now. After extracting a feeble promise from Cam to call Donna that very morning, Lucy hung up the phone, made a couple of quick notes in Donna's file…and waited for the next disaster to strike.

She didn't have to wait long. Lucy had just returned from her own late lunch and was receiving a pile of message slips from Gabby when Cam stepped through the door.

"Oh…hi!" she said, turning to him with a start. She folded her arms awkwardly across her chest, trying to appear detached and composed. Gabby grinned like an idiot. "Cam, you've met my assistant?"

"Just briefly." Cam nodded. But his attention was not on Gabrielle. His eyes were filled with frustration, and he stepped to Lucy's side. "May I speak with you privately?" he said in a low voice.

"Of course." Feeling like she'd just been called to the principal's office, Lucy excused herself from Gabby and led the way to her office. Cam didn't even bother to sit down once they got there. He pushed the door partway closed, leaving it slightly askew, then turned to Lucy. As usual, he was dressed comfortably, in black corduroy jeans and a stone-colored polo. He looked anything but comfortable now, and he began to pace the room like an expectant father.

"Cam?" Lucy knew what was coming. Clearly he was fed up.

"Well, we're two for two," he announced wryly.

"Excuse me?" She watched helplessly as he wandered.

"I had my second date today, at lunch," he explained.

"Really?" This caught Lucy by surprise. For a man who

wasn't interested in finding a wife within a month, he sure was keeping busy. She tried to push back the suspicious thoughts. "That was fast."

"Well, I promised you I'd call her, and she wanted to get together right away," he said.

"That's nice, isn't it?" She tried to sound optimistic. "What happened?" She couldn't imagine why he was so shaken.

"What happened is…" Cam stopped, turned, and gave her an offended look. "Donna proposed to me!"

"She *what?*" Lucy gaped. Gabby had painted a picture of the woman as desperate…but this? He had to be kidding. It was clear from Cam's expression, however, that he was not. "I don't know what to—" She tried to keep her composure this time, but a tiny smile began to play on her lips.

"Would you stop laughing at me?" Cam said testily. But as his eyes met Lucy's, he, too, began to smirk. "It isn't funny," he insisted, even as the smile grew.

"I know. It's not," Lucy agreed, a grin on her face. For the second time that day, they laughed until their sides ached. After several long minutes of this, the door opened a crack as Gabby peered inside.

"Just checkin' to make sure you two are okay," she explained, then threw Lucy a knowing look and disappeared once again.

Sobered by the interruption, Cam wiped at his eyes and gave Lucy a solemn look. "Okay," he said at last, "all humor aside, would you please tell me what's going on here? What these dates are all about? Because I'm afraid I can't take much more of this."

Lucy shrugged. "I don't know what to tell you," she said honestly. "I've never been this bad at this. I guess I've known all along that these women weren't right for you, but I couldn't resist setting you up."

"As a joke?" Cam looked at her hard. He didn't seem to think it was funny anymore.

"Oh no," she quickly reassured him. "It's nothing like that. I just—I didn't want you to quit, and I felt like I had to come up with somebody or you would leave."

Cam's dark, thick eyebrows furrowed as he took a step toward her. Lucy felt suddenly very aware of his presence, and the room seemed suddenly much smaller. "You didn't want me to leave? You wanted me to stay?" Lucy felt drawn in by the intensity of his eyes. She took a tiny, halting step in his direction. *Go on, Lucy. Tell him the truth,* she told herself. *You've been thinking of him ever since he first came here. It's obvious to everyone. You might as well just come out and admit it.*

"I—" she opened her mouth to speak.

Just then the door opened, and a beautiful blonde poked her head in the door.

"Lucy," she began in a gentle, songlike voice, "please don't let me interrupt. Gabby's on the phone, and I left a check on her desk. I just wanted to say hi while I was here. Are you—? Oh!" The woman broke off as her wide violet eyes landed on Cam. "I'm sorry. I didn't realize you had company." She smiled sweetly in Cam's direction.

Cam smiled back.

Lucy's heart sank. She opened her mouth to speak, swallowed hard against the dryness of her mouth, and tried again. "Janie, this is Dr. Campbell Howard. Cam, Janie McCallister." Her voice was listless, colorless.

Just then Gabby stepped through the door and eyed the group with a look of delight. "Well! It looks like you two have met at last," she said to Janie and Cam, then threw her boss a broad wink. "What a coincidence. Lucy and I were talking about the two of you just the other day…"

Five

"What on earth did you do that for?" Lucy complained bitterly. It was several hours after Janie and Cam had left, and she'd been moping about all afternoon. Finally, just before leaving the office, she'd been unable to contain her displeasure with her assistant any longer.

Gabby frowned. "What do you mean? I just suggested that Cam and Janie might want to go out for coffee or something." *Or something*, Lucy thought bitterly. She happened to know Cam had invited Janie to meet him at a new restaurant, the Winter Place, that very evening. "I certainly didn't force anyone into doing anything he—or she—didn't want to," Gabby insisted.

"It wasn't any of your business," Lucy said stiffly. She hated the way she sounded: crabby, bossy, controlling. "I'm the one who's supposed to make the matches around here!"

"Oh, right. And you're doing such a fine job of it too." Gabby rolled her eyes.

Lucy stared at her.

"What?" Her friend's look of innocence was a bit too forced. "Why are you looking at me like that?" She wriggled in her seat, at least having the decency to look uncomfortable. "Oh, all right," she confessed. "I listened in on a couple of minutes of your conversation with Cam. It's not like you two were being soooo quiet about it."

Shari MacDonald

Lucy turned away, wanting only to go home, crawl up in bed, and pull the covers over her head until the whole mess went away. Now Gabby knew what a terrible failure she had become. Soon the whole world would know it too.

"I don't see why you're so upset about this," Gabby complained. "You're the one who said you didn't want the guy for yourself. You should be happy for him and Janie. They seemed to hit it off. Maybe they'll actually end up together."

"Maybe." It was true. That was what she'd wanted, wasn't it? A match for Cam? So why did she feel like crying?

"Then again—" Gabby paused. "Maybe you like him more than you thought." Her swivel office chair was pushed slightly back from her coal black desk, allowing her to prop her feet up amidst the mass of papers on her desk. She considered her boss carefully.

"I don't know." Lucy stood uncomfortably in the doorway, frustrated with Gabby's question but unable to deny the truth any longer.

"Am I right?" Gabby didn't sound saucy anymore; she was genuinely concerned.

Lucy started to pace. Did she like Cam after all? It was a legitimate question; she just wasn't ready to give a legitimate answer. "Maybe I don't want to make myself a match," she suggested halfheartedly in one last desperate attempt to deflect Gabby's interest. "Maybe I just want it to happen."

"Oh, I see." Gabby's head bobbed up and down, like one of the dolls Lucy used to see in the back of station wagons. "So matchmaking is good enough for your clients, but it's not good enough for you?"

"That's not what I said," Lucy whispered. "You're twisting my words."

"I'm just trying to make you think. You act so confident, Luce. But are you sure you know what you really want?"

100

No, I'm not sure. I'm just doing the best I can. "I'm fine," she assured her assistant, keeping her expression as noncommittal as she could.

"If you say so." Gabby reached into a side drawer of her desk, pulled out a box of wheat crackers, and fumbled with the inner plastic wrapping. "You're so stubborn," she said fondly but with a touch of disapproval. "Not every man is like Rick, you know. I hope you don't regret letting this one go."

The words echoed hollowly in Lucy's heart. *I hope so too.*

Gabby chewed thoughtfully on the crackers. "You know, it's not too late to do something about it.

Lucy's heart skipped a beat. Of course it was too late... wasn't it? "But—" she protested. "No, I—I can't," she faltered. "He's...he's..."

"He's what?"

Lucy took a deep breath and set her lips in a grim line. "He's taken. As of five-thirty this evening, as a matter of fact. Cam didn't ask Janie to coffee. He asked her out for dinner. And I have a feeling he won't be coming back tomorrow with another dating horror story."

"Oh." Gabby considered this. Even she looked a bit defeated. She shrugged. "I guess you'll just have to wait and see what happens."

"I guess so," Lucy said with regret. But now the thought was planted in her mind. Maybe it wasn't too late after all. She wasn't yet ready to tell Cam how she felt. Not if he really liked Janie. And if he was as fickle as all that—flirting with her one minute, with Janie the next—there wasn't any point in trying to make it work. But maybe the two wouldn't hit it off. She had to see for herself. She moved toward the coat rack.

"Hey! Where are you going *now*?" Gabby leaned over her desk, trying to catch her.

Lucy stopped and threw a quick look over her shoulder. "I'm just going to get a little peek," she confessed. She knew it was ridiculous, yet she couldn't seem to stop herself. "Just to make sure they're doing okay. I feel responsible. I wouldn't be able to sleep at night, knowing I had sent Cam on one more disastrous date. Okay?" But before her assistant could either agree or disagree, she had grabbed her coat and was headed out the door.

By the time Lucy arrived at the Winter Place, it was five-forty, and the after-work happy-hour rush was at its peak. Perhaps a hundred men and women of all ages, races, and backgrounds had crowded into the front bar section of the restaurant where some appeared to be nursing their second and third cocktails of the night.

The crowd was boisterous and loud, but for once Lucy didn't mind. It simply gave her the cover she needed to execute her plan. On the far end of the room a wide doorway opened into a more spacious, and most likely more quiet, section of the restaurant. She set her sights on it and began her scouting mission.

The bar was so crowded it took her nearly ten minutes to work her way across the room. By the time she got to the other side, she had already been splashed by several excitable cocktail wavers who were telling loud stories while motioning with hands that clutched drinks containing olives or little umbrellas. Lucy frowned as a swaggering businessman splattered a bit of hefeweizen onto her sleeve. She couldn't imagine Cam liking this place. It was too aggressive, too out of control. Not in his character at all. She wondered if he and Janie had even stayed once they walked in the door.

When she peeked into the dining room, however, she quickly spied Janie, looking elegant and regal at a table by herself about halfway across the room in the center section. Lucy watched, mesmerized, as the woman pulled a delicate gold compact from her alligator-skin purse and proceeded to dab at her nose with pressed powder. A moment later she withdrew one of her expensive lipsticks from her makeup bag and painted her wide, full lips a rich raspberry red.

Lucy glanced around the dining room, but Cam was nowhere to be seen. Had he gone to the rest room? Or was he simply running late?

Suddenly it occurred to her how ridiculous she was being. It wasn't any of her concern where Cam was; his absence was Janie's problem.

Lucy looked again. Janie, for her part, appeared unconcerned about being alone. In fact, she seemed quite content as she sat at her table, sipping dark liquid from a crystal glass. Lucy watched as she leaned forward and pointed her delicate nose in the direction of a large flower arrangement at the center of the table. Filled with asters, lilies, and freesia, the bouquet was quite gorgeous.

Something nagged at the back of Lucy's mind, but she couldn't quite put her finger on what was bothering her. It certainly couldn't be anything important. Things seemed to be going along swimmingly, even if Cam wasn't actually present. Of course, perhaps that was why everything was going so well.

It couldn't hurt to stick around for a little bit until he arrived, just to make sure everything was going all right.

She scanned the room for an empty table. Mercifully, she saw one in the far right corner.

The layout of the room was perfect; she couldn't have planned it better if she'd tried. To her delight, the dining area was divided into two basic sections: an inner eating area with six small tables, immediately surrounded by a ring of plants and free-standing fish tanks filled with fresh lobsters and other edible sea creatures, then an outer eating area with another twenty tables positioned along the perimeter of the room. From her location at the table in the far right corner, Lucy would be hidden by dim lighting and the cover of aquariums, yet would still have a decent view of what was happening at Janie's and Cam's table.

It was perfect.

Pleased with her plan, Lucy grabbed a menu from the abandoned hostess station, held it over the right side of her face—between her and Janie—in what she naively hoped was a fairly inconspicuous manner, and quickly skirted the length of the dining room floor.

By the time she reached the empty table, her palms were damp and she had received a number of curious stares—thankfully, none of which came from Janie, who appeared to still be busy admiring her flowers.

With a sigh of relief, Lucy dropped to the chair and glanced around to see if anyone was staring at her. Fortunately, most of the restaurant's patrons had already turned back to their meals. However, one man seemed to be captivated by her actions—or, to her horror, by *her*.

He was dressed all in black. Slim, blue-eyed, and with a mop of dark, wavy hair that fell below his ears, the man seemed to have taken great pains to adopt an artist's persona. Yet Lucy could not help but feel that the whole image was an act. Instinctively she could tell there was something false about him. Perhaps it was the look in his eyes as he sized her up or the way he leaned forward, a bit too eagerly, and leered at her. He was the sort of man Lucy chose to avoid at all costs.

Unfortunately he sat only three tables over. He was alone. And he was definitely interested.

Without meaning to, Lucy made eye contact. Immediately the man winked—a broad, obvious gesture that left no question as to its meaning.

Lucy felt her skin crawl. She gave a polite, halfhearted smile and quickly turned away, hoping he would catch the hint. The last thing she needed now was to fend off some deluded, would-be Lothario. Thankfully, at just that moment, an official-looking member of the restaurant's staff approached her table.

She glanced at the pile of dirty dishes left by the previous diners. "Thanks!" she said appreciatively. She hadn't really wanted to sit at a dirty table, but it was the only choice she'd had. "That was quick. Let me just get out of your way." Lucy leaned back to give the man room to do his job.

The man gave her a disparaging look. "I'm not the busboy," he said disdainfully. "I am the host. And as such, it's my job to tell you that you can't sit here."

"But—" Lucy looked about her helplessly. "There's nowhere else to sit."

"Exactly," the host said evenly, looking at her as if she were an imbecile. "Which is exactly why we have a waiting list, miss. I'm afraid you'll have to find a seat in the bar and wait until we have room for you."

"But—" Lucy tried again. "Can't you just…" She glanced around, feeling at a loss. Several feet away a party of three sat at a table that could have easily held four or more. "Maybe you could just ask—" she began hopefully.

"I don't think so." The man looked down his nose at her—literally.

"Oh, all right," Lucy said crabbily. It was probably a bad idea, anyway—spying on Cam and Janie. Whatever would they think of her if they found out? This was a blessing really. It would get her out of the restaurant, away from the annoying man who was still trying to make eye contact, and out of a potentially humiliating situation altogether. She certainly didn't need any more humiliation this week!

"Miss?" the host prodded.

"I'm going…I'm going." Lucy grabbed her purse and, resisting the urge to give him the withering look she'd practiced on Daphne all these years, rose to her feet. Pointing her shoes in the direction of the door, she took one step and came to an abrupt halt. "I'm…not going." She plopped back down with a thud. For it was exactly at that moment that Dr. Campbell Howard had chosen to make his entrance. Her heart nearly stopped as he looked in her direction and waved. Instinctively she lifted her voluminous black-and-gold menu and held it over her face once more. Only the realization that Cam was waving at Janie, and not her, kept her from going into cardiac arrest.

"Excuse me?" The host stared at her as if she had just announced she was about to give birth.

"I…I…I can't," she said, as if that explained it. Only her eyes showed above the menu. She felt like the infamous Kilroy. Unlike the strange little character, however, she did not feel like announcing that she "was here."

"I assure you—you can leave," the man said dryly.

"But I—" Lucy implored him with her eyes.

"No 'buts.'"

"You don't understand. I—"

"*Tst.*"

Lucy stared at him. *Tst?* That was the best threat he had? *Tst?* He'd have to come up with something better than that. If it was a choice between facing Cam's shock or the host's *tst*, she'd take the *tst* any day.

She let the menu drop slightly, taking the great risk of revealing her nose as well. "I'll make it worth your while," she whispered conspiratorially.

"Miss," the man began in a weary voice, "I am not a member of the Mafia. I do not want a bribe. I want this table. There are ten couples patiently waiting who came in at least half an hour before you did. Now are you going to leave quietly, or do I have to call the police and have you forcibly removed?"

Lucy thought about this. Leaving quietly was definitely the preferable option. Being forcibly removed sounded like something that would attract a great deal of attention. Including Cam's. Unfortunately, there was still a strong chance that he'd see her even if she did leave quietly. She wondered how long it would take the police to arrive.

"Oh, all right," she grumbled at last. The waiter started to reach for her menu but stopped at the menacing look Lucy threw him.

He shrugged but made no move to step away. Clearly, his patience was pushed to its limits—not that he had much to begin with. She couldn't buy any more time.

Lucy paused for a moment, eyes over menu, as she tried to determine which way Cam was headed. He had stopped at the doorway to speak to the hostess now manning the station, apparently asking for something. Lucy waited impatiently. She didn't care what Cam needed; she just wanted him to sit down so she could finish making her escape.

When he had finished speaking with the waitress, Cam looked up in Lucy's general direction. A curious look came across his face, and for a moment she feared the worst. She quickly held the menu up over her eyes and walked forward with her face covered.

"Ouch!" she cried out automatically as she ran into somebody's elbow.

"Why don't you watch where you're going?" a disgusted male voice complained.

"Sorry." Lucy felt sheepish at causing the accident. But figuring she'd rather be sheepish than thoroughly mortified, she kept the menu pulled up over her head as she continued to shuffle her way toward the door.

Deciding it was worth the risk, six or seven steps later, she let herself peek over the top edge once more. To her dismay, however, Cam had completely disappeared.

She looked frantically to Janie's table. Not there.

Back up to the hostess desk. Not there either.

It was then that she sensed someone approaching from behind. Horrified, Lucy turned first to the right, then to the left, desperate for even the most unappetizing of escape routes.

Which was exactly what she found.

Just three feet away now, her would-be admirer waggled his eyebrows, offering an obvious invitation to his table. With no other choice in sight, Lucy made a split-second decision and lowered herself into the empty chair. She leaned forward, putting her face much closer to the stranger's than she would have normally allowed.

"I'm Lucy," she said in a low, husky voice, hoping that Cam could not hear. "Don't ask any questions. Just follow my lead."

"I'm Oliver," the man replied delightedly, matching her tone. "And I'll be delighted to follow you anywhere. But why are we whispering? Not that it bothers me, mind you."

"Lucy?"

Her head snapped around as she looked up at the man addressing her, while grinning like a lunatic. The look of concern in Cam's eyes was clear.

Ignoring the feeling that she was getting in way over her head, Lucy inhaled deeply and took the plunge.

"Oh, Cam! Hi." She raised one hand and gave him a little wave, then realizing she looked ridiculous, let it drop like a dead fish to her lap. "I wondered if I would run into you tonight, but I couldn't remember what time you said you were coming. After you mentioned this restaurant, I just couldn't resist trying it out." Cam looked pointedly at her companion. "Er, I mean, we. We couldn't resist trying it out, could we, uh—" Despite the last-second introduction, Lucy drew a blank on the man's name. "Uh—hon?" she finished lamely.

Cam's eyebrows shot up at that. "I don't believe I've met your…date." The word fell from his lips as though he had spit out a bad grape.

"My…date." Lucy cleared her throat. Her skin was starting to crawl again.

Her companion, however, could not have been more delighted. Grinning from ear to ear, he reached out and took Lucy's hand in his. His palms were pale and clammy. Lucy felt as though she were being held by a mackerel. It took all her willpower not to snatch her hand away.

"Of course. How silly of me," she ground out through clenched teeth. "Cam, this is…" Her eyes implored the man to help her. To her dismay, however—whether because he was amused or simply was too dense to catch the hint—the man remained silent. It had an *O* in it, she remembered, and an *L*. "…Lothario," she said helplessly, uttering the first name that came to mind.

"I see. Lothario," Cam said calmly. Lucy looked away, waiting for the laughter. But he didn't even question it. She couldn't imagine why. Surely Cam knew that Lothario was the young seducer in Nicholas Rowe's play *The Fair Penitent*. He wouldn't believe that was really the man's name. Would he?

From his blank expression, it seemed he was unaware that the name referred to men determined to seduce women. Maybe he just assumed it to be a strange name.

Somewhat consoled by Cam's lack of reaction, she turned to her companion, fully expecting him to react negatively to her comment—perhaps even deny that he knew her after all. She almost hoped that was the case. As humiliating as it would be, she was beginning to think that coming clean would be preferable to playing out this entire embarrassing charade.

To her surprise and dismay, however, Lothario—Oliver, she now remembered too late—seemed actually flattered by the moniker she had given him. Didn't he know it wasn't a compliment? Lucy watched him puff out his chest with pride.

Apparently not. As far as he was concerned, she had nicknamed him Don Juan.

Looking from one to the other, Cam seemed to be sizing up the situation. Feeling like a child on trial for stealing cookies from the jar, Lucy tried to look as innocent as possible. When her eyes met Cam's, however, her steady look faltered, and she was forced to turn away.

"So…Lothario. May I call you Lothario?" Cam said innocently.

The man gave him a rather smug nod.

Lucy felt like crawling under the table.

"I wasn't aware that Lucy was seeing anyone."

"She is now." The words were spoken overconfidently. Lucy tried to kick the culprit under the table but missed.

"I see." Cam's eyes narrowed as Oliver gave her hand a possessive squeeze. "Where did you two, uh, lovebirds meet?"

Lucy felt the bile rising in her throat. *I think I'm going to lose my lunch.*

"Here," she mumbled dully. Both men looked at her in surprise. "I mean…uh, here!" She forced a brightness into her tone. "Sorry. I'm nursing a bit of a headache."

"Oh, Lucy." Oliver simply oozed with sympathy. "Why don't you let me take you home?"

"No!" The word was out before she could stop it. "I mean, we just got here."

Cam looked down at the other man's half-finished plate of food and the empty place in front of Lucy. "I mean, uh...I just sent my food back. I don't want to leave until I get it." Lucy bit the inside of her lip. She couldn't tell if Cam was buying her story.

"But you just said a minute ago that you wanted to try this restaurant," Cam challenged her. "How could you and your man, Loth, have met here?"

"*Your man, Loth...*" Lucy had the distinct feeling that Cam was toying with her now, but she couldn't be sure. There was nothing to do but finish this dance now that it had begun.

"Oh, I just meant that we'd met in the...uh, bar."

Cam scowled outright. "I'm sorry. I had the feeling that you didn't drink."

Lucy wanted to cry. He was right. She *didn't* drink, but she certainly smelled of alcohol from being jostled in the bar earlier. "I don't," she admitted this one truth, then continued with her lie. "I was with friends. I had juice."

Oliver looked at her as if she were some strange, new species of bird. Feeling like she'd suddenly gotten a bit of a break, Lucy seized the opportunity to set the guy straight once and for all.

"Remember how cute you thought it was, honey, when I told you I was having apple juice? When I said I prefer not to drink alcohol?" she said, smiling sweetly and batting her eyelashes in his direction. Oliver's mouth hung open, just slightly, as he absorbed this new bit of information. "And how I told you I never go home with strange men? Ever, ever? And if one tried to force me to, he'd learn the hard way that I'm a black belt in Tae Kwon Do?"

"Oh, right." The man wasn't looking so elated anymore. On the contrary, he was looking decidedly nauseous. Lucy felt a tiny thrill of victory, then realized she was blowing her cover. For Cam's benefit, it might be time to change the subject.

"Well, Campbell," she said, turning back to him with a gracious smile, "it's been nice seeing you. I'm sure you'd like to get back to Janie, however."

Cam ignored her dismissal and focused on her companion. "So what do you do...Lothario?" he said, still digging.

Nervously Lucy studied Cam but could not tell if he knew it was all a lie. He spoke in a completely normal voice, yet insisted on saying the man's name over and over.

And, by the way, what *did* Lothario do? Lucy turned her attention back to him, afraid of what might come next. *Oh, please,* she thought, as if wishing could make it so. *Don't be something horrible, like the president of the Society Against Behavioral Psychology.*

"I'm an architect," her date said proudly, his cockiness returning. He seemed glad to be the topic of conversation once more.

Lucy breathed a sigh of relief. At least he hadn't announced that he was a mass murderer.

"Oh." Even Cam seemed surprised that the man's occupation was something so normal. "That's great. Where'd you go to school?"

"USC," the man replied proudly. "Six years. I had to work my way through."

Lucy started to breathe more normally as Cam gave a nod of approval. "Wow. I'm impressed," he said. "That must have been tough." She sat back, pleased that disaster had been averted. Now that things had settled down a bit, she had a moment to realize how parched she was. She glanced around the table. Oliver's crystal goblet of water seemed untouched. Deciding to take her chances, she reached for the water.

"I've had worse gigs." The words dripped from Oliver's lips like honey. Lucy looked at him closely, her skin crawling again.

Was that a leer on his face? She raised the glass of water to her lips.

"Excuse me?" Cam shook his head, not understanding.

The man leaned forward and gave him a broad wink. "I worked my way through school as a dancer. A male dancer, if you know what I mean."

Lucy sputtered, spraying tiny droplets of ice water onto the man across from her.

"Hey!" he protested, glaring at her outright for the first time.

A stripper? She closed her eyes and sank back against her seat, wishing madly that she might somehow disappear. How lovely. More than a hundred people in the entire establishment, and she had to pick the one with the most questionable character.

Unable to continue the charade any longer, Lucy grabbed her purse and climbed to her feet. "Look, I'm sorry," she said to Cam, ignoring Lothario and not bothering to explain to Cam exactly what she was apologizing for. "But I think it's just about time for me to go home."

Taking that as his cue, Oliver jumped up and grabbed her by the elbow. Dumbfounded and frozen with shock, Lucy could do nothing but stare at him. He couldn't possibly be serious! She'd made it abundantly clear that he wasn't her type. How could he think she would actually leave with him? Or was he just being polite, trying to help her out of her scrape? Her mind raced. She could walk out the door with the guy, then ditch him. At least she wouldn't have to explain everything to Cam.

She knew that wasn't a realistic possibility, though. It was too dangerous—who knew what the guy would do when they got out on the street? It was hardly worth the risk. Besides, as embarrassing as it was going to be to admit to Cam this had all been an act, it was better than letting him think she'd actually date a guy like Mr. Chippendale.

Before she could compose herself enough to set Oliver straight, however, Cam took her by the hand and pulled her out of the man's clutches.

"Excuse us," he said to Oliver. His voice was low and harsh, and the look in his eyes held an obvious warning.

Raising his arms in a gesture of submission, the man sat back and began picking away at his pan-fried oysters.

Firmly but gently Cam pulled Lucy several feet away. While Oliver's actions toward her had been blatantly possessive, she noticed, Cam's were subdued and protective. Though he held her tightly, his grip was loose enough that it didn't hurt her. The look in his eyes, however, was much more harsh. Accustomed as she was to seeing the playful, teasing, and gentle expressions on his face, Lucy was completely taken aback by the anger she now saw there.

At six-foot-two, he towered over Lucy's five-foot-six inches, making him appear more ominous than he was. Instinctively she shrank back, although she knew in her heart she had nothing to fear from Cam. It wasn't his physical presence that alarmed her but the complete transformation of his warm, comforting personality. The look he gave her was pained. He pulled no punches. "Look, Lucy, if you think I'm letting you leave with this guy, you're out of your mind." He appeared completely distraught.

Lucy blinked at him. That was it? She'd thought he was going to call her on the carpet for lying to him, for making a ridiculous scene at the restaurant, for spying on him and his date. But...he really thought she was leaving with Oliver?

"I...I'm not letting him take me home, I promise." Lucy's heart raced. She knew she had to tell Cam the truth. But when she looked into his eyes and saw the hurt there, she couldn't bring herself to say anything further. Hadn't she already made a big enough mess of things? He must hate her by now. She couldn't blame him a bit.

"Lucy—" Cam began, then stopped and thought a minute. "I have to say I'm very surprised. And quite honestly, pretty disappointed."

Lucy looked at her shoes as tears threatened to spill from her eyes. Cam was disappointed? Not any more than she was. Her heart ached as she choked back the words she longed to speak. *I'm so sorry, Cam. I feel like such an idiot. I didn't mean for this to get out of hand, didn't mean to lie to you. I just wanted to...* Lucy wiped at her eyes with one sleeve. What exactly *had* she wanted to do? When she'd left the office, she'd felt so certain, so self-assured. Now she just felt ashamed.

Reaching out with one hand, Cam gently lifted away a stray curl that had fallen across her eyes.

"Hey," he said gently, sounding vaguely reassuring. Lucy lifted her eyes hopefully. But the message of comfort ended as abruptly as it had begun. Cam looked restless, uncertain. His lips were stilled. He had nothing else to say.

"Hey yourself," she said, trying to make the word sound lighthearted. "I gotta go."

Cam's eyes held hers, and for a moment she couldn't tear herself away. But as he searched her expression for some explanation, she knew she had none she could give.

Withdrawing her arm from the protection of his grip, she spun on one cross trainer-encased heel and ran across the dining room and through the bar, sprinting as quickly as the crowd would allow.

Six

Morning dawned lazily, deliberately—and to Cam's anguished mind, more slowly than it ever had before—with pale light gradually covering the sky before blossoming into something stronger that could finally be recognized as day. Cam was awake to see it all. All night he'd lain with his bloodshot eyes open, considering what he should do. Lucy wouldn't take his calls. He didn't know if she was angry with him, embarrassed, or…what? Why was she hiding? Could it be that she actually did feel something that she was afraid to let him see? It was too much to hope.

One by one, he replayed in his mind the events of the previous days—the emergency trip to the hospital with Lucy; his first, horrific date with Monica; his subsequent lunch with the desperate Donna; and the lighthearted laughter he had shared with Lucy after each disaster.

Lucy. Sweet, crazy Lucy. He didn't know what to think. Since the day he'd first laid eyes on her, Cam had been smitten. He'd tried to move slowly, to give her time to get used to the idea that he might be good dating material for *her*. He'd given her the opportunity to see that he wasn't out to snag a wife just so he could get his inheritance. If that had been his motivation, surely he would have jumped at Donna's offer to marry him.

But with every turn in the path, just when he thought it might be time to make his move, Lucy insisted on setting him up with another date! The day before, he could have sworn she was finally about to admit having feelings for him. It had taken every bit of self-control he had not to step out, wrap her in his arms, and press his lips against her own. He had waited for her sake to give her a chance to speak the words that had formed there.

But once again, disaster had struck. First Janie, then Gabby, had broken in and distracted them. After Janie's arrival, Lucy had retreated even further into her emotional shell. Turning away, she had brightly wished Cam and Janie good luck on their date, then excused herself from the room. He might have deduced from that that she was uninterested, that she didn't care who he went out with after all—if it weren't for her bizarre appearance at the restaurant that same night.

Strangely, her arrival at the Winter Place hadn't surprised him. He had enjoyed the brief conversation he'd had with Janie when he first got to the restaurant, before excusing himself to answer a page from Dr. Bernard at the university. But when he saw Lucy sneaking around the restaurant, trying so hard not to be seen, his heart had melted. He'd decided to play along with her little game but then had become confused when she introduced him to her date. She'd seemed perfectly willing to leave with the smarmy man. It was more than Cam could handle. He'd become protective and upset, which had proven to be his fatal mistake. Lucy had bolted from the restaurant, and in shock he let her go. Now she wouldn't talk to him, wouldn't let him explain. If only he could get her to listen!

Cam kicked his feet free of the bedcovers, grabbed the telephone book from its spot in the corner of the room, and flipped through the white pages. It was almost daylight. His decision was made. Now that he knew what he had to do, he couldn't get started soon enough. Thankfully, the information he needed was in the book, though if it hadn't been, he would have found a way to get it.

He moved into the kitchen and put on a pot of coffee to brew.

And by the time the sun had fully risen, Cam was out the door, in the truck, and on his way.

"Lucy, come on. Snap out of it. You know, you're going to have to get out of bed sometime." The words were pointed but muffled, coming as they were from the other side of the mass of covers Lucy had pulled over her head.

"Says who? Is there a law somewhere? Show me where it says I have to get out of bed. I dare you." Lucy tightened her hold on the heavy wool blankets that covered and smothered her. She hoped Daphne would hurry up and leave so she could poke her head out and breathe. It was getting awfully hot in here. With one eye open, one shut, she groggily considered her fetal position, wondering if it created an air pocket that might help her survive an extended hibernation. How long could a person go without air, anyway?

"If you're expecting me to make you get up," Daphne said conversationally, "you're thinking of the wrong sister. Cat's already at work, no doubt. I'm headed there myself, but I figured I'd check on you first. Frankly, I don't care if you go into the office today or not. I'm just concerned that you might be suffering from oxygen deprivation."

"Well…" Truth be told, things were starting to get a bit fuzzy, but Lucy wasn't willing to admit to her discomfort. "Maybe I am getting tired of staring at my own belly button." Pulling her comforter down below her nose, she took a deep, cleansing breath of the fresh air coming in through her open bedroom window.

"That's better," Daphne said, employing Cat's motherly tone. She sat on the edge of the bed wearing a lightweight, berry-colored charmeuse blouse and long, flower-patterned skirt in the sort of fabric that was *meant* to look wrinkled: a favorite of Daph's, who hated ironing even more than she hated living according to other people's expectations. At the bottom of Daphne's skirt, Lucy could see just the rounded toes of her clunky black boots. "Good girl. Good Lucy." The young woman seemed pleased that she had decided to make an appearance. Coming from their eldest sister, such words elicited feelings of comfort; from twenty-four-year-old Daph, they just sounded silly.

"Glad you approve, wee one," Lucy grunted and forced herself into a sitting position. "But I'm not a puppy, you know. What time is it, anyway?"

"Time to face the music," Daphne said brightly. "Aren't you glad you asked?" She reached into her shirt pocket and pulled out several scraps of pink note paper covered with her loose, loopy script. "You've had three calls this morning from Campbell Howard, and it's not even ten o'clock yet. Plus, he called four times last night before I was forced to turn off the ringer."

"Ugh. Don't remind me." Lucy could still hear the persistent ringing in her head. "I told you I didn't want to talk to him." She stared at the pieces of paper Daphne offered her but made no move to take them from her.

"I remember," Daphne said defensively, tossing her dark curls. "And did I make you talk to him?" she sniffed. "No, I did not."

"For which I am forever in your debt."

"Don't mention it," Daphne said generously. "But I wish you'd call this guy back sometime before he drives us both insane."

"I'm afraid it's too late for one of us." All morning long Lucy had lain awake replaying the previous night's events in her mind, seeing herself creeping furtively throughout the dining room, trying to make her escape. What was she thinking? She'd never acted this way around a client before. What had happened to her sense of protocol and etiquette? Throughout her young life, she had considered herself creative, artistic, and unique, but she'd never thought of herself as an actual lunatic. "I knew we should have gotten an unlisted number," she grumbled.

"Yeah, well," Daphne agreed, "unfortunately, Dr. Howard's got it now. And you're going to have to deal with him." She shifted on the bed so that her hips were positioned just to the right of Lucy's. One hand reached out to rest comfortably on her quilt-covered arm. "Do you want to talk about it now?"

Lucy started to pull the covers back over her head, but the look of genuine sympathy—and curiosity—in her sister's eyes stopped her.

She sighed. Daphne deserved an explanation. The night before, Lucy had stormed in the front door and marched straight to her room, informing Daph as she blew past the kitchen that she was dead to any callers. If anyone were to ask for her, she ordered, Daphne was to say that she was a thousand miles away, at a home for the criminally insane.

Naturally, Daph had followed her to her room to ask what had happened. But exhausted from the night's events, Lucy had begged for a reprieve, telling Daphne that she would explain in the morning.

Now morning had broken. "Well, I wouldn't say I want to talk about it," she said honestly.

Daphne shrugged. "You don't have to. But it might help."

"I," Lucy said with great certainty, "am beyond help."

"So you say." Her younger sister considered her thought-fully, remaining silent for several moments while she considered the problem. "Look," she said at last. "I don't know what this is about, exactly. But I doubt it's as bad as you think."

"Oh, Daphne," Lucy moaned. "It is soooo much worse than that."

"So tell me." Daphne folded her arms resolutely across her chest.

"Oh, all right." Lucy sat up straight and pulled the covers up to her chin. She tried to imagine some way to present the facts in a neat, little, organized package—one that Daphne could open and pronounce either "a tragedy" or "not so bad." But she couldn't imagine where to start or how to end—and so she started talking wildly, confusingly, word over word, until sentences and ideas and feelings all mangled together, the victims of a communications accident.

As she spoke, she wrapped her arms around her flannel-pajama-covered body and squeezed hard, comforting herself. Talking about feelings was supposed to help, at least that's what she'd been told. But as the words spilled forth, Lucy felt herself becoming more and more distraught.

At last she fell silent, not sure that she had explained herself in any meaningful way, but not knowing what else to say. Daphne said nothing at first—simply stared out the window as sunlight poured in from the east, bathing the bedroom in shades of gold. Her face was unusually drawn, and she looked as though Lucy had just informed her that she was suffering from some dread disease.

"Wow," she said at last. "You really do like him."

The words hit Lucy hard in the chest. She sucked in her breath and held it. "I'm sorry, Luce." Daphne looked genuinely remorseful. "I didn't realize it was like this. I shouldn't have teased you."

Lucy blew out her breath in a rush. "Don't be silly," she snapped irritably, punching her thick feather pillow for effect. She cringed at the sound of her voice but couldn't help the sharpness of her reaction. "Of course you're going to tease me; you always tease me."

"Yeah, but not about anything like this." Daphne shook her head. "This is really serious, isn't it?"

"No," Lucy said a little too quickly. *It wasn't, was it?*

"Come on, Lucy," Daphne urged. "Why can't you just admit it? You like this guy. You like him so much you're acting like a teenager in love. Or maybe a junior high student," she said, considering the evidence. "But that's beside the point."

"Love?" Lucy closed her eyes as the room started to spin. "Now you're the one who's off her rocker."

"Suit yourself." Daphne had been called crazy more than once in her life; it would take a lot more than that to offend her. "Deny it all you want. But I'd wondered when you'd get around to dealing with all your emotional baggage. I can't imagine a better time than now."

"What do you mean, my baggage? You and Gabby are a couple of amateur psychologists."

"Maybe we are," Daphne admitted. "But at least we're trying to help you figure things out. You won't even try to help yourself."

"But—" Lucy felt unexplainably forlorn. Since when had she ever had to take advice from her wacky, ungrounded little sister? The woman who had tried to elope, sending eldest sister Catherine in a round-the-world chase to save her from her own impulsiveness? "I don't even know what I need help with. I've never felt like this before."

"Maybe you've never been in love before," Daphne suggested.

"This isn't love." How could people think such a thing?

"It isn't even 'like.' I hardly know the man." With her lips she protested, though in her heart she recognized there was a shred of truth to what Daphne was saying.

"And you're not going to get to know him any better by hiding from him."

"I am not hiding."

Daphne gave her the look.

"All right, I'm hiding. But not because I'm in love. I'm just humiliated."

"So why do you care about what happened last night? Since when have you worried about what other people think? The Lucy I know would just laugh and figure it would make a good story—which it does, by the way."

"But I don't *want* a good story." She gave the pillow one more jab, then stuffed it behind her back where it could no longer tempt her.

"Fair enough. What do you want?"

Lucy looked away from her sister's penetrating gaze and traced the pattern in her quilt with the white half-moon of one fingernail. What did she want? She wanted her dignity back. She wanted to travel back in time and behave in a way that wouldn't leave Cam feeling disappointed in her.

"I want him to think I'm normal. Likable." That didn't sound quite right, though. She wanted more somehow.

"That sounds like pride talking, to me." Coming from Daphne, it didn't come across as a judgment.

"Is pride always a bad thing? Maybe I'm just taking care of myself. You know, learning from my mistakes." After all, a certain amount of pride had to be healthy. But the excuse sounded hollow, even to her own ears.

"Now who's the amateur psychologist?" Daphne pulled her legs up under her, tucking her Doc Martens under the crinkly folds of her gauzy skirt. "Besides, I find it hard to believe you're learning from your mistakes, considering that you won't even talk to the guy," she said dryly.

Lucy set her lips, determined not to be baited. Daphne studied her for a moment, then gave a small sigh and said, "Look, I know this isn't going to go over well with you, but I think it's time I told you what I see." Lucy opened her mouth to protest, but Daph waved one small hand in the air, shushing her. "Now, now. Let me have my say. It's not often I tell one of my sisters what to do; goodness knows I have enough trouble keeping my own life in order."

"You can say that ag—"

"Silence." Surprised by the forcefulness of her sister's order, Lucy stopped talking. A quick look, though, showed her that Daph's eyes were twinkling, and she wasn't really mad.

The youngest Salinger wriggled herself into a more comfortable position on the bed, and Lucy felt as though they were small children again, snuggled up together to share secrets in the privacy of their small green-and-white bedroom. Though Daphne no longer wore pigtails, it was hard for Lucy not to see her as her baby sister. She looked at her sister a second time, and for a brief moment she saw Daphne differently— as the beautiful and surprisingly sensible young woman she was becoming. She settled back against her pillows, ready to listen—for a time.

As if realizing her window of opportunity was small, Daphne chose her words carefully. "I guess there's no point in beating around the bush, Lucy. I suppose you know by now that Cat and Felicia and I have been worried about you."

Lucy blinked at her. How strange to hear Daphne say she was worried about her. All Lucy's life, she and the other girls had conferred about flighty Daphne's well-being. Since when had the sisters starting having such clandestine meetings about *her*?

125

"I don't know what you mean," she said flatly. "I'm doing great. My life is great."

"Yes, it is," Daphne agreed. "And it's very full of family and friends and work and faith. Why, I'd have to say it's full of everything—except a man."

Lucy rolled her eyes and shoved one foot at her sister. "Oh, please! You three are out of control. Just because you're out of the dating market, you're trying to live your life vicariously through me. If you're in such a hurry to get me married off, why don't you just gift-wrap me and leave me on the corner and see what man gets me?"

Daphne grabbed her foot through the covers and held it. "I'm not playing around, Luce," she said seriously. "You've been alone for a really long time."

"Ouch. Thanks a lot." Lucy wriggled her foot away from Daphne's hold and glowered at her. "You make me sound like a leper. I could have a boyfriend if I wanted one, I'll have you know."

"I'm sure you could," Daphne said easily. "So why don't you want one?"

Lucy wriggled uncomfortably in bed. Why didn't she want a boyfriend? She'd never really thought about it in those terms before. In college she'd dated Rick for nearly a year and a half. He hadn't been ready to make a long-term commitment at first. It had taken him more than eighteen months to make up his mind. And once he did, Lucy was ecstatic. She had happily planned the wedding of her dreams. Rick was sweet, intelligent, charming—all the things she wanted in a man. But as it turned out, he hadn't really been ready for a commitment. Lucy had waited at the church for him for several hours on what was supposed to be the happiest day of her life. She cried all afternoon. But once she left the church, she determined to leave Rick—and all men—behind her.

It was an extreme reaction, but it seemed like the right thing for her. Lucy wasn't ready to take another risk—wasn't ready to fall for a man who didn't really want to commit to her. Felicia's current troubles simply assured her that she'd been right. Robert, Fee's husband, had been a reluctant fiancé like Rick had been. No, if there was one thing worse than having no husband, it was having a husband who didn't really want her. That was one reason she was so careful, so prayerful in her approach to helping men and women find each other.

Even as she thought about this, however, Lucy was overcome with feelings of guilt. She hadn't been careful with Cam. Not once since he came into her office had she prayed about him, as was her practice with all her clients. Instead of working through the process slowly and methodically, she had acted on impulse, reacting emotionally to the situation based on her own feelings and needs—not Cam's.

And what were those feelings? Interest, pleasure, curiosity, discomfort...and a general nervousness that had kept her off balance ever since they'd first met.

Lucy looked up, hoping that perhaps Daphne would be staring out the window, that her mind would have wandered and she'd be ready to talk about something more benign, like politics or taxes. Daphne looked at her, though, like a bird dog with its eyes on a quail. There was no way out of it. Lucy would have to face the question that her sisters had raised: Was she or was she not in love with Dr. Campbell Howard?

She pictured herself crouching behind her big, black menu, jogging through the city streets in her Donna Karan suit and Nike cross trainers, hiding under the covers as the telephone rang incessantly. Who was she kidding? Of course she was completely enthralled with the man. For no one else would she have made such a fool of herself—so many times. That didn't mean she was going to do anything about it.

"It's just hard to think about sharing my life with anyone," she offered lamely after several minutes. "It takes so much energy. I've been putting all my time into building my business. And I don't regret it," she said, forming her defense before Daphne's offensive even began. "It's very fulfilling, I'll have you know."

Daphne screwed up her face, looking puzzled. "Why? What's so fulfilling about it?"

"Are you kidding?" Lucy felt her burden lighten slightly, as she remembered some of the couples she had brought together: Leo and Bess, Anna and Garvey, Randy and Linda...Ed and Velma, the older couple who had become like a second set of parents to her. "There's nothing better than love," she said confidently. "The way they look into each other's eyes, the way they commit to working things out no matter how difficult things get, the promise to be there for each other through all the struggles life brings..." A twinge of longing tugged at her heart.

"Sounds wonderful," Daphne said quietly.

"I get it." Lucy frowned. She'd backed right into that one. "You want to know why I don't want all that for myself, as well as for them."

"Aren't you the least bit curious?"

Lying back against the pillows, Lucy pondered the patterns of golden sunlight that were thrown against her ceiling. She never would have admitted it to her sisters until now—she'd hardly even admitted it to herself, in fact—but she had, on occasion, wondered if she would ever find her own perfect match.

For some reason it was difficult to imagine that happening. She enjoyed men, enjoyed their company a great deal, and found herself extremely attracted to many of them.

That wasn't enough to send her in search of a mate, however.

"I've been down the path of romance once before, you know. I can do it if I have to. It hurt a lot to say good-bye to Rick after a year and a half, but it wasn't nearly as painful as, say, losing Mama. I can handle the hurt of losing a man again. I just don't feel like putting myself through it right now. Maybe in the future, when I feel more settled, when I feel more ready—"

"Say that again," Daphne broke in.

"What?" Lucy tried to think what her sister might mean. "Maybe in the future—?"

"No, what you said about Mama. This is about more than just Rick, isn't it?"

"That's silly." She sounded more confident than she felt. Of course, Lucy had missed her mother greatly while growing up. But at least she'd enjoyed her for a short time, hadn't she? She treasured the few memories she had. And of course she'd had two loving older sisters who had doted on her while she was growing up. Lots of people had it worse than she had. There was nothing to complain about. It certainly wasn't still affecting her, particularly her love life.

"Lucy," Daphne began carefully, "have you ever stopped to think that maybe—just maybe—you're afraid of getting close to people because if you do, you might lose them?"

Lucy's head began to swim. It sounded absurd. But what if Daphne was right? What if she was pushing Cam away not because it was unethical for her to date him, not because she didn't want to date him, but because she was afraid to?

"I think it's time for you to talk to him." Daphne spoke so quietly Lucy almost didn't hear her. Yet the voices in her heart were telling her the exact same thing.

"But I don't know what to say!" Lucy tried to visualize herself confessing to Cam. *Sorry about spying on you and your date the other night. It's just that I like you so much I'm not behaving like myself anymore. You seem to have turned my world upside down, my heart inside out.* But the image dissolved as quickly as it formed. She couldn't imagine it; it could never happen. It didn't make sense that she should like Cam so much, so quickly. She'd humiliate herself—yet again—if she tried to say anything.

"Why don't you start by thinking about what's in here," Daphne said, placing a small hand over her own heart and indicating with a nod that Lucy should do the same. "After you know what you feel, then maybe it'll make more sense up here." She tapped her skull with one finger.

Moving with her customary grace, she slid off the bed and, after pausing just long enough to drop a quick kiss on Lucy's forehead, clomped her Doc Martens-ed feet toward the door. "Coffee's on," she threw over her shoulder casually, as if she had not just turned Lucy's world upside down. "And the paper's on the floor by your bed. I'll call you this afternoon to check on you."

"Thanks," Lucy said desolately.

Daphne smiled brightly, blew her another kiss, then disappeared.

That girl's just too smart for her own good, Lucy thought grumpily. *But at least she made coffee.* Pushing their conversation to the back of her mind, she decided to focus on the here and now. She'd deal with Campbell later, after she'd had her morning jolt of java, after she'd read the morning cartoons…after she had a foolproof getaway plan and a one-way ticket to Siberia.

Wishing Daphne had actually brought her a cup of coffee, Lucy resigned herself to the fact that she was going to have to get out of bed to get it herself. *Hmm…that Daphne's a lot trickier than she looks.* Oh, well. She'd make a quick run to the kitchen, pour herself a cup of strong, French roast—thick enough to stand a spoon in, no doubt, if Daphne made it the way she usually did—and hop back under the covers before her sheets had even lost their warmth.

Cold toes slapped against even colder hardwoods as Lucy raced to beat her internal, imaginary clock down the hall, across the living room, into the kitchen, and back again.

"Thirty-four seconds!" she announced triumphantly to her empty bedroom. Carefully she placed her steaming mug on the bedside stand, grabbed the thick, heavy morning paper from the floor where Daphne had dropped it, and crawled back under the security of her covers.

Once she was settled, she reached for her drink and wound both hands around the mug, as if protecting it from some imaginary coffee snatcher. *There,* she thought contentedly. *Now I can just sit back and forget about Cam—for a few minutes at least.* She was almost successful too—almost—until she unfolded the paper and a battered copy of C. S. Lewis's *The Lion, the Witch, and the Wardrobe* fell out.

Lucy stared. No wonder the paper had felt so big. She looked at the cover illustration with its depiction of the book's four protagonists: Peter, Susan, Edmund, and Lucy…for whom she had been named. Her eyes welled up with tears as she opened the battered cover and saw Cam's name on the title page. It was his personal copy. A page of crisp white note paper fell out.

Heartfelt and plainly worded, it simply read:

> *Dearest Lucy,*
> *Meet me by the lamppost.*
> > *Love,*
> > *Cam*

Lucy ran her fingers lightly across the pages. Could this be for real? As a child, she had read this book perhaps a hundred times, delighting again and again in the adventures that began at the infamous lamppost for the four Pevensie children. She'd mentioned this to Cam the night he'd accompanied her to the hospital, where she'd spied a child reading a copy of the book. But what did Cam mean by the note? What lamppost could he be talking about? There were thousands in the city of Los Angeles, thousands surrounding her home in Malibu alone.

Her heart caught in her throat. Not even caring that she was spilling coffee all over her prized comforter, Lucy struggled to free herself from her bedclothes, untangling one knotted-up foot at a time, and scurried to her bedroom window.

As she looked down to the street below, Lucy hardly dared to take a breath. It was only seconds, though, before she saw him. Standing casually with his back indeed to a lamppost on her street, Cam waited patiently. And from the determined look on his face, it appeared that he was prepared to wait all day.

"I think it's time for you to talk to him." Daphne's words echoed in Lucy's heart like a blessing.

Or a curse.

With that twisted benediction echoing in her mind, Lucy sprang into action. Grabbing a gray, zip-up sweatshirt, faded blue jeans, and canvas sneakers to throw on between her room and the front door, she prepared to do what she had been dreading all night, all morning—perhaps her entire life.

Like it or not, Daphne was right.

It was time to face the music.

As she approached Cam, still leaning with his back to the lamppost, Lucy felt almost like singing. It wasn't that she felt any better about what she had to tell him. Still, it felt wonderful to see him there on her street, waiting for her. As ridiculous as it sounded, she felt hopeful, as though he might actually be able to understand, even to forgive her for her oddball behavior.

She continued to approach him at a walk, though her feet itched to run. Twenty feet away now, he still hadn't seen her. His gray eyes were staring into space, not watching anything in particular it seemed, yet Lucy couldn't help but feel that he saw a great deal. He had seen that she needed to talk to him, even when she did not. He had known that he was a part of this...this...whatever it was she was experiencing. After all, he was a behavioral psychologist. From the very beginning, he must have noticed how he threw her completely off kilter. Had he found it funny? Had it frightened him? He certainly didn't look frightened now. If anything, he looked concerned and, at the same time, strangely calm.

Though the Southern California sunshine poured down upon the beachfront side street, the air still held a hint of chill. Cam was prepared, however, in his camel-colored Shetland sweater over a white T-shirt, khakis, and loafers. A section of blond hair flopped over his bespectacled eyes, and he looked more like an over-the-hill skateboarder than a distinguished psychologist.

Allowing herself to look at him closely for the first time since admitting her growing feelings, Lucy paid special attention now to the distinguished arch of his nose, the comfortable curve of his mouth, the powerful strength of his jaw line.

Good grief. Why on earth did he have to be so attractive and so likable?

Her steps faltered even as she closed the gap between them. Her sudden confidence quickly fading, she struggled to find the right words. As she approached, Cam turned to her, his gray eyes lighting up with recognition.

Giving him a timid smile, Lucy came to a halt directly in front of him and opened her lips to speak, not knowing what would come out when she did.

She took a deep breath. "Nice lamppost," she said, wishing she could have come up with something more witty. The look Cam gave her, however, was one of complete delight, as if she had just uttered the most clever phrase in the world.

Lucy bit her lip, wondering what he would say in return. But Cam responded only with an approving smile.

She shifted uncomfortably under his gaze. "I want to apol—" she began, but Cam reached out and laid one strong finger softly across her lips.

"Hush," he said in a voice that made her nearly forget what she had to say to him.

"But I need to tell you—" she tried again.

Cam, however, was having none of it. "Not now," he said firmly and reached out with one hand to spin her around in the direction of the street. "I have other plans," he informed her.

"What plans?" More curious than alarmed, Lucy found herself being propelled in the direction of a silver Toyota truck.

"Plans I should have made long ago," Cam said with great certainty. He dug into his pocket for his keys and unlocked the door. Opening it, he gave a half-bow, indicating that Lucy should get in. Which she did.

"And those plans would be…?"

"Ah. Plans for you, my dear," Cam said with a look of great satisfaction. "You see, I made a very big mistake yesterday."

"You did?" Lucy felt herself turning five shades of pink.

"I did." Cam leaned casually on the edge of the doorframe. "I allowed you to set me up with Janie McCallister when I had someone else on my mind."

"You did?" Lucy whispered again. Her stomach started to turn little flips. Did he mean what she thought he meant? She hardly dared hope. "But who?"

"Please." Cam made cluck-clucking noises with his tongue and shook his head disapprovingly. "Such modesty. You know very well who. As if I had to tell you, Lucy Salinger, Queen of Hearts."

Lucy closed her eyes, unable to face him until she knew for sure. *Oh, please tell me, please. I don't dare guess wrong and make an idiot out of myself again.*

Cam leaned in then and brushed one hand against the softness of her cheek, as if smoothing away her anxiety. "You know, don't you, that I've had a crush on you ever since I laid eyes on you, Lucy Salinger?" Lucy dared to open her eyes then. She shook her head slowly, unable to believe what she was hearing. "Well, I have," Cam said roughly. The playfulness was gone from his eyes now, something equally tender but much more powerful in its place. "And I am determined to get to know you better. Which brings me to today's mission."

The lightness returned to his voice, and he slowly pulled away—a good thing, since Lucy was having a hard time keeping herself from reaching out and touching the softness of his hair, to make sure he was truly real.

"'Today's mission'?" she repeated dumbly.

"That's right." Campbell stood back and placed both hands on his hips, looking like an eager genie preparing to grant his very first wish. "Lucy Salinger," he said, "you're coming with me."

Lucy opened her mouth to protest. But before she could say a word, Cam stepped forward, clamped one hand gently over her mouth, and grinned at her in a way that would have made her willing to fly to Tasmania, had he asked her to go.

"I mean it," he said with all the seriousness of an under-taker. "And I hope you're in the mood to have some fun. Because I believe it's time you and I had our very first date— whether you like it or not!"

Seven

"So where exactly are you taking me for this, uh, date?" Only partially recovered from her initial shock, Lucy leaned back against the truck's comfortable interior and focused on the road ahead of them. She still couldn't believe she was actually here.

"Truthfully?" Lucy looked at Cam but couldn't quite decipher the expression on his face.

Was he kidding? If there was one thing they didn't need, it was more falsehoods between them. "Truthfully," Lucy said with utter conviction.

"Well...I—"

She glanced at him again out of the corner of her eye. Both of Cam's hands gripped the steering wheel. He looked about as nervous as she felt.

"Actually, I hadn't gotten around to making any real plans," he admitted, throwing her a guilty schoolboy look. "Part one of my plan was focused on getting you to come out and talk to me. I didn't think I'd even get to part two."

Lucy arched her eyebrows in a look of amazement.

"Don't give me that look," Cam protested as he came to a halt at a stop sign and smoothly turned right. "I didn't think you'd actually come outside. You wouldn't take my calls, remember?" His voice held the slightest hint of frustration and hurt.

"I remember." Outside the passenger window, Lucy spied a small group of teenage girls, laughing as they headed for the beach. Skipping school, she guessed. She tried to focus on them and not on her feelings of embarrassment. She hoped that Cam wouldn't be too hard on her and wished there was some way to explain why she had been so reluctant to talk to him.

"Whoa. Too much shame, huh? Sorry." Her face must've been like an open book. Cam reached over with one hand and squeezed her arm gently. "That was a cheap shot. I wasn't going to talk about that yet. Can we just forget about last night and focus on each other for now?"

"Sure," Lucy said bravely and flashed him a smile that seemed to convince him. Cam turned his attention to the road, the conflict apparently forgotten.

"So I guess that means our schedule is fairly open," Cam said. "I'll be happy, though, to whip up some elaborate plan. But if you don't mind, I'd really prefer to just spend some time together—just being with each other and talking."

Lucy glanced around at the crowd of people—young and old—heading down to the sand. She enjoyed the familiarity of her community, the playful, relaxed attitude of the city. "I would kind of like to stick around here," she said honestly. There was nothing more soothing to her than a day at the beach. Besides, if she got too uncomfortable, she could always walk home. That, she thought, glancing down at her casual appearance, and the fact that she wasn't exactly dressed for an honest-to-goodness formal date.

"Perfect!" Cam appeared thoroughly pleased. "I wanted to spend the day getting to know you, not getting all wrapped up in some particular activity. What better way to do that than by prowling around your stomping grounds?" He had let the vehicle slow to a near crawl, but now, with an actual destination in mind, he stepped on the gas and drove purposefully toward the beach.

Lucy sat quietly, considering his words. They were comforting—it helped to know that he still wanted to get to know her even after she snapped at him—but she still felt vaguely uneasy. She wasn't convinced that this was a good idea, even though she'd been unable to refuse him. There was still the not-so-little matter of an inheritance to consider. Cam was being so nice to her, showing so much interest. But what if it was all an act? What if he was simply using her? Lost in thought, she refrained from speaking as Cam drove a few more blocks, then pulled into a public parking area just off Pacific Coast Highway.

Once the engine was turned off, Cam turned and, with one arm over the back of her seat, asked gently, "Are you okay, Luce?"

At the sound of the nickname used only by her sisters and closest friends, Lucy felt a rush of pleasure that warmed her clear down to her toes. She reached up and patted Cam's hand. Rough and warm, it gave her comfort somehow. They would talk later, isn't that what he had said? For now—for the length of their date—she would try just to enjoy being with him.

"Okay," she assured him, and the smile she gave him was genuine.

As they climbed out of the car, it struck her as silly that they had driven the short distance. She lived only a half-mile from where they now found themselves, just south of Malibu Pier. North of the pier, she knew, was a lagoon where they might see pelicans, ducks, and herons. And even farther north, at the junction of Pacific Coast Highway and Webb Way, lay the Malibu Country Mart—filled with little shops and cafés—a perfect place not only to shop, but to go stargazing, since so many famous actors and actresses lived in the area.

The Hollywood glitterati, however, was the farthest thing from her mind this morning. The only people watching Lucy wanted to do today involved a certain behavioral psychologist. And from the shy glances he kept throwing her way, she had the distinct impression that she was being watched too.

She borrowed Cam's cell phone to call the office before they went out to hit the beach. Gabby was, of course, out of her mind with curiosity and thoroughly frustrated when Lucy refused to tell her what she was doing that day.

"Daphne called to tell me you wouldn't be coming in," Gabby said. "She told me what happened last night and said you might be taking on a new identity in some foreign country. The way she talked I thought you were miserable. But listen to you now! You sound positively chipper. What's going on?" she asked, suspicious.

"Does anything have to be going on for me to sound chipper?" Lucy said evasively. She waved cheerfully at Cam, who was politely waiting about fifteen feet away, allowing her to conduct her conversation in private.

"As a matter of fact, yes, it does," Gabby said, sounding as if she meant it. "At least this week it does."

"Well. I hadn't realized I was making things so very dull for you," Lucy told her, her voice dripping with regret. "Consider my absence today a personal gift to you."

"Are you at least going to let me do some of the *real* work while you're gone?" her assistant wheedled. "I can go talk to some professional female softball players and see if any of them would be a match for Tiger Mason," she suggested, referring to the local pitching ace who had recently signed up with their agency. "Or I could—"

"I'd prefer that you just take calls and keep an eye on the office," Lucy told her.

"Grinch," Gabby grumbled. By the time they got off the phone, she was complaining bitterly about being left out of the loop, but at least she agreed to field calls for the rest of the day.

Once Cam's phone was safely locked up in the truck, Lucy felt ready to leave the rest of the world behind them.

"Where do you want to start?" Cam asked, gesturing around them.

"Mm...why don't we just walk?"

The suggestion seemed to please him, and as they headed north along the stretch of sand, Lucy felt first startled—then secretly delighted—as Cam took her hand and tucked it companionably into the crook of his arm. The gesture was intimate, yet not too invasive. And though it did, indeed, go against her rules about getting too close to her clients, Lucy knew that she was in too deep to turn back now.

"So tell me, Ms. Lucy Salinger," Cam said in a soft voice, "exactly how you got started in this matchmaking business in the first place."

Other questions might have felt too personal, but this...this was something that Lucy could handle. Breathing a sigh of relief, she allowed herself to lean against him as they walked. She explained how she had become known as a matchmaker even as a child and how it had seemed so very natural to follow that course after college. When the matchmaking service became an overnight hit, some said it was luck, others, God's blessing upon her. The local columnists had been intrigued with her agency, and with the fact that a young college graduate was doing the sort of work commonly attributed only to elderly Russian women. Retro was 'in' these days, they'd said. Lucy knew that her instant popularity could fade at any moment. But for now she felt that she was doing what God had called her to do.

"That's very important to you, isn't it?" Cam observed. "Following God's call for you?"

"Yes, it is. In fact, I—" Lucy faltered. Though her faith was an integral part of her life, she'd felt farther away from God than normal over the past few days. She thought it was important to take her concerns to the Lord, but she hadn't spent any time talking with him about how Campbell's appearance at Rent-a-Yenta had impacted her life. She hadn't allowed herself to admit to anyone—not her sisters, not herself, not even God—that she cared about Cam. Now that it was clear she did, she realized how much she needed to talk about it with people who understood her, including the One who loved her most of all. The fact that she hadn't done so left her with a distinct lack of peace.

"Look, can we sit for a minute?" she asked. "I know you said we should talk about things later, but it's hard for me to focus on *now* when I'm still so worried about *then*," she admitted.

"All right." Cam glanced at the open beach around them. Though there were a number of truant teenagers scattered here and there and an occasional mother and toddler, for the most part, they were alone. He pulled his sweater over his head—leaving just the T-shirt underneath—and, laying it down on the cream-colored sand, offered Lucy a place to sit.

Her heart swelled as she blinked back the water that stung her eyes. The gesture made her feel important, valued, and incredibly special.

Touched by his tenderness, she sat. Cam planted himself on the sand beside her. Then, as naturally as if he had done it every day of his life, he reached out, took her hand in his own, and rubbed it gently between his palms, warming it.

"Go ahead, Luce," he said kindly. "I'm listening."

His action was distracting, and for a moment Lucy could hardly even speak. "Cam," she said after a moment. She paused, but from that point on the words came out in a rush; she knew if she didn't just blurt it out she'd never find the courage to explain. "Before we say anything else, I have to apologize to you for the way I've handled your account." As the words spilled from her lips, she saw him straighten up stiffly and realized that was exactly the wrong thing to say. "Not that I see you as 'an account,'" she hastily amended. "Or at least *just* as 'an account.' You're not *just* that to me. But that's how you came to me first. You asked me to help you find someone, and I...I..."

Lucy struggled to find the right words. For a moment she stared out at the crashing waves that brought her comfort. Assured by their quiet roar, she took a deep breath and tried again. There was no point in beating around the bush. She might as well just come out and say it.

As Cam listened attentively, Lucy continued with her torrent of words. "I need to face the truth, Cam. I haven't treated you the same way I have every other client." Her face burned as she made her confession. "I can't explain why—well, maybe I can, but I'd really rather not," she said honestly. "But for one reason or another, I've acted crazily, impulsively, with you."

He smiled at this. Lucy's brow furrowed. Cam didn't see that this was a bad thing. Obviously further explanation was needed. "Do you remember the day we met?" she said patiently.

"I do."

"Well, I told you then that I pray about—and for—all my clients. But—and I'm embarrassed to say this—I haven't prayed about you," she said. "Not one bit. And now everything's a mess! *I'm* a mess." Maddeningly, Cam just smiled at her. Lucy groaned in exasperation. "Don't you see? This is

143

your life we're talking about here," she said dramatically. "Your entire future. And I'm running around, playing Russian roulette with it!"

"Don't you think that's a bit of an overstatement?" he said gently. "I don't think our God is the kind who would ever punish you for not praying. He's patient and loving, and he wants to talk to you. Right? But he's not waiting with a big stick, ready to rap your knuckles when you make a mistake. So you haven't prayed about this yet, and obviously you feel it. But now that you feel the need to, you'll pray for me, for you…for us."

Us. Lucy liked the sound of that. She tried not to let it show.

"Besides," Cam said, "you're not solely responsible for my entire future and well-being, you know. It was only a couple of dates. You can't make me marry someone I choose not to," he reminded her. "And, by the way, no offense to your services intended, but I do choose *not* to marry Janie McCallister, thank you very much. Nor, for that matter, am I the least bit interested in Monica or Donna, in case you're wondering."

For some reason, that little revelation both pleased and disconcerted her. "I know, I know," she said miserably. "Those were bad matches. I felt terrible about them. And then Gabby practically pushed Janie on you, and you didn't resist. I felt bad, for so many reasons." Cam's eyebrows shot up, but he said nothing. "And then I went to spy on you."

"Yes. You did." His lips turned up at the corners, but he didn't seem surprised by this confession.

"You knew?"

"Of course I knew. You think that little act of yours fooled me? Lothario? Please."

Lucy hung her head in shame. "Well…you seemed to buy it at the time."

"I'll admit, you had me worried for a moment or two," Cam confessed. "But I knew it couldn't be real. That...that man—"

"Oliver," she supplied.

"Thank you. That Oliver was as far below you as a man could ever get. Do you think I could actually know you, Lucy, for more than thirty seconds and believe that you would be satisfied with that, uh..." Words failed him again.

"That Lothario?" she suggested.

Cam's eyes brightened as understanding dawned on him. "Ah. It all makes sense now," he said. "I wondered where you'd come up with that one." The look of enlightenment was fleeting as his expression hardened with the return of the memory. "You know, I'm not a violent man. But I have to admit that even I was tempted to poke a few more holes in that bit of Swiss cheese. I think he knew it, too, because the minute you walked out the door, he started confessing."

"He did?" It figured. "How gallant."

Cam nodded. "He told me all about how you'd dropped in at his table, that he didn't even know you. He said you were looking for some place to hide. That helped me put a few of the puzzle pieces together."

"I don't know why I thought spying on you would help," Lucy offered weakly. "Maybe I thought I could stop the date, change things, get another chance to make things right for you—" *And for me.* She pushed the wayward thought away. "I'm not sure what I was trying to do," she said firmly, trying to convince if not Cam, then at least herself. "But I do know that I've acted like an idiot all week long. And I'm sorry. Please, I want you to know that I haven't done it on purpose. I just feel totally out of control these days."

Ever since I met you.

Cam accepted this little outburst as calmly and matter-of-factly as if she had just explained the law of gravity. Lying on his back, he turned his face skyward and closed his eyes against the grains of sand that blew across, getting trapped in his tawny lashes.

Lucy wanted to join him. But feeling uncertain about his response to her impassioned confession and recognizing the intimacy of being that close, side by side, she remained frozen in place with her arms wrapped around her knees—finding contentment instead in simply watching Cam.

For a long time, he lay like that—thinking, Lucy was sure, of ways to berate her for her foolishness. Though he had been kind to her all along, she was still surprised when he finally reached out with one hand and fondly squeezed the toes of one of her sneakers.

"Tell me more about you," he said at last. Lucy wondered if her ears had filled with the blowing sand. Surely she couldn't have heard him correctly.

"But, Cam! You just said you knew that I was spying on you. That I—"

"I know what I said. And I heard what you said." He didn't sound angry. Only curious. "But I'm not concerned about what you've done. I want to know more about who you are. I want details. Tell me about your family. Your last boyfriend. What it's like to be Lucy."

She stared at him as if he had just asked her to explain life from the perspective of a Slinky.

"Are you sure you're really a behavioral psychologist?" she asked dubiously. "And not one of the nut bars themselves?"

"No," Cam laughed. "I'm not sure at all. Now, enough stalling." He turned his head, opened one eye, and pointed a finger at her while demanding regally, "Speak!"

With few other options open to her, Lucy decided to comply. She began with a brief explanation of her childhood and the subsequent loss of both her parents—her mother to

146

leukemia when Lucy was five and her father after a heart attack just a year ago. But though she started with every intention of giving Cam nothing but the bare facts, she soon found herself relating details that she hadn't remembered in years—both painful and joyous. Soon she was sprawled out on the sand beside Cam, regaling him with ridiculous tales from college and what her sister Daphne had dubbed the "Rick Years."

She told him about how she'd fallen in love during college and had been thoroughly convinced that Rick was the one—until he stood her up at their wedding. She recalled how she had used the airline tickets to Tahiti that were still in her overnight bag and had taken off on the prepaid, ten-day vacation with Daphne, all at Rick's expense. And she sadly remembered how she had spent those days alternately numb and tearful as she mourned the loss of her first true love.

"It must've really hurt you to have been left like that." Cam sounded sincere, concerned.

"It was hard," Lucy admitted. "I felt so betrayed. It took me a long time to get over it, to learn to trust people again. Rick had seemed so right for me—I really loved him…" Her words trailed off as the sad memories floated back to her. They sat in silence for a few moments; it wasn't an uncomfortable silence but an easy silence, respectful. Finally Lucy cleared her throat and said, "Well, enough of that." And they soon resumed their lighthearted talk.

Occasionally Cam responded with a frown, a look of compassion, or a boisterous laugh—depending on the point of the story. And from time to time, he asked questions to clarify. But for the most part, he simply listened. It was the first time in years that Lucy could recall someone taking the time to really get to know her, as she daily tried to do with each of her clients. It surprised her how good it felt to be known by Cam, even in such a small way. She was soon sharing personal details willingly, as Cam made it clear that she could trust him with the secrets of her heart.

By the time she had finished telling him about Daphne's recent almost-elopement and Cat's subsequent marriage, the sun was high in the sky and her stomach had begun to rumble softly.

"Oops. Sorry," she said as a tiny growl escaped. "How unladylike."

Cam grinned at her.

"What?" Lucy looked at him suspiciously.

Cam shrugged. "You're just so cute." The transgression seemed only to endear her to him even further.

This pleased Lucy more than she was willing to admit. She bowed her head, unable to meet his eyes. "Stop." She'd been having so much fun talking with him, she'd forgotten how much was at stake. It was hard to listen to such things, especially if they were only temporary.

"Luce? What's the matter?" He sat up and caught her hands between his own.

Instinctively she started to pull away. In such close proximity, he seemed incredibly strong, terribly powerful. She felt herself becoming swallowed up in the urge to know him as more than a casual friend, just as he was beginning to know her. But she could not bring herself to ask the questions of him or to allow herself to be truly vulnerable. If she felt so drawn to him now, how much more difficult would it be when he left after she had come to know him on a deeper level?

"Please? Tell me." He sounded like he cared.

She tried to pull her hands away, but he held them tightly, and she finally gave up.

"I'm not cute," she said at last. It sounded pouty, childish. But she didn't know what else to say.

"What?" Thankfully, he didn't laugh.

"I mean…I'm not fishing for compliments. I'm not even talking about what I look like."

"I hope so. Because I would think that you'd know how adorable you are physically." Cam frowned as she tried to pull away once more. "Sorry. I didn't mean to offend you. If you're not talking about your appearance, what are you talking about then?"

"I just don't feel cute," she said, trying hard to find a way to explain. "I feel…bad."

"Tell me what you mean. What's that bad feeling like?" He spoke just like a psychologist, which of course he was. Part of Lucy wanted to reach out and poke him with one finger; the other part wanted to run and hide.

"I wish I could explain, but I don't think I can." She uncrossed her legs and switched to a kneeling position, as if preparing to flee. "It just feels bad to me that you're being so nice and calling me cute and listening to me, but you're not getting the fact that I've really blown it with you," she said heavily.

"Why is it so important to you that I get it? Don't you like me?" Cam's eyes bored into her. "Don't you want me to forget those things that you think are so horrible?" There was a strange intensity about him now that Lucy had a hard time reconciling with his usually easygoing personality.

"I'd prefer you figured it out now rather than later," she explained carefully, ignoring the second part of the question about liking him. She tried not to meet his eyes, but he kept his gaze trained on her until she looked at him again.

"Why?" He wasn't so gentle now in his pursuit of answers. Lucy could hear a hard edge in his tone. "Why does it matter to you when I figure it out? What do you think I'm going to do?"

"What do you mean, what do I think you're going to do?" Lucy stared at him incredulously. For such a brilliant man, he sure asked some obvious questions. "You're going to be disappointed in me, like you said you were the other day. And you're not going to want to be around me anymore." The words echoed in her ears as she clambered to her feet in an attempt at escape.

"This is ridiculous." Lucy was half-laughing now, a laugh with no real humor to it. How absurd! She was worried about a relationship that didn't even exist.

Spurred into action by her withdrawal, Cam stood to his feet even before she did. "Why do you say that?" His eyes and voice both demanded an answer. "What's so ridiculous about it?"

"Me," she said helplessly. "You. This whole thing! Listen to us, talking like an old boyfriend and girlfriend. Cam, we hardly know each other. It shouldn't matter to me what you think of my behavior. And you shouldn't care whether or not I return your calls. It doesn't make sense for us to be this emotionally involved in something that hasn't even happened."

"Happened? What needs to happen?" There was a spark in Cam's gray eyes now, but his mouth was still drawn into a look of intensity.

"I didn't mean—" Lucy faltered. "I just meant—" Her knees felt weak, and the heat from the sun seemed to increase as Cam put his arms on her elbows and pulled her close. Incredibly, she saw what was coming, knew it was probably a bad idea, but made no move to resist.

"Is this what you're talking about?" The words were whispered. His arms around her were more gentle. Cam was grinning now.

A sigh of relief escaped Lucy's lips. The old, familiar, teasing Campbell was back. And as he drew her close, she realized that despite all her worries and concerns, she was smiling too.

As kisses went, it was one of the best ever. Not that Lucy was extremely practiced at the art, but she knew beauty when she experienced it. Soft and gentle, passionate and pure, it was the kind of kiss against which all others were compared. And as she stood in the circle of Cam's arms, gazing out together at the crashing surf, she knew it was one that she would remember for the rest of her life.

"There now." Cam spoke the words against the back of her head, the sound muffled as he brushed his lips against the softness of her hair. "Are you convinced now that you're cute?"

"All right," she conceded, her voice playful and saucy. "If you say so. I'm cute."

She could feel the approving curve of his lips as he planted another kiss at her temple.

"Do you understand, too, that I do care about you? And that this does matter?" He slipped his arms from around her and turned her around to face him. "Because it does matter. A lot. I don't care if it makes sense. This is how I feel. And if that kiss was any indication, it's how you feel too."

"Aha!" Lucy forced a mock glare. "So this was a setup! You were gathering evidence for your case against me."

"Perhaps." Cam gave a playful leer and started to reach for her. "Perhaps we should try that again, just to make sure."

Deftly Lucy stepped away, narrowly escaping his embrace. Her heart skipped a beat. Every nerve was calling for her to kiss him again. But not yet. She wanted to take things slow, to be sure.

"Sorry, but you have to feed me first. My stomach is complaining. Remember the noise that made you decide how cute I am?"

"Your stomach isn't the *only* cute thing about you," Cam grumbled. He made a great show of appearing disappointed but obediently took her by the hand, looking content to wait.

"There are some little cafés down at the Country Mart," Lucy told him. "Some friends of mine run one of them, if you're interested." Ed and Velma, the restaurant's proprietors, were like family to her. It struck her, strangely, that it was as if she was taking Cam home to meet Mom and Dad. The thought unnerved her. Yet at the same time, it felt terribly right to give Cam a glimpse into this part of her life.

He perked up visibly at the prospect. "Friends of yours, you say? Perfect. After all, isn't that what this day is about? Getting to know you?"

"So I've been told," Lucy said dryly. "And you seem to be doing a good job of it so far." She could still feel the pressure of his lips on hers.

"Well then!" Picking his sweater up off the sand, Cam shook it vigorously, tied it around his waist, and took Lucy's hand once more.

The walk to the Country Mart was brief, and they strolled in silence, perfectly happy for the moment simply to enjoy each other's company. When they arrived, five or six children were romping on the picturesque playground around which the collection of shops and restaurants were centered.

Normally Lucy would have enjoyed stopping to watch them for a while—she loved kids and still hoped that someday she would have some of her own. But today her growling stomach took precedence, and she led Cam directly to one of her favorite hangouts, Ed and Velma's Beach Sidewalk Café.

Wisely, he didn't argue.

For nearly two years she had been coming to Ed and Velma's, ever since the two had become a couple, thanks to her matchmaking, or—as Ed liked to call it—her "blessed meddling."

Unlike most other couples, Ed and Velma had received the benefit of Lucy's wisdom not because they were clients, but because they were friends. Velma, a spirited, white-haired woman of sixty-two, had been one of Lucy's English teachers in college, and the two had remained in touch over the years, getting together approximately every six months. Sixty-year-old Ed, on the other hand, was the widowed father of Emily, one of Lucy's girlfriends from high school.

One day during a visit with Emily to Buena Park, where Ed had lived with his son since being widowed, he spoke with Lucy about how much he still missed his wife. Touched by his loneliness, Lucy determined to find him a companion for his later years. Four months later, during her next visit with Velma, it hit her. She became a woman with a mission. Introductions were made despite the elderly pair's reticence. And miraculously, one year later, the two were married—with Lucy, appropriately, serving as one of Velma's bridesmaids at the lovely August beachfront ceremony.

Like Lucy, Ed and Velma shared a deep and abiding love for the sea. Which was one of the primary reasons that six months after their wedding, they decided to settle in Malibu, where they opened the tiny café.

A passionate, if not highly skilled, fisherman, Ed had insisted on decorating the two-room restaurant with authentic fishing paraphernalia: enormous nets hung from the ceiling, filled with starfish and Japanese floats but, thankfully, no actual dead fish. On the walls, rods and reels hung at odd angles, punctuated by an occasional fly, all in a kaleidoscope of bright colors.

As they walked in the door, Lucy found herself overcome with the feeling of home.

"Well, I'll be!" Velma beamed at them from behind the counter and raised her dishrag, which she waved enthusiastically in greeting. "Ed, get out here," she called in the general direction of the kitchen. "Our girl is here!"

"Which one?" The voice wafted lazily from an open door behind her. As far as he was concerned, he had three daughters: Emily, Margaret—Velma's only child—and Lucy.

"You'll just have to come out and see for yourself, won't you?" She grinned mischievously at Lucy and Cam as they joined her at the counter. "Impertinent, aren't I?"

"As ever," Lucy said lovingly and leaned across the counter to plant a kiss on the woman's papery cheek. "Velma, I'd like you to meet Dr. Campbell Howard. He's a..." She started to say "friend of mine" but on impulse stopped herself and said with a sheepish grin, "He's my date."

Cam reached over and put his arm around Lucy's waist, squeezing her gently. Then before she had time to feel self-conscious about it, quickly released her.

"Oh, I seeee. Your date." *Calm down, Velma,* Lucy thought, her embarrassment genuine. *You're practically salivating.* Like her sisters, Velma had been concerned about Lucy's marital status, though she'd been even more verbal about it. *"Ed!"* She hollered again over her shoulder, louder this time, then smiled demurely at Cam. "It's such a pleasure to meet you."

Cam turned to Lucy, his lips twitching in amusement. She grinned back at him, delighted that he saw the humor in the situation and did not appear to feel like a bug under a microscope—which he essentially was.

"The pleasure is all mine," Cam said dramatically as he turned his attention back to Velma. Lucy stifled a laugh as their hostess literally squealed with delight when Cam took her hand and squeezed it warmly. She'd never seen Velma respond like this to anyone—except Ed, of course. She looked like a smitten schoolgirl. Lucy leaned her body way over the white Formica counter and shouted, "Ed, you old dog, are you gonna come out here, or do I have to go back there and drag you out myself?"

"Who are you calling an old dog?" As Ed came around the corner, however, spatula in hand, Lucy could not help but think that he did resemble an old, lovable bulldog. Round-faced and jowly, he beamed at Lucy with the pride of a parent.

"And what exactly are you doing here? Don't you have work to do, young lady?" Despite his playful reproach, he was obviously delighted to see her.

"I'm taking a personal day, actually," she explained, ignoring the look of innocence Cam was throwing at her.

"Yes. Personal," Cam said seriously. "Very personal."

Lucy gave him a little frown of disapproval and reached out to give him a playful swat on the arm, but he danced away just out of her reach. Velma watched the exchange with wide-eyed interest, while Ed turned his attention to Cam.

"Who's this guy?" he asked rather unceremoniously.

"He's—" Lucy began.

"This," Velma interrupted, "is little Lu's date." She looked thoroughly pleased.

"Campbell Howard, actually," Cam supplied, extending his hand to Ed.

At first Ed didn't respond. To Lucy's chagrin, he simply looked Cam up and down. Several times. For a moment she thought he might actually ask Cam to proclaim his intentions. Eventually, however, Ed put down the spatula and took Cam's hand in his own, fierce grip.

"How d'ya do?" he said, pumping Cam's hand up and down. He gave Cam another searching look. "Want some trout?" he said at last. "It's today's special. Fresh caught."

Cam didn't appear to think twice. "I'd love some," he said, sounding like he meant it.

This appeased Ed, and he disappeared into the kitchen once more. After a second, his rotund face appeared back around the edge of the doorframe. "Lucy?"

"The same," she said, knowing how Ed loved sharing the food he had personally caught.

"Grnh." The response was unintelligible, but Lucy could see from the look in his eyes that he was pleased.

"Why don't you two have a seat?" Velma said amiably and stepped out from behind the counter to show them to their table.

Since it was still early, they pretty much had their pick of the place. Taking charge, Cam nodded at a tiny table in one corner. Lucy was delighted with his choice. Flanked by windows on both walls, it gave them a view of the sidewalk outside, allowing them to people watch and drink in the warm California sunshine.

The table was small, and as Lucy scooted her chair forward, her knees bumped up against Cam's. Shyly, she gave him a sideways glance, wondering if he had noticed.

From the way he was grinning, she guessed that he had.

Oblivious to their flirting, Velma grabbed a chair from a nearby table and pulled it up to join them. She began to ask questions and to share stories with Cam about the fresh-faced, college-age girl Lucy had been, and Lucy began to relax, enjoying the distraction. Certainly, it was easier to talk to Cam in Velma's presence. Feeling less threatened by the intense feelings that came with being close to him, Lucy was able to lose some of her self-consciousness. As the three talked and laughed and shared, the time passed quickly, and Lucy was surprised when Ed came out and deposited enormous plates filled with crispy, golden potatoes and pan-fried trout on their table.

"Well, I suppose I should let you young folks eat your lunch," Velma said with regret and pushed her chair back from the table. "But you two come back soon. Do you hear me?" She waggled one finger in front of Lucy's eyes.

"Yes ma'am."

"'Cause we like this boy of yours," she said with conviction. And despite his gruffness, Ed didn't argue.

I like him too, Lucy found herself thinking, as the two puttered away. *This boy of mine...that is, if he really is mine.*

If he was bothered by the label, Cam didn't show it.

"May I say grace?" Cam said.

Moved by the gesture, Lucy nodded mutely and allowed him to take her hand in his as he bowed his head and prayed. "Dear Lord," he began, "thank you for my lovely companion, for this gorgeous day, and for your continual presence. Please be with us today, and bless our time together. We thank you for this meal and for all that you provide, including relationships with those we care for. In Jesus' name, amen."

Lucy wondered at the words he uttered about relationships but could not bring herself to ask what he had meant. She wasn't ready yet to tackle the questions that needed answering, so she focused on the plate in front of her and happily scooped the tender meat into her mouth, letting its buttery sweetness melt against her tongue.

Throughout their meal, Cam skillfully steered the conversation to harmless topics like school and work and even past dating relationships, though he kept the stories light. By the time her stomach was full, Lucy was feeling relaxed and content in Cam's presence.

Finally, putting down his fork, Cam turned his attention back to their earlier conversation, as Lucy had known he ultimately would.

"Now," he said, taking her hand once more in his. "We've had a little room to breathe, which if I'm not mistaken, you needed."

Lucy nodded, waiting wordlessly for what would come next.

"And I want you to know I heard everything you said this morning," he said, gently smoothing the soft skin of her fingers with his own rough hands. "But now, I want to tell you what I've been thinking about all this. And I *have* been thinking about it—about you—since the moment we first met."

Struggling to assimilate this bit of information, Lucy simply blinked at him.

"You seem so embarrassed about how you handled my account, as you put it," he observed. "And I can understand why. You're a professional. I can see why you feel you've made mistakes, setting me up with someone who wasn't right for me."

Stung by his words, though she knew they were true, Lucy steeled herself for whatever was coming next.

"But," Cam said, his voice and expression softening, "I wouldn't have wanted you to be any more professional than that."

"But why?" Lucy grappled with the absurdity of his statement.

"'Cause if you had been, you might have actually set me up with a good match—but one who wasn't *you*. It would have meant that you didn't care about me. But you do care, don't you?" He seemed fairly certain, yet his eyes held just a trace of doubt.

Memories of that morning's tender kiss flooded Lucy's mind, stirring her senses. "Of course I do," she said in a low voice. There was no sense in denying it now.

"And you did from the beginning?" Cam pressed.

Lucy hesitated. That was a bit harder to answer. Certainly she'd felt attracted to him, had felt nervous in his presence. But had she cared for him, even that first day, as she cared for him now? As she was caring for him more and more with each passing moment?

"I felt...something," she admitted haltingly. "But I'm not sure what it was. I don't even know what I'm feeling *now*, exactly," she said, although it was becoming clearer.

Cam appeared satisfied with that. He began to play absentmindedly with her fingers, stroking each nail of her right hand with the callous pad of his thumb. The gesture was exciting and endearing and thoroughly distracting. Lucy put her left hand over his, stilling him. But with both her hands on his, the moment felt even more intimate.

"The truth is, Lucy," Cam said, his voice thick with emotion, "I felt something too. I told you why I came to your office that first day—it was a favor to my sister. Alex talked me into it, and I wanted to make her happy. I didn't really expect to meet someone I could care for. But I did. I met you." He shook his head in amazement. "The matchmaker herself—who'd have thought it?" He laughed, a familiar rumble that somehow comforted Lucy's soul. "Don't you see? I didn't want you to fix me up—not because I didn't trust you, but because I didn't want anyone else but you. That's why I came to see you a second time when I saw you out, uh, running." He laughed. "I wanted to tell you that I didn't want to be set up with anyone but you. But by then, you had this whole other plan figured out. It hurt my feelings to know that you had someone else in mind for me. I didn't know what to say. But I know what to say now. I don't want anyone else, Lucy. I want *you*."

Cam sounded for all the world as though he meant it.

"But why?" She tilted her head to study him. Hadn't he been paying attention? Didn't he realize that she was a basket case? Maybe they should try dating later, when she was more together, more composed, more prepared for a relationship. "I drool, remember? I jog in my suit. I spy on men in restaurants. I'm a complete lunatic, in case you haven't noticed. A 'nut bar,' I believe you called it."

But Cam didn't appear in the least concerned. "As a behavioral psychologist, I can testify that, yes, you have acted a bit strangely since we first met," he agreed good-naturedly. "I think I can handle it, though."

"But—" Lucy tried to offer another protest.

"Listen to me, Lucy." Startled, she hung on to her chair as Cam put one hand on its back and dragged it close to him, so that they were sitting with their noses almost touching. Up close like that, Lucy could see every wrinkle, every line of his dear, sweet face. "You may be a nut bar," he said fondly. "But I'd like you to be *my* nut bar."

Lucy laughed in spite of herself. "I should probably be offended by that," she said. "But you actually make it sound like a compliment."

Cam, however, wasn't laughing anymore. "I know you're used to dealing with long-term commitments in your job," he said carefully. "And maybe that scares you because you know you're—we're—obviously not ready for that. But relationships don't have to be all or nothing, you know. I can't commit to marrying you right now, and I don't think you'd even want me to if I could. But I *do* promise to stick around for a while, to get to know you, to learn all I can about you, and to show you that I care."

I promise to stick around for a while. It wasn't much of a commitment. It was a temporary promise, at best. And yet, as Cam looked at her earnestly, expectantly, waiting for her answer, she knew she could not turn him down. Even if the relationship wasn't going to last, it would be worth letting him into her life—for a while.

She smiled tremulously. Taking this as his cue, Cam reached out and took one of her hands between both of his.

"Lucy Salinger," he said in his most formal voice. "Make me the happiest man in this restaurant. Will you be my girl-friend?"

Lucy took a deep breath, nodded slowly and—pushing her doubts to the back of her mind—answered him with great simplicity and utter sincerity. "I will."

Eight

From the moment she agreed to be Cam's girlfriend, Lucy felt a perplexing mixture of delight, apprehension, and something deeper—something unidentifiable, that she was certain she'd never felt before. Had one of her clients come to her with a list of the symptoms she now experienced—clammy hands, nervous stomach, loss of appetite, and the extraordinary feeling that the world was suddenly a new and wonderful, though somewhat frightening, place—Lucy would have triumphantly proclaimed the man or woman "in love," stamped the client's file NO LONGER AVAILABLE, and started shopping for an appropriate wedding gift.

When it came to her own life, however, Lucy felt curiously reluctant to succumb to the throes of romance, regardless of how unbelievably enticing the prospect was with Cam as the object of her affections.

After their lunch together at Ed and Velma's café that day, Cam had gone with Lucy into at least a half-dozen nearby shops, content simply to browse together until his eye landed on a brightly colored gold-and-scarlet kite. From that point on, he would not be satisfied until Lucy joined him on the beach, where they spent the next two hours playing with his toy. Though the air at Malibu could be dead calm during the long summer months, the tail end of spring still brought a constant invasion of breezes ranging from mild to tempestuous, all of which served to further their enjoyment of the day.

Finally the sun sank low in the sky, the temperature dropped, and Lucy longed for a chance to rest. As the growling of their stomachs resumed, she and Cam climbed back into the truck, drove just north of Malibu, and continued their date with a light Mexican dinner at Carillo's, located right off of Pacific Coast Highway, where they dined heartily on seafood tacos and chili rellenos. This was followed by a late evening walk along the more isolated El Pescador beach, where more sweet, gentle kisses were added to her memory of their first, convincing Lucy that what had happened earlier that day was not just a lovely, unrepeatable dream.

That night she slept peacefully.

And in the morning, her first thoughts were of Cam.

That weekend and the following week their relationship continued to unfold much as it had begun: with laughter, new revelations about each other, and not a little trepidation on Lucy's part. Though Cam asked her repeatedly about the tiny furrow that appeared occasionally on her brow, Lucy insisted it was nothing, assured him that she was greatly enjoying his company—which she was—and focused on enjoying the time they now spent together.

Though she felt a bit uncertain about their future, Lucy did, however, manage for the most part to live in the here and now, thoroughly enjoying herself as Cam escorted her to a Dodgers game, to an authentic black gospel concert in downtown L.A., on a stroll through Westwood Village—even to Disneyland, which she hadn't visited since she was a small child.

Most of the days slipped by peacefully, happily, without incident. Cam was the very picture of the devoted beau, showing up at her office with voluminous bouquets of wildflowers, calling her twice a day, and offering thoroughly convincing reassurances that he would always be there for her. Like a wildlife veterinarian coaxing an injured squirrel to safety, Cam offered one delicious nut after another—time, attention, promises, and affection—until Lucy felt relatively secure in the safety of his arms.

The following Tuesday afternoon, Lucy was sitting at her desk, mulling over a stack of client profiles when Cam called to say he'd be late for dinner that evening.

"I know we said six o'clock," he said apologetically, "but I have a meeting that's going to run at least until five-thirty, and after that I'd really like to go running."

That last comment surprised her. Lucy gripped the receiver firmly in one hand and wrapped the spiral cord around the fingers of the other as she tried to remember if Cam had ever mentioned to her that he liked running. She remembered their little running fiasco when he'd bumped into her in front of her building—he'd been winded then. It was obvious that he was making this up now. "Of course," she said smoothly, masking the hurt feelings that tugged at her heart. She couldn't help but wonder if maybe he didn't really want to be with her tonight. They'd spent a great deal of time together in the past week. Maybe he just needed to get away from her.

"You need to take that time for yourself," she reassured him, sensing that was what she was expected to say. Deep inside, though, she wished that he would tell her he'd rather take the time to be with her. Obviously, she decided, the first bloom of romance was fading. A week ago Cam couldn't wait to be with her and would drive straight from work to her office. Now he'd rather breathe in drafts of stinky, exhaust-filled air as he pounded his way down the busy city streets during rush-hour traffic. "It sounds nice," she lied.

She could see that it was all happening again, just it had with Rick. First the little excuses, wanting to get away from her more and more, then long spells without so much as a phone call. Well, she wouldn't be blindsided this time. She could see the handwriting on the wall. Why did she always choose the wrong men? As she sat stewing, she remembered how devastated she'd been by Rick's rejection, and the feeling reemerged as if the events had just happened. She couldn't let herself go through that again—she just couldn't.

"Thanks." Cam sounded relieved. "I was afraid you'd be mad."

"Mad?" she said lightly. "Don't be silly." *Try hurt, disappointed, worried, afraid.* "I'll see you at what? Seven, then?"

"How about seven-thirty?"

Lucy's heart sank, but she refused to let it show. No matter what, she wouldn't let him know how much he was hurting her. She forced a smile onto her face, even though he couldn't see it.

"Seven-thirty would be great."

By the time Cam finally showed up at almost seven-forty-five, Lucy had worked herself into an emotional state. Twice she'd had to remove her eye makeup and reapply it because her watery eyes had caused her mascara to run, and there was a distinct puffiness under her eyes.

Even her attire for the evening had caused her anxiety. At first she'd put on a soft, gray, ribbed turtleneck tucked into stylish hound's-tooth trousers and oxfords. Then, deciding that was too dressy, considering Cam's snub, she changed into jeans and a T-shirt that read "I'm with Stupid," a gag gift she'd picked at the white elephant party she and Daphne held last Christmas. On second thought, however, that seemed too rude—even to Lucy—and she switched to a Pacific blue corduroy shirt, which she paired with jeans and navy suede clogs.

When Cam finally rang the bell, Lucy opened the door and greeted him with a wary look. And when he leaned over to kiss her, she offered not her lips but her cheek. It wasn't that she was trying to be nasty; she just didn't feel like being affectionate.

Cam accepted all this without any reaction but a raised eyebrow. Clearly, he noticed the signs. It was obvious she was upset; there was no point in trying to hide it. Yet for some reason, she did. Leaving him in the living room to entertain himself, she retreated into the kitchen and flitted between it and the dining room until their meal was on the vast farmhouse table, homey and warm with its painted red legs and polished pine top.

The food itself looked irresistible, even if the mood of the evening was ruined. Piled high in a brick red bowl was an enormous mound of corkscrew noodles. Steam rose from the spicy sauce, still in its pan on a hot pad. In yet another bowl, crunchy dinner rolls were wrapped in a soft blue kitchen cloth, folded over to keep the heat from escaping. And a green salad added the perfect complement of color to the table.

Politely Cam waited until Lucy was seated before pulling out his own chair. Then after offering up a quick prayer, he attacked both his meal and her change in attitude.

"What's the matter, Lucy?" he said as he twirled his fork around in a pile of tangy pasta and marinara.

"Nothing," she said, trying to sound like she meant it.

Cam wasn't fooled. "Obviously, it's something."

Lucy shrugged and said nothing. Cam's eyes flickered over her face, then focused back on his plate as he worked on his meal. After two denials, he stopped asking, and the two of them finished the rest of their meal in silence.

This is it, she thought, biting down on a forkful of crisp, romaine lettuce and Caesar dressing. Mentally and emotionally, she tried to prepare herself for the breakup that she was

165

certain would come. Sure enough, after the last noodle was gone from his plate, Cam looked at her soberly, took her by the hand, and led the way into the living room, saying quietly, "Come here, you. I think we need to talk."

Lucy followed reluctantly. She plopped down against the green-and-white ticking couch and grabbed a soft, emerald chenille pillow to comfort her, holding it close against her chest.

Cam sat down beside her, two feet away, his face twisted in an expression of worry. "You look like you think I'm going to hit you," he observed sensitively.

Lucy shook her head. "That's not what I'm afraid of. I know you'd never hurt me." *Not that way anyhow.*

"So what are you afraid of?" He looked and sounded sympathetic. But how could she ever explain?

"Look," she said, trying to sound calm and composed. "I realize that you're mad. You wanted to go running this afternoon, and I made you feel bad about it."

"What?" Cam broke in. He lifted his arms in a gesture of helplessness. "That's what this is about? You didn't make me feel bad about going running." He looked at her as though she'd lost her mind. "I thought you didn't even care. You said it sounded like fun." He seemed completely bewildered.

"You have every right to go running if you want to," Lucy affirmed, even though his decision still stung.

"But you said it didn't bother you."

"Why should it bother me?" Lucy responded lightly. She hoped she came across as independent and brave.

"I'm not saying it should." Cam studied her features carefully. He appeared less bewildered now. In fact, he looked as though he had just made a great discovery. "I'm saying that it *did*. Have you been crying, Lucy?" She tilted her head away, but he put one finger to the side of her chin and turned it so she had no choice but to look at him. "You have, haven't you?"

She blinked back the tears that she'd been struggling to hide and tried to pretend otherwise.

"Oh, Lucy." Cam gave a great sigh, leaned over, and pulled her into his arms. At first she held her body stiff but could keep it up for only so long and finally fell limp against him. Soothed by his embrace, Lucy relaxed a tiny bit. Finally the tears spilled out. She let out a tiny, hiccuplike sob, then, appalled by her outburst, tried to regain control once more. "Don't you know that it's all right to tell me how you feel about things?" Cam whispered against her hair. "I want to know when you're upset."

"You...you do?" Lucy hiccuped again as she wiped her eyes. It sounded hard to believe. "I thought all men hated that."

"I'm not 'all men,'" he chastised gently. "Don't believe all the stereotypes you hear. There will be times when I hate hearing that you feel bad about something, especially if it has something to do with me. But that doesn't mean I don't want to know about it. Trust me." Cam wiped away one dark curl that had fallen over her eyes. "I'm not going to run away at the first sign of conflict." He smiled. "Obviously."

His smile warmed her, and Lucy burrowed even deeper into the comfort of his arms. Cam wanted to stay and talk things through with her—it made her feel almost willing to try.

"Well, it did make me feel bad," she admitted. "But I didn't think it was okay to say so. It seemed silly. I didn't want it to bother me."

"So you decided to act as though it didn't?"

"I suppose." As Cam held her, Lucy struggled to put words to her feelings. And even though the conversation lasted more than an hour, he did not seem to want to let it drop until they had talked things through completely. Ultimately she confessed how badly she had felt when he said he didn't want to come right over that night. She told him how she had worried that he wasn't as interested in her anymore and that she'd wondered if the story about running was simply a convenient excuse to get some time away from her. And after a great deal of coaxing, she finally was able to talk a bit about the feelings that went with those thoughts: fear, guilt, anger, and anxiety.

With each word that she spoke, Lucy expected him to pull away or to get angry. But to her surprise, he didn't respond defensively. He simply listened to her, asked some questions, and then, after she had finished sharing her feelings, asked if he could explain his own position.

"You're right about one thing," he said when she nodded her assent. "I didn't feel as eager to come over tonight as I have before. But that isn't about you. I just feel tired."

Lucy searched her heart. She wanted to believe him.

"We've been running around all week," he said. She knew it was true.

"I just wanted to slow down and spend some time alone. I didn't make up the story about being a runner, though," he assured her. "Maybe I don't run every day like a lot of people do, but I am fairly consistent about it—I go out at least twice a week. I like it. It gives me time to think, to regroup, to figure out what I'm feeling. And that's important to me." His words were calming, soothing—a balm to her soul. "I do need to spend time alone. But not because I want to get away from you. I just need that if I'm going to really be all here for you. Does that make sense?"

Lucy nodded cautiously, wrapped her arms around Cam's slim waist, and pressed her cheek against the rough fabric covering his strong, firm chest. In her head, what he said did make sense. But in her heart, she could still feel the sting.

Still, she tried to see things from Cam's perspective. Of course he deserved to have time alone. It made her feel insecure, but then lots of things did. She would just have to learn to trust him. Besides, she hated fighting and was more than willing to kiss and make up.

Which worked out well, since kissing Cam was quickly becoming one of her very favorite things.

As the days unfolded, Lucy began to trust Cam more and more with her thoughts, with her feelings…with her heart. Every day she felt closer and closer to him. There wasn't any mistaking her emotions any longer: It was love she felt, pure and simple. And from all indications, Cam was pretty well smitten with her.

They had been dating for nearly three weeks when Lucy decided to call Alex and ask her about Cam's upcoming birthday celebration. After much deliberation, Lucy had decided upon a simple dinner for two, followed by a night on the town with Cam's sister and brother-in-law: the perfect combination of romance and family. Wanting to surprise him, Lucy decided to ask his sister what Cam might enjoy the most. A live theater performance? An art opening? A concert—and if so, what type of music?

Lucy placed the call at around ten o'clock on a Thursday morning; Alex called her back by 10:05.

"Hello, Alexandra," she said warmly, still uncomfortable using Cam's nickname for the woman. Though she still felt a bit awkward with Alex, Lucy knew it was important to make every effort to reach out to the sister of the man she loved.

"Oh, hellllloooo, Lucy," Alexandra gushed. "What a nice surprise!" Something about the tone of her voice made it sound as if she wasn't surprised at all. Lucy swallowed hard, feeling vaguely uncomfortable.

"Yes, well…" she began carefully, "I just wanted to check with you about Cam's birthday." Alexandra tittered. Lucy blinked and stared at the telephone receiver in her hand. What on earth? "I, uh, sort of have some special plans—"

"Oh, I know!" Alexandra interrupted, unable to contain herself any longer. "And Wallace and I couldn't be more thrilled!"

"You couldn't?" Lucy glanced at her day planner, looking for an escape. Didn't she have to be somewhere soon?

"Of course we're delighted for you and Cam," Alexandra said happily. "Things couldn't have turned out better if I'd arranged them myself…which I rather like to think I more or less did."

Lucy decided that her original assessment of Alexandra was correct; the woman was crazy.

"Great," she said dully. She had no idea what Alex was talking about and didn't particularly want to know. Leave it to Alex to take all the fun out of her plans. "Well, Alexandra, I'm afraid I'm going to have to go now. Maybe we can talk about this later?" Suddenly she felt desperate to escape.

"Of course! Just tell me where it's going to happen and how I can help," the woman said with relish. "If you need money for anything, please, don't hesitate to say so. Flowers, photography…they're yours, my dear. Money is no object. All you have to do is say the word." She was practically salivating. "I'm sure once you and Campbell receive Daddy's inheritance, you'll have more than enough to pay us back."

"Where 'it's' going to happen?" She shook her head as if trying to clear it. Flowers? Photography? What on earth was the little nut talking about? Surely she couldn't possibly think—?

Lucy nearly dropped the phone. She stared at it as if it were a snake. Of course that's what Alex thought. It was obvious.

"Alexandra, really," she said reproachfully. "Cam and I aren't getting married, if that's what you're implying."

"Don't be silly," her would-be sister-in-law said in a pouty voice. "Of course you are. But don't worry. I'll keep your little secret. I should have known from what Campbell said that you wouldn't want to say anything."

Cam? He planned for them to get married? For his birthday? So he could get his money after all? What was he planning to do—slip her another antihistamine, shove her in the car, and head off for Las Vegas?

Lucy bit back her tears. "Alex—I've got to go," she said brusquely, then hung up without another word.

She couldn't believe it. All this time she'd thought Cam had been sincere, but it had been an act. And she'd been stupid enough to fall for it. Hadn't this been the very reason she didn't want to take him as a client? And now instead of some poor ignorant girl being his victim, she was the victim.

He'd put on such a convincing performance he should've been nominated for an Academy Award. Even feigning patience and understanding with her little insecurities. Now it all made sense. It wasn't out of love for her; it was for that wretched inheritance money.

That night Lucy joined Cam at his Westwood Village apartment, just as they had planned. Cam had suggested renting a movie or just watching a little TV and vegging. But though he didn't know it yet, Lucy thought to herself, Cam's plans had changed.

Lucy showed up at seven o'clock on the button. Cam opened the door, wearing well-worn jeans and a gray Harvard T-shirt. He smiled, clearly delighted to see her.

Of course he's happy, Lucy thought morosely. *I wonder if he's really seeing me or dollar signs?*

"Hi there, gorgeous," he said, giving her a playful wink.

"Hi there yourself," Lucy answered quietly. Cam's brow furrowed at the obvious lack of enthusiasm in her response, but he didn't comment.

"Dinner's in there," he said, jerking his head in the direction of the kitchen. "I picked it up at Luigi's," he said, mentioning their favorite pizza place. Lucy nodded and went to sit on the couch.

Lucy looked around the room sadly. She'd loved Cam's apartment ever since she first saw it two weeks before. The furnishings themselves were pleasing enough. No thrift-store specials here; Cam had outfitted his home with some of the finest furniture she'd ever seen in a bachelor pad. Positioned at the center of the large living area was an attractive yet masculine sofa marked by alternating stripes of gray and white in between wider strips of navy blue. Half of it was covered with a dozen or so items of discarded clothing.

Soft velvet throw pillows of cream and cobalt were tucked into each corner of the sofa—a present from Alexandra or perhaps a former girlfriend? A matching ottoman sat in a far corner, where it sagged beneath a frighteningly tall stack of *National Geographics*. Along the far wall, a well-used piano provided a home for several long-deceased houseplants, brown and dry, positioned one after the other along its top.

At either end of the couch were pine end tables, each piled high with battered manila file folders, books with names like *Perspectives in Human Development,* and a grim-looking family of old fast-food wrappers and Coca-Cola cups. A chocolate brown leather chair stood kitty-cornered to the couch, covered with a large pile of unopened newspapers. Beneath the entire grouping was a cheerful blue-and-white-striped woven rug that helped make the entire mess feel somehow like home.

Cam sat beside her on the couch and opened the pizza box over his knees. "Care to join me?"

"I'm not really that hungry," she said truthfully. She wanted desperately to leave, to not have to say the words she knew needed to be spoken. But there was no way out of it now. "I'd really rather just talk. And then I'm going to have to leave."

"Okay." Cam gave her a strange look.

As she tried to collect her thoughts, Lucy felt an awkwardness, a distance between them she hadn't felt before.

"All right. What is it, Lucy?" It was the same question he'd asked on Tuesday night. This time, though, he didn't sound as if he really wanted to know.

Lucy's eyes stung. It wasn't supposed to be like this. "I just—" She faltered. "Cam, I can't do this anymore. I can't—" Her voice caught in her throat. "I don't trust you anymore," she forced out.

Cam closed his eyes. He didn't even move. "I see." He sat quietly for a moment, then asked simply, "Why?"

"Because I know now that you're using me." Lucy watched Cam through heavy-lidded eyes. How could he just sit there like that, not even looking at her? "I know you just want to get your inheritance. I know you don't...you don't really love me." Lucy took one last look around Cam's living room. It was the last time she'd ever see it, she was sure. "I know that now, and nothing you say can change it." As the words spilled out of her mouth, his transgression seemed more and more unforgivable. It was clear what she had to do

"Cam," she began in a broken voice. "I don't think this is working."

His eyes opened at that, and he regarded her with disbelief, as though he couldn't fathom what was happening to him. "This is about the inheritance?" he said dully. "You've known about it from the beginning."

So he'd assumed she would go along with his plan from the start! Lucy had expected him to at least try to deny it. She pulled back as if she'd been slapped. "Cam," she began again, struggling to keep her voice even, "this is over."

He paused, then said levelly, "You're sure this is what you want?" His voice was completely devoid of emotion.

Lucy didn't feel sure. But she knew that she had to be. "I am."

He sat up straight, finally. "Where did this come from?" She could tell from the look on his face that he truly didn't get it. Well, she wouldn't tell him. There was no point in bringing Alexandra into this. It didn't matter now.

"You know I've been worried about this all along," she hedged. He'd only deny the whole thing. "I wasn't sure it would work."

"Yes, but—"

Lucy turned away from the fury in his eyes. He was angry now, she could tell. Pretty soon he'd try to convince her to go through with it after all. Maybe he'd even say that he really cared about her. She wasn't sure she could withstand that. "I'm serious, Cam." Her lips trembled as she spoke. Knowing that she would soon dissolve into a puddle of tears, she grabbed her purse and stood. To her surprise, Cam made no move to stop her.

"This is crazy, Lucy," he said, shaking his head. This time he wasn't coddling her, begging her to open up to him. It was too late for that. He was letting her go.

She turned away before he could see the pain in her eyes.

"It's not crazy, Cam," she assured him. "It makes sense for us."

"Not for me," he said, his voice dull and emotionless.

That stung. Lucy spun back around and stared at him. He stood in front of the sofa, the pizza box abandoned on the cushion beside him, looking as though she had just sucker-punched him in the stomach. Of course it didn't make sense for Cam. He wanted the money after all. And she had ruined his plan.

"Well, it makes sense for me," she said quietly, anger renewing her strength.

"Well." Cam just looked at her, the spark gone from his eyes. "I guess that's your decision then, and I'll just have to live with it." There was no mistaking the anger in his tone. "Won't I?"

For a split second, Lucy thought he might actually be in pain. She longed to go to him, to wrap her arms around him and tell him that she didn't really mean it. But she stopped herself. She knew the truth about him, about why he really wanted to be with her. She wouldn't give him the satisfaction, though, of knowing how deeply he'd hurt her.

"I'm sorry, Cam." It was all she could think to say. She crossed the floor unsteadily, put her hand on the front door knob, and pulled hard.

Cam's voice stopped her before she made her way through the door.

"By the way," he said raggedly, "you should know that I love you."

Lucy spun around, her heart racing. "What?" Her mind was a jumble. *It's a lie, Lucy,* she told herself. *Don't listen.*

"That's right." He sounded hollow and bitter now, not himself at all. "Since we're broken up now, I figured you might as well know the way it was." He said it with great finality.

Lucy nodded mutely as she wiped at the tears that had begun to stream down her cheeks. *Since we're broken up now.* Cam had accepted her decision. There was no going back now.

"I'm sorry," she repeated. The words sounded so weak.

"I'm sorry too." Cam held her eyes with his own for several long seconds, then turned away.

The spell was broken.

Lucy was free.

She turned back to the door, and without hesitating again, walked straight through—out of the apartment and out of Cam's life.

She had been sure, completely certain, that it was the right thing to do. But as she stepped out into the chill of the evening breeze, Lucy could not help but feel she was making the biggest mistake of her life.

"Hello, Kit-Cat?"

"Wh—? Lucy?" Catherine's voice sounded drowsy and muffled. "What is it?" It took just seconds for her motherly instincts and take-charge attitude to kick in. Lucy could practically picture her sitting up in bed, reaching for her robe and car keys. "Are you all right? Has there been an accident? Where's Daphne?"

"Oh no. No!" Lucy quickly assured her through her sniffles. "It's nothing like that." She couldn't blame Cat for jumping to conclusions. Lucy rarely turned to others except when in desperate need. The last time she had called Cat in the middle of the night, she'd been twenty-one years old and stranded at a downtown nightclub.

"What is it, honey?" Even through the phone line, Cat's voice oozed with concern. Lucy wriggled under her bedcovers for a more comfortable position as she listened to the soothing sound. Cat loved her no matter what.

Unfortunately, she realized too late Campbell had too.

"Cam...and I...broke up," she cried, haltingly, through sobs that racked her chest.

"What? But you two were getting along so well! Weren't you?" Cat waited as Lucy blew her nose. "Oh, sweetheart. I'm so sorry."

In the distance Lucy heard a male voice mumble, "Huh? What's going on?"

"Shh." Catherine covered the mouthpiece with one hand, Lucy could tell, but she could still hear what was going on. "It's Lucy, hon," she told Jonas, her husband of nine months.

"Well, is she all right?" Lucy felt both tender and resentful at the sound of Jonas's voice. Though she loved him like a brother, and he obviously felt the same way about her, it grated against her emotions to imagine her sister and brother-in-law cuddled up in the shelter of each other's arms. She was happy for them but hated the reminder that they had something she didn't—and now probably never would.

Once Jonas was mollified, Cat came back on the line. "Sorry about that," she apologized. "Jonas sends his love."

Feeling like an ungrateful monster, Lucy mumbled back, "Thanks."

"Do you want to tell me what happened?" The question was purely ceremony. Cat was always interested in the minute details of her sisters' lives, whether they wanted to share them or not. The fact that Lucy had called her simply made things much easier for the eldest Salinger sister.

This time Lucy didn't have to be asked twice. Not knowing where else to turn, she had called the first person who came to mind: the sister who had been as unlucky at love as she. Felicia, of course, had had the worst luck of all—but she had enough problems of her own without having to deal with Lucy's. Daphne, on the other hand, collected men like shiny coins—until meeting Elliott a year before. Admittedly, most of them had broken her heart, but she never had any trouble finding a new man after the previous one disappeared. That woman did not understand loneliness. If there was one person who would understand her predicament, it was Catherine.

Until she had met Jonas the previous June, Cat had been not just single but extremely single for a number of years, not dating for most of that time. Once or twice she had confessed to Lucy that she feared living out the rest of her life alone—although that stopped when Lucy cheerfully threatened to set her up with one of her clients.

Between running her ad agency and meddling in her sisters' lives, Cat had no time to pursue love. She found Jonas only as a result of his pursuing her.

At least she had found the right one, though. When she was with Cat and Jonas, Lucy was constantly amazed at how loving and devoted the man was to his wife. It was obvious to everyone who saw them together how much he adored her. And that was what Lucy wanted too. She doubted that Jonas ever went jogging after work just to avoid seeing Catherine. And he certainly hadn't gained a hefty inheritance when he'd married her.

These were the thoughts that went through her mind as she explained to her sister what had happened that night. Though she started out crying, she finished feeling angry—certain that Cam had been plotting all along to use her to get his wretched money. Even without Catherine saying a word, Lucy felt better about her decision. She was about to say so, and to let Cat go back to sleep, when her sister lowered the boom.

"Wow. You must feel terrible," Cat said unnecessarily.

"Well, yes, I do," Lucy said dryly, wishing she had said it a bit more sensitively. "And thanks for noticing. But I'm more sure than ever that it was the right thing to do." She sounded more certain than she felt.

"Oh, really?"

Lucy bit back an insolent retort. She hated it when Cat took that superior tone with her. But in all fairness, it was after ten o'clock at night, and she had awakened her early-to-bed, early-to-rise workaholic sister from her beauty sleep. Cat was entitled to take a bit of a tone if she so desired.

"Are you so certain that Alexandra can be trusted?" Cat asked.

"Well, yes, I suppose. I mean, no. But I'm pretty sure I know what was going on there. Wasn't it obvious? She had talked with Cam, and he told her to keep the whole thing a secret."

"Lucy," Cat said kindly. "I'm afraid you may have jumped to conclusions. How can you know the truth if you don't ever give him a chance to explain?"

"But…but I don't want to feel uncertain about our relationship all the time." Lucy sighed. "I want what *you* have, Cat," she said with feeling. How on earth could her sister argue with that? It would be selfish of her to even try. "Jonas loves you so much! It isn't so *hard* for you two all the time."

"It's not?" Cat sounded surprised at this.

"That's right. It's not," Lucy said flatly. What was Cat thinking? Lucy had seen the two of them together; she knew the score. "Are you kidding? You two get along well. Your communication is great. You even have the same interests." Lucy hoped the envy she felt wasn't as obvious as she suspected it might be. "With Cam and me, it was just one struggle after another."

"Like what? Besides this whole inheritance thing, what happened that seemed so horrible?"

"Well." Lucy thought about this. "He didn't pay as much attention to me. He seemed to need more space all of a sudden." She listed off his offenses one by one, not bothering to mention that she was afraid it would end up as her engagement to Rick had. "It just wasn't the same anymore, Cat," she finished at last, feeling more justified than ever.

"Of course it wasn't." Cat spoke in a crisp, professor-like tone. "It's obvious what your basic problem was."

"What's that?" Lucy sat up straight. She'd hoped that Cat would have some insights; she hadn't thought Cat would be able to put her finger directly on the core issue.

"Don't you see?" Catherine dropped her voice to a whisper. "Lucy, I hate to be the one to tell you this, but you…" she spoke slowly, "were going out…with…a *man*."

"Oh, har-de-har, har, har." Lucy flopped back against her pillows. She should have known it was a mistake to call. "Very funny. Go ahead and laugh at my expense."

"I'm serious, Luce," Cat insisted. "I'm not trying to be insensitive. But you're describing exactly what every woman I've ever talked to has gone through."

"And you do realize," Lucy observed, "that the majority of the population is divorced."

"So?"

"So maybe there's a reason."

"Lucy—" Cat began in a chiding voice.

"Don't get me wrong. I'm not saying divorce is right. I'm just saying that your argument is illogical. If what you say is true, and most women complain about the things I just shared with you, then that proves I did the right thing, don't you think? Obviously, this is enough of a problem that it can seriously affect interpersonal relationships. Don't you think I'm right to put the brakes on things with Cam before it gets that far?" There was a touch of desperation in her voice, and she couldn't decide which way she truly wanted her sister to respond.

"What I think is, you're the one who's going to have to live with your decision, so you're the one who needs to determine what's right," Catherine said simply. "I do think, however, that it takes more than a few weeks to know if someone is going to work out."

"Ha!" Lucy snorted. "You and Jonas eloped after less than a week!"

"Yes," Cat admitted. "But we had dated before that. We had a history. I knew what kind of a man he was. I knew that at one time, we had been compatible. I knew he was a man of character. And I knew that I loved him. That made it all worth the risk. But even with all that, I was surprised by how hard it really was for us after the wedding."

"You?" Cat had to be joking. "You and Jonas? The poster children for marital bliss?"

"The very ones."

"But you practically light up when he comes in the room."

"What can I say?" Cat laughed. "The man lights my fire."

Lucy ignored the quip. "And he watches your every move," she insisted.

"Lucy," Cat said more seriously, "that may be true. But it's only part of the story."

"It is?" Lucy had the sinking feeling that she was going to get the rest of the story whether she liked it or not. And something told her that she wasn't going to like it one bit because it might just make her question the biggest, and potentially the worst, decision she had ever made in her life.

"It is," Catherine assured her. "Who do you think forgot my birthday in January and had to make it up to me with flowers and dinner not one, but two nights later?"

"Hey!" a muffled male voice mumbled from the background.

"Don't worry about it, love," Catherine whispered to her husband so Lucy could barely hear. "You're still forgiven. I'm just making a point."

"Not Jonas?" Lucy was appalled. "I find that hard to believe."

"So did I," Cat said dryly. "But it happened...believe me."

"So he made *one* mistake," Lucy ventured.

"I wish." At the sound of Cat's voice, Lucy knew she was fighting a losing battle. "My dear, sweet husband has also been known to steal the last brownie; forget to take out the trash on a weekly basis, leaving it for me; leave whiskers in the bathroom sink every morning; and argue about whether we should spend two hundred dollars on a more expensive printer for our home computer."

"Well, I can see that those things would bother you," Lucy admitted. "But that doesn't mean—"

"I'm not finished," Cat interrupted. "Jonas also sulks when his feelings are hurt, says insensitive things sometimes in order to get me to react, and tries to talk me out of things that he knows I really want. Not to mention the fact that he goes mountain biking twice a month—instead of spending the time with me, even when we've been too busy to really take time together—simply because he needs that time of solitude. And if you think we haven't argued about *that*, you've got another think coming. In other words, honey, this ain't paradise."

"Um…," Jonas began again in the distance, "I think I resent that."

"Whoops." That, at last, put an end to Catherine's preaching. "I think I may have shared just a little too much," she said sheepishly.

"I'll say," Jonas grumbled.

"The point is," she said after murmuring something vaguely consoling to her husband, "that nobody's relationship is perfect because people aren't perfect, and we shouldn't expect ourselves to be. Life is good for Jonas and me because we work at it, Lucy. We have our problems like everybody else, but we promised each other that we'd stick it out even when it got ugly. And we have. We do."

"Are you saying I was too hard on Cam?" Lucy hated the direction this line of reasoning was taking her. "But what about the money?"

"I don't know," Cat admitted, unusually hesitant to give advice. "It may be true that he was using you; it may not. But you'll never know unless you talk to him about it. Things aren't as simple as they sometimes seem. As far as the rest of the situation goes, of course, you're right—you do want to find someone you're compatible with. I wouldn't want you to force something that isn't meant to be. But if you're looking for perfection, for something easy that isn't going to take any work, then I'm afraid you're just in for a lot of disappointment. 'Cause it just doesn't happen that way."

"Not even for the poster children for marital bliss?"

Cat sighed dramatically. "Not even. And now, if you'll excuse me, I do believe the man I love is pouting. I'd better go apologize."

"Okay." Lucy wanted to but she couldn't find it in her heart to be mad at Catherine. "Thanks for being willing to offend your husband for me," she said weakly.

"Don't worry about it. It's not the first time it's happened," Cat said with a laugh. "And it won't be the last."

Nine

The following Friday dawned bright and beautiful. The sky was blue and cloudless, the L.A. summer haze not yet visible. The sidewalks were thick with in-line skaters and skateboarders, exhilarated by the fresh spring air. And the beaches were filled with young couples looking like deer caught in headlights as they gaped, open-eyed and open-mouthed, at each other—captivated by each other's charms.

It seemed the whole world was in love.

Lucy thought she might actually be sick.

As she dressed for work that morning, she considered calling Gabby and pretending that she had the flu or something. She might as well. It had been days since she'd felt like getting any real work done. Ever since her breakup with Cam, her mood had ranged from weepy to crabby. And as she headed for the office, her disposition was the nastiest it had been all week. Angry with Cam for using her, upset with Alexandra for spilling the beans, but mostly furious with herself for falling for his scheme, she longed for some release for her pent-up feelings. She halfway considered stopping by the kick-boxing gym but feared that in her emotional state she might thoroughly annihilate her opponent.

Her ire had been building all week. Despite what she knew about the money, Lucy couldn't help but wish Cam would call. She had expected him to do so right away and had prepared herself to resist his explanations. When he didn't call in the first twelve, then twenty-four hours, she decided that he was giving her time to think things through, and she continued to wait. After three or four days, however, it became clear that he wasn't going to call at all. Now that a full week had passed, she had given up hope of ever talking to him again. Now more than ever before she felt terminally alone. She had already plotted in her mind which assisted-living community she'd go to, to live out her retirement years surrounded by crossword puzzles and thirty cats. Lucy didn't even own a cat. But time was passing quickly. She figured she'd have to get one soon.

It was after ten o'clock when she finally slunk in the front door of the office. Gabby regarded her with one eyebrow raised. "You're late," she said unnecessarily.

Though instantly defensive, Lucy figured Gabby did deserve an explanation.

"Sorry," she said flatly, dropping her briefcase to the floor with a thud. "I went for a walk on the beach this morning. And you know what I discovered?"

Gabby shook her head. "No," she said. "I don't. And I really don't think now is the time to—"

"I'll tell you what I discovered," Lucy cut in. Both hands were on her small hips now. She was ready for battle. "Tst...tst!" She hushed disapprovingly when Gabby tried yet again to break in.

Gabby registered this behavior with a look of shock, her mouth hanging slack. "Luce—" she said warningly. But Lucy just shook her head. Maybe Gabrielle didn't want to hear what she had to say. But it was time she faced the music—just as Lucy was doing. Why, what she was doing was...well, a public service of sorts. Enlightening the naive.

"I found out that love is highly overrated," she announced with finality. Her words were sharp, biting.

"Lucy, honestly!" Gabby glared at her. "Would you please—"

"I'm serious, Gabs!" Lucy wriggled out of her coat and slung it over a chair by the door. "I mean, think about it! Every day they're out there: men and women on the street, hanging on each other, making kissy faces. I've seen it; you've seen it. You can't pretend you haven't."

Gabby just gaped at her.

"Those people all think they're in love!" Lucy continued, barely stopping for a breath. "But it's only temporary, you know." She pointed one finger at Gabby and wiggled it furiously. "Most of them are going to find out they're incompatible and then break up before they even reach a serious commitment stage. But it's even worse for the ones who do! Because those are the ones who really start to depend on each other before, *boom*, their whole world falls apart!"

Gabby's eyes had a glazed look now. She glanced around the room nervously, as if looking for an escape. Lucy felt a fleeting twinge of regret. It was too bad really. She hated to burst Gabby's bubble. But, hey, someone had to do it. Better her than some handsome behavioral psychologist—or whoever—who would someday steal her heart. Gabrielle would thank her someday.

Besides, she was on a roll now. "If you ask me, love is nothing but a commercial concept sold to the general public by greeting-card companies, florists, and other members of the wedding industry," she said, her voice rising in pitch. "And I for one am tired of being a part of the machinery." *Can I get an amen, sister?* Lucy felt more like a preacher than a bitter single woman with an ax to grind. "As far as I'm concerned, there's no such thing as a happy ending." She was nearly shouting now. "And anyone who thinks there is...is...a...sap!" she finished triumphantly.

Only then did she notice the frantic, cut-throat gestures Gabby was making. Too late, she saw the reason when her eyes landed upon a timid-looking woman standing in the doorway of her office, just fifteen feet away.

"I'm sorry," the woman said, clutching her coat to her chest. "I'd, uh, forgotten that I had, um, another appointment this morning. So I'll just be going now. Thanks for your time." She sidled past Gabby's desk, tiptoed her way around Lucy as if fearing that one false move might rekindle her anger, and slipped gratefully out the front door.

Lucy turned to Gabby in dismay.

"That," her assistant said with a battle-weary sigh, "was your ten o'clock."

"Oh." Lucy looked long and hard at the empty doorway. "She seemed nice," she said at last.

"Mm," Gabby grunted a general agreement. "Very funny, Luce. Very humorous indeed. I don't think it'll be such a riot when neither of us is getting a paycheck anymore." The look she gave Lucy was dark and ominous. "Don't you think it's time you dealt with what happened between you and Cam before you single-handedly destroy the business it's taken you four years to build?"

Lucy sank into the chair by the door, ignoring the coat she had thrown there. "So I'm having a bad day," she admitted. She didn't need Gabrielle telling her she'd made a mess of her life. It was a fact that haunted every minute of the day and—as her nightmares would testify—night.

"Honey, you're having the worst of all weeks," Gabby corrected. "But that doesn't give you an excuse to sabotage your entire future."

"I'm afraid it's too late for that. That's already done," Lucy mumbled under her breath. *So much for happily ever after.*

"What's that? What did you say?" Gabby pounced on that last comment, but luckily Lucy had spoken low enough that she hadn't been able to hear clearly.

"Nothing." Gabrielle had given her a hard enough time before she started dating Cam. If Lucy admitted how she felt about him now, after the relationship was over, Gabby would never let the matter rest. And Lucy desperately needed to find a way to leave what had happened in the past if she was ever going to find a way to make peace with the present. The future was something that would have to take care of itself.

"Oh, come on, Luce," Gabby pressed. "Why don't you just come clean? Admit it. You love this guy, don't you?"

By the way, he had said, *you should know that I love you.* Did she really love him too? Still? After all that had happened? Lucy wanted to deny it, but every cell in her body cried out that it was true. "It's too late to worry about that, Gabby," was all she could manage.

"Phooey! I can't believe you're willing to just give up so easily." Gabby got up and walked over to the metal file cabinet in the corner. "You see this thing? It's filled, and I do mean filled, with information about some of the handsomest, richest, and most interesting single men in the entire city of Los Angeles. And from everything you've told me," she said, "there's not one of them that could hold a candle to Dr. Campbell Howard."

"Gabby, you don't know." Lucy couldn't take much more of this.

"No," her assistant admitted. "I don't. You're the one who knows him best. But I do know how your face lit up every time you talked about him. And that didn't have anything to do with his looks or his money. I know you, Lucy. You have a good heart, and you wouldn't be drawn to a man who wasn't really something wonderful."

"I don't know about that." Lucy wanted to believe what Gabby said was true. But history just didn't support her theory. "Rick wasn't any real prize. I'm afraid my judgment's not as great as you'd like to think."

"I disagree." Gabby argued. "In fact, I'd guess that your judgment is a whole lot better than you'd like to believe."

"What?" Lucy glared at her.

"Well, isn't it?" Forceful and determined to take control, Gabby was quite unlike her usual self. Lucy would have given anything at that moment to have her easygoing, noncommittal assistant back; this passionate stranger was almost more than she could deal with. "It's a lot easier to pretend you can't handle something than it is to actually face it," Gabby said pointedly. "If you tell yourself you can't face Cam, that you don't even love him, that you're not willing to fight for him...well, then, you don't even have to try, do you?"

"Gabby," Lucy said quietly, doing her best to control the angry words she wanted so badly to speak. "I know you're only trying to help. But this is just making me feel worse. So just stop now, okay?"

Gabby shook her head fiercely, a blatant refusal. "Sorry. I can't do that. I wouldn't be a friend if I encouraged you to let go of the best thing to come into your life in years."

That did it. Lucy jumped to her feet. She couldn't just sit there and take it anymore. "Well, if you think Cam's so great," she said hotly, "why don't you go after him? Maybe he's *your* perfect match. The two of you will hit it off, run away together, and have a half-dozen children. And then maybe everyone will leave me alone about it!"

"Fine. Maybe I should go out with him," Gabby said just as heatedly. "But if I did, I can tell you one thing: I wouldn't let go of him so easily. Because if he's as great a guy as you seemed to think, then he deserves a lot more than a kick in the pants on his way out the door."

"Why, you…I…I didn't kick—" Lucy sputtered. She tried desperately to think of a clever rebuttal but was still floundering when the phone started to ring.

She looked at Gabby.

Gabby looked at the phone.

Lucy looked at Gabby looking at the phone. "Are you going to—?" she started. Her assistant gave a dramatic sigh and reached for the receiver.

"Rent-a-Yenta," she said in a decidedly unenthusiastic voice. "Making all your dreams come true." She looked pointedly at Lucy and mouthed, "Except yours."

Lucy was still trying to figure out how much unemployment compensation she'd have to pay after firing Gabby when the next words caught her ear.

"Oh, Alexandra. Hello." As Gabby turned to her, Lucy waved her arms frantically and tiptoed across the room, as if heading out the door. This was one call she was simply not prepared to take. "No," Gabrielle said after a moment's consideration, mercifully intervening. Maybe, Lucy thought, she wouldn't fire her after all. "I'm afraid Ms. Salinger is not available right now. But I'd be happy to take a message."

Hoping to make peace, Lucy threw her a thumbs-up sign. Gabby rolled her eyes and turned away.

"Uh-huh. Mm-hmm. Really?" Lucy shifted her weight from one foot to another, then back again, like a toddler in desperate need of a potty break. "You don't say?" Gabby continued. "Mm-hmm. Right. Of course, I understand."

Understand what?

Lucy waited impatiently for her assistant to finish the call, wishing Gabby would have the decency to at least offer some clue as to its nature, as in *"Why, yes, Alexandra. I understand perfectly that Campbell is missing Lucy desperately and has asked you to step in and ask, on his behalf, if she would even for a moment consider coming back to him."*

As it turned out, that wasn't really too far off the mark.

"Excuse me, Alexandra, I need to put you on hold for just a moment." Gabby punched a red button on her telephone console and turned bright eyes to Lucy. "Okay," she said in her battle-plan voice, "the wacko is calling because she says she's worried about Cam. Not because of the money, but because he's been rather depressed lately."

"He has?" A tentative smile crept onto Lucy's face. Immediately she wiped it off. "I mean...he has?" She didn't know how she managed to sound sorry when her heart was singing. "She actually said depressed? That's too bad."

"Yes. Well." Gabby eyed her curiously. "She said she realizes it's an awkward situation, but she was wondering if maybe we'd be willing to set him up on a date or two. You know, to help him over this hurdle?"

Lucy caught her breath. Surely Alex couldn't be serious? After all she and Cam had been through, his sister just expected her to throw him into another woman's arms? "Why, that's—" She took a gulp of air. "I couldn't possibly—" Words caught in her throat. She stumbled to her feet but couldn't make herself go over and pick up the phone.

"Never mind. Don't worry about it." Gabby waved both hands at her, shooing her out the door. "Why don't you go downstairs and get a drink of water? Or better yet, take the whole day off. You've already bitten my head off once, so your work here is done. You know you're not going to be any good here, anyway." From the way Gabby smiled, Lucy knew she wasn't really mad. "I'll handle this. I'll handle everything. You go get some rest."

Lucy didn't have to be told twice. Picking up her coat, she gratefully did as she was ordered and headed for the door. *Whatever had she been so upset about earlier?* she wondered as she headed for the elevator. Lucy knew she never would have made it through that entire conversation with Alexandra. Gabby was a godsend. A saint, even. Saint Gabby.

She was still trying to think up creative ways of rewarding her angelic assistant when the office door closed behind her just as Gabby picked up the phone again and intoned forebodingly: "All right, Alexandra. Cards on the table. Let's get this thing settled once and for all."

Lucy delighted to let Gabby "settle things" for her. There was no doubt in her mind that Gabrielle would set Alexandra straight. If only things with Cam could have been fixed as easily.

Smoothly she guided her Honda down Santa Monica Boulevard toward Felicia and Robert's elegant home. Not knowing what to do with an entire day off, she'd instinctively pointed the nose of her car in the direction of her sister's house. It was only natural, of course. Misery loved company. And Fee certainly was a miserable creature. More miserable, perhaps, even than she—if that were possible.

Lucy had called Felicia several times over the past week. Her sister had responded slowly, in dull tones, as if she were in shock—which, of course, she probably was. From time to time, Lucy could tell from the nasal sound of Fee's voice that she'd been crying—especially on the occasions when she called late at night after the children had already been tucked into bed.

She thought about the children: nine-year-old Dinah, precocious, smart, and fully aware of the struggle between her parents; and six-year-old Clifford, trouble enough to be five children and not one. Each was wonderful and difficult in his or her own special way. And yet how well her sister handled the challenge of motherhood! Lucy hoped she'd be half as loving and understanding when she became a parent someday. It was so tragic, so bewildering, so brutally unfair for Felicia to have lost her husband's love. If anyone deserved happiness, it was her generous, open-hearted sibling.

She had nearly made it to their street and was about to turn in when it occurred to her that Fee might not be home. Thankfully, though, Fee's minivan was parked in the driveway. Lucy glanced around to see if Robert's snazzy red Miata was nearby, but it wasn't anywhere in sight. That made sense. Fee had told her that Robert had moved some of his things into an apartment earlier in the week. Fee might not see him for a month or more, until he needed more of his belongings and came back to claim them.

Lucy shuddered. How ugly. How utterly wrong. This was what she wanted to avoid at all costs. Losing Cam at this stage of the game was painful, but at least it was a manageable pain. She didn't know how Fee made it from one day to the next.

She pressed one finger to the doorbell and held it, making the chimes peal over and over again—a practice she and her sisters had begun years ago as their own little signal that it was one of them. Robert, of course, had hated their habit. It made Lucy smile to think that for once she could play their game and not worry about the complaints that Felicia would have to suffer through afterward.

"Lucy!" Felicia opened the door and gave her sister a smile. Lucy was glad to see that Fee looked well put together. Today was clearly one of her good days. Her long, dark hair was combed to a sheen and pushed back over her shoulders. Despite the extra ten pounds Fee was carrying, her black jeans were not overly snug, and she looked comfortable and warm in her white cotton turtleneck, covered with a white cable sweater. In her own navy stretch pants, boots, and fitted almond V-neck, Lucy felt overdressed and wished she'd had a change of clothes in the car. Today was a lazy day. Why, she might just plop herself down on Fee's couch and stay there for the rest of the day. Who—or what—was there to stop her?

"Hey, Feebs," she said. "Can I come in?"

"Of course." Felicia stepped back graciously and waved her in the door. "I was just wishing I had company. Dinah's at school and Clifford's down for his nap. Robert usually stays home with me on Fridays. At least, he used to. But then, it's been awhile since I've been able to count on that," she admitted. A flicker of sadness passed over her gentle eyes.

"Well, today you can count on me," Lucy said reassuringly, locking arms with her sister and leading the way into the sitting room. "What do you have planned for the day? Nothing important, I hope. I was thinking maybe we could rent a movie, pop some popcorn, and lie in front of the television until our minds rot."

"Mm. That's appealing." Felicia considered it. "But don't you have work to do?"

"Not today." Lucy fell back against the cushions of Fee's navy-and-white, slipcovered couch. "My assistant gave me the day off," she said brightly, drawing her knees up onto the sofa.

"How nice. What's the occasion?" Felicia wrinkled her brow.

"I think she just wanted to get rid of me," Lucy said, poker-faced. "Right now the little vulture's rummaging through all the client files: getting phone numbers, addresses, and vital stats on all the male doctors, lawyers, and stockbrokers who've ever come to our agency."

"Seriously." Fee might be feeling a bit better, but she obviously wasn't in a joking mood. "I don't remember you ever taking a day off during the week. What's going on?" She lowered herself into a nearby armless slipper chair covered in folds of soft, creamy fabric.

"Well…" Lucy couldn't hide anything from Fee. "I just couldn't go in today. I tried. But I'm too depressed."

"Campbell." Felicia nodded knowingly. "This has hit you really hard."

"I guess." Lucy shrugged, trying to pretend it was nothing. "Not any harder than this thing with Robert has hit you."

"Maybe. But that doesn't make it any less painful." Fee leaned against the soft back of her chair and gazed upward at the light streaming in through one of the room's skylights. Painted in a cheerful butterscotch yellow, the room was one of the most inviting in the house. Lucy knew it was Felicia's favorite; it was hers as well. It was the perfect place to relax, to let go of life's problems and just *be*.

Neither of them spoke for a while. Unlike Daphne, Felicia did not feel the need to prattle on simply to avoid silence, and in her presence, Lucy didn't either. It was a comfortable stillness, one that did not need to be punctuated with the noise of words nor with the comforting music of cups and saucers. It was enough simply to be together.

After some time Felicia turned to Lucy, wearing an expression of compassion that went beyond the furrow in her finely arched eyebrows and involved her whole face.

"You really loved Cam, didn't you?" she asked quietly.

At that moment Lucy could do nothing but tell her the truth.

"Yes," she said plainly, wondering at how amazingly simple it was to express what she'd been trying so hard to hide. "I did. I still do."

Felicia nodded wisely. "I know you do. I can see it in your eyes." She looked around the room where she had spent so many afternoons and evenings with her husband. "I don't have a choice, you know," she said. "Robert chose to leave me. But you, Lucy…you can do something about Cam. You can get him back. If you want him."

"Of course I want him, Fee." Lucy turned both palms upward. "I just don't trust him."

Fee looked at her curiously. "Are you sure it's Cam you don't trust…or is it yourself?"

"What do you mean?" Something about the comment rang true. Lucy twisted in her seat.

Fee blinked, took a moment to collect her thoughts, then continued. "It just seems strange that you wouldn't even talk to him about it. It's almost as if you weren't willing to find out the truth either way, even if it meant he wasn't using you to get the money." She thought for a moment. "I think you were scared, Lucy," she said at last. "You were scared that he'd hurt you then, and you were scared that he'd hurt you in the future. Like Rick did. Most of all, you were scared that you wouldn't be able to take the pain again, or that you wouldn't be able to protect yourself. So you took the easy way out. But it doesn't feel like there's anything easy about it now, does it?"

"Do you blame me for wanting to avoid the pain?" Lucy asked helplessly. "I don't want to go through what you're going through with Robert. It's just so hard for you."

"But you'd handle it," Fee assured her quietly, "just like I'm handling it. God would give you the strength. You're wise not to want to go through it. It's important to think things through, to be careful when choosing a mate. So many people jump into marriage too quickly." She shook her head again. "Marriage is hard, you know. And Robert's and mine was especially hard. If it hadn't been for Dinah and Clifford, I don't know if we would have made it this far."

"It doesn't matter if it was," Lucy said angrily. "Robert should have stayed."

"That's right." Felicia nodded. "But he didn't," she said simply. "Sometimes I wonder if I could have predicted it. But it doesn't matter what I thought I knew. You know as well as I do: Lots of seemingly doomed marriages make it, and other picture-perfect relationships collapse. It doesn't matter whether or not two people have all the skills they need to make it. What matters is whether or not they're willing to stick it out. Robert wasn't." She looked at Lucy point-blank. "Neither were you."

Lucy pulled back as if she'd been slapped. "What?" Tears rose to her eyes. She couldn't believe Felicia—of all people— had said such a thing to her. The worst part of all was, it was true.

Fee rose and moved gracefully to her side. Sitting close to Lucy on the couch, she wrapped one arm around her little sister's shoulders. She was the comforter now instead of the comforted. "I didn't say that to make you feel bad," she said, her voice soft and low. "I'm just afraid that you're making a terrible mistake."

"You do? I thought you of all people would understand."

"But I do," Fee assured her, patting her arm with one hand. "I understand that you're afraid. Good for you. You'd be out of your mind if you're weren't scared. Fear can be a good thing too. It can help protect you. But protecting yourself and hiding are two completely different things."

"It doesn't matter, Fee," Lucy said. One tear leaked out of the corner of her eye and traced a crooked path along her cheekbone. "It's been too long. Cam's not going to forgive me now."

"Maybe," Felicia said, wiping the tear away with a delicate white finger. Two more tears quickly followed. "Maybe not. His birthday has come and gone, right?"

"Yes..."

"Well, if he wanted you for the money, the deadline has passed. Now you can be sure that if he takes you back it's for you and not some old inheritance. There's only one way to find out."

"You think?" Lucy sniffed, looked around for a Kleenex, then wiped her nose on one sleeve. For the first time since leaving Cam's apartment in shame, she felt a trace of hope.

"Oh, Lucy. That's disgusting." Felicia crossed the room and grabbed a box of tissues for her. "Use one of these," she said, handing her the package. "I'm glad I'm not doing your laundry. Clifford's is bad enough."

Lucy laughed at that. It felt good.

"Do you really think he'll listen to me?" she asked timidly. "It's going to be so hard, going back, hanging my head in shame."

"Well, for goodness' sake, don't do that." Fee looked appalled. "How unattractive could you possibly be? You need to go back to him in both confidence and humility."

"You're right," Lucy conceded. "Head hanging: bad. Positive approach: good. But what else am I supposed to do? I want to tell him I'm sorry. Am I supposed to shout it from the rooftops?"

"Nooo." A mischievous look crossed Felicia's features, the first Lucy had seen in years. "But listen. I've got an idea." She grinned, her gray eyes actually sparkling with excitement. "There's more than one way to get Cam's attention," she said. "Have you got a pen and a piece of paper? It's been awhile since I took a poetry class, but I think I remember the basics."

Dumbfounded, Lucy watched as Felicia jumped up and began to retrieve the required items from around the room. Lucy knew she was in real trouble when Fee looked at her and gleefully asked, "By the way, how's your singing voice? And do you know if Daphne is at work?" Grabbing her cordless phone from a nearby end table, Fee began to dial. "Because she has this friend who owns a costume shop…"

"I cannot be*lieve* they talked me into this," Lucy muttered as she eased her car into the university's parking lot.

How did the song from *A Chorus Line* go? *But I can't forget what I did for love....* Well, that was the understatement of the year. If she spent the rest of her days trying, Lucy was certain she'd never be able to erase from her memory the complete and total humiliation of showing up at Cam's office dressed as a giant nut. If only she'd known what Felicia was asking when she posed the question "Did Cam have any pet names for you?" What on earth had possessed her to confess that he referred to her as "my little nut bar"? Couldn't she have said something like princess, duchess...or even buttercup? She'd rather have shown up encased in petals than dressed as a giant peanut.

When they'd arrived at the Costume Palace, Lucy had actually thought it was a good thing that there were no huge nut-covered ice cream bars in their stock.

Now Lucy cursed her naiveté. How innocent she'd been. She'd actually thought she'd been granted a reprieve. But Felicia and Daphne, who had happily skipped out on her afternoon appointments to join them, were determined she should go through with Fee's plan.

Daphne had been violently opposed to letting Lucy drive to the university any way but in costume. Which was why Lucy now found herself trying to force her enormous peanut head out the driver's side door of her Accord. Once, twice, three times she tried to push her way through before finally accomplishing her goal.

As she stood, she felt her big, nutty head for damage. It seemed a bit bent, but she was sure it would regain its shape eventually. Perhaps that was how babies felt immediately after birth. She put her hands on both her sides and tried to readjust her costume, peering out the eyeholes in order to get them positioned right. When she looked out, she was horrified by what she saw.

Two students, one about twenty-five years of age, the other maybe twenty-two—both male and both, of course, gorgeous—were approaching. At first they didn't seem to notice her. But it didn't take long. Giant nuts, she discovered, had a tendency to draw a crowd. The boy to the right, a redhead, saw her first and nudged his companion with an elbow poke to the ribs.

They were far enough away that Lucy couldn't hear what they were saying. But she could imagine what it was, and those imaginings did not please her one bit. With great effort, she managed to look down at her legs, which were covered in black tights, and her feet, tucked into soft black slippers, trying to see what they must see. Her arms, too, were covered in black, the only part of her cotton turtleneck that showed. The shell itself was not hard, like a real nut's. Rather, it was soft, made of a feltlike substance, which began at her knees, and continued up approximately one foot over her head. Thankfully, her face was fully covered by the costume. Only her eyes appeared, occasionally, through the holes that had been cut into the fabric.

Unfortunately, those holes were not particularly big, and Lucy's costume kept slipping so that they were at her chin. In the car, she'd managed to maneuver the peanut head into just the right position so that she could see—and being wedged in there as she had been, it hadn't moved a centimeter while driving. Thankfully, the costume shop was just blocks from the campus, so the driving hazards were minimal—though if she'd known the difficulty she would have, she never would have tried it in the first place. Mark that down as just one more thing to thank Daphne for.

Lucy carefully placed two hands on her hips and lifted upward so she could see out the eyeholes. To her dismay, the two men were still standing there, laughing now, and several of their friends had joined them.

"Hey!" she hollered. She wasn't in the mood for this at all. "What's the matter? Haven't you guys ever seen a big nut before?"

This simply inspired a whole new batch of guffaws. "I'm not even going to touch that one," the first guy laughed.

"Too easy," his friend agreed.

Lucy stamped her foot on the ground, making them chortle even louder.

"Wonderful," Lucy muttered. She considered abandoning her mission right there on the spot, but the thought of messing up yet another opportunity to work things out with Cam quickly stopped her. "Hey!" she called again after the students, who had begun to disperse. "Where can I find the behavioral psych lab?"

The students looked at one another and broke into all-new fits of laughter. "Looking for commitment papers?" one suggested.

"I figured she was a nut job," another commented. "But I had no idea she knew it too."

The witticisms continued to fly as Lucy stood, uncomfortably shifting her weight from one foot to the other.

"I'll show you," a pleasant female voice finally broke in.

Oh, thank you, Lord. Lucy tried to lift her nut body enough to view her heroine but overcompensated and only managed a glimpse of bare, tanned legs and Birkenstock shoes. That was enough of a reference for her. "Oh, boy. I really appreciate it," she said gratefully. With one hand, she reached out and pawed at the air until her new friend took her arm.

Step by step, the woman led her into a nearby building and up so many flights of stairs Lucy lost count. "Which office?" the voice inquired politely.

"Dr. Campbell Howard's." It was getting close. Soon she and Cam would be face-to-face—more or less—once again. Lucy's arms and legs were starting to tremble. She was so nervous.

According to Fee and Daphne's theory, her little performance would break the tension, Cam would laugh, and they'd actually be able to talk about what had happened between them. But what if Felicia and Daphne were wrong? What if Cam didn't see the humor in the situation? Or even worse, what if he did indeed laugh but then told her there wasn't anything left for them to talk about? She hadn't heard from him all week. Surely that meant something. Whatever it was, it couldn't be good.

Blindly she followed her leader until the woman stopped abruptly, causing Lucy to run right into her.

Oof. "Sorry," Lucy said.

"No problem," the woman told her. "You're here. We're in front of the office door. I'm looking in the little window, but there doesn't seem to be anyone there."

Lucy let out the breath of air she'd been holding. "That's okay," she said. She'd been hoping for a chance to gather her wits before seeing Cam anyway. "I'll just wait here."

"All right." The woman was silent for a moment. Lucy stared at the inside of her costume. "You okay?" her companion finally asked curiously.

"Absolutely," Lucy assured her. Nut bad. Never butter. Nutting to worry about. "Thanks for everything."

Perhaps figuring it was none of her business, the student responded with an indifferent "Okay" and headed back to class or wherever she'd been going before she'd come to Lucy's rescue.

Alone now, Lucy leaned against the hallway wall, trying to look inconspicuous. After several minutes she heard the slap-slap-slap of feet in the distance. Instinctively she grabbed for Cam's doorknob and pushed, fully expecting the door to remained locked and closed. To her surprise, however, it opened easily, and she found herself standing in the midst of his office.

She breathed in deeply, relishing the smell of chalk and musty books and Cam himself. She lifted her costume enough to see out the very top of the eyeholes. In this way she managed to see the top half of Cam's office: shelf after shelf lined with textbooks; several cheap wooden cupboards; and a framed picture of Alexandra, looking more relaxed and positively happy, with her arm around a short, balding man Lucy took to be her husband. Both of them were beaming at the camera. Lucy turned her attention from Alex's face to the books on the shelf; intermixed with the books about psychology were several titles by C. S. Lewis and Frederick Buechner. This glimpse into Cam's inner life warmed her heart and momentarily strengthened her inner resolve to go through with Fee's crazy plan.

Somewhere in the distance she heard a murmur that sounded like voices.

"Oh!" Lucy jumped, and in the process lost her grip on the costume. It fell to its natural position, leaving her completely blind once more.

She froze, listening, keen as a hunter. Was it Cam? Would he come? She silently mouthed the first words of her song/poem, refreshing her memory. The murmuring noise was closer now and getting louder by the second.

"Hold on," she heard a male voice call out. "Let me just get those notes."

Her adrenaline was high; she was poised to jump. When the door opened, Lucy took a deep breath and without even stopping to think, leaped into the center of the room and started singing to the tune of "I Wish I Were an Oscar Mayer Wiener":

> *"Oh, I know that, Cam, you think I am a*
> *nut bar.*
> *I don't really blame you much, you see.*
> *But if you see me as your little nut bar,*
> *Maybe you could try to for-give me."*

Lucy heard a throat clearing but pressed on before she could lose her nerve.

> *"I never had the guts to say I love you.*
> *Never trusted that, my dear, you'd stay.*
> *And so I left, not knowing that I loved you,*
> *'Til this nut cracked up and ran away!"*

By now the throat clearing was joined with a nervous foot shuffling, but Lucy was on a roll and headed for her big finish.

> *"I've never known someone that I could*
> *love so.*
> *Never known a man as good as you.*
> *I'm sorry, dear, and I will always love you.*
> *Tell me you forgive me, darling, do."*

To her dismay, her performance was met with nothing but silence.

Inside her costume she was sweating profusely. Winded by the effort of dancing around her fifteen-pound shell and nervous about Cam's reaction, she stopped to catch her breath before raising the costume up to see his face. After taking several breaths, she finally ventured to peek out the eyeholes. She was greeted with a small sea of six or seven blank-looking, unfamiliar faces.

"Errrr." She was the one clearing her throat now. "Um, I'm looking for Dr. Campbell Howard," she said, trying to sound as though it were perfectly normal for a giant nut to have personal business with a behavioral psychologist.

"So we gathered." The strange face closest to the front—belonging to a portly, white-haired gentleman—regarded her with a mixture of amusement and disbelief.

"Is this his office?"

"It is." The man wasn't volunteering any information. None of the others had spoken or even moved. Lucy guessed they were still in shock. She knew she was.

"Is he...with you?"

"Why, no," the man said regretfully. He half-turned and gestured toward his companions. "I'm Campbell's associate, Dr. Bernard, and these are Drs. Flynn, Andrews, Olafson, Tobias, and Pascal. We just stopped to pick up some notes he left for us concerning his recent business trip. You just missed him actually. He stopped in at the office for the first time this afternoon after being out of town all week."

"He's been gone?" Lucy felt tremendous relief at this. Her spirits started to rise. Perhaps he hadn't been avoiding her after all. "Do you know where he is now? Where I can find him?"

The small cluster of psychologists crowded together and murmured amongst themselves.

"I think he said something about going up to Big Bear this weekend," one of them said.

"That's right," another chimed in. "Something about a woman."

Lucy felt as if someone had kicked her in the stomach. "What?"

"Oh yes," a third agreed. "She called this afternoon. What was her name? Gilly? Goldie?"

The big peanut shell started to sway as Lucy said, almost in a whisper, "Not...Gabby?" It couldn't be. Her friend would never betray her like that.

"That's it," the man nodded. "Gabby. Big Bear. This weekend. Cam seemed awfully excited about it too."

But Lucy never heard the details of what Cam was excited about because at exactly that moment, the room began to spin, she and the peanut toppled, and she found herself looking out of the eyeholes at last—directly up at Cam's ceiling—before finally, mercifully, everything went black.

Ten

"Is she…dead?"

Lucy heard the voice as if coming from a long distance away.

"Honestly, Harv. What a thing to say! Of course she's not dead." The reproach was muttered in hushed tones.

For a moment Lucy wished that she were. Could it be possible that she, dressed as a giant nut, was actually lying on the floor of Campbell Howard's office at the university, surrounded by a handful of his closest associates?

She opened one eye and groaned.

It was. She was.

"See!" voice number two cried in triumph. "I told you."

One of the men leaned over her, studied her for a moment, then raised a clipboard to his face and scribbled something furiously. Lucy could only imagine what he was writing: *Subject exhibits signs of paranoia, schizophrenia, and a lack of lucidity. Suffers from delusions of peanuthood.*

"I'm fine." Grunting in a very unladylike manner, she pushed herself up on her elbows.

"We should really get her out of that thing," someone whispered.

"Oh, I don't know if that's such a good idea." Lucy could almost hear the embarrassment in the man's voice.

"Come on," another voice broke in. "Look at her arms and legs. Obviously she's fully clothed under there."

After much discussion, the group of men pulled Lucy to her feet, held her by the arms, and tugged the peanut costume up over her head—leaving her in nothing but a black turtleneck, black shorts, and black leggings and slippers. Her mind, however, was on other things.

Cam and Gabby? But Gabby was one of her best friends! She would never do such a thing to Lucy. Gabby knew that Lucy loved him...didn't she? *"Come on, Luce. Admit it. You love this guy, don't you?"* Gabby had said. Lucy's heart sank as she remembered her reply: *"It's too late to worry about that, Gabby."* How could she expect Gabrielle to understand that she loved Cam when she hadn't even been willing to admit it herself? Lucy had denied it up until that very morning. Hadn't Cam's associate said that Gabby had called that afternoon? Maybe she had taken Lucy up on her offer.

"If you think Cam's so great," Lucy had told her, *"why don't you go after him? Maybe he's your perfect match."*

"Fine. Maybe I should."

Even though Gabrielle had always begged for a chance to date the good ones, Lucy hadn't thought that her assistant actually meant it.

So much for Saint Gabby.

Her eyes pooled with tears of self-pity. She had practically thrown the two together. She had only herself to blame.

The men gathered around her, like protective brothers.

"Are you all right?"

"Do you need some water?"

Concerned, but at a loss to know what to do, they blinked at her.

"I'm fine." Lucy took a deep breath and struggled to her feet as they took her by the arms and helped her to rise.

"Just mortified. But I'll get over it." Embarrassment, at least, was one thing she could recover from. Losing Cam—to her closest friend, no less—was another thing altogether. "I don't suppose you know what time he left?"

"About an hour ago, if that," a young, dark-haired psychologist volunteered.

"Was he going home, do you know?" Lucy bent over and lifted her nut costume with both arms.

"I think he said he was going up to Big Bear this afternoon. He didn't say anything about stopping anywhere first. But I didn't ask."

Lucy stepped to Cam's desk and, shifting the costume to one arm, dialed the number of his apartment. Getting no answer, she tried her office. *Please answer, Gabby. Please.*

The machine picked up.

Lucy dropped the telephone receiver into its cradle. She stared at it. *"Don't worry about it,"* Gabby had said, shooing her out the door. *"I'll handle this. I'll handle everything."* She certainly had. Unfortunately Lucy hadn't realized that what Gabby planned on handling was Cam.

As she stood there considering what she should do next, Felicia's words echoed in her head: *"It doesn't matter whether or not two people have all the skills they need to make it. What matters is whether or not they're willing to stick it out."*

Wasn't that practically the same thing Cat had said? *"Life is good for Jonas and me because we work at it, Lucy. We have our problems like everybody else, but we promised each other that we'd stick it out, even when it got ugly."*

Well, Lucy thought. It didn't get any uglier than this.

Dragging her fingers through her rumpled curls, she turned to the small crowd that still surrounded her. "Gentlemen," she said, more confident now, knowing at last what she had to do. "Thank you for your assistance. You've been very kind."

She hoisted the heavy costume up higher in her arms and walked forward as the men parted like the Red Sea. "And now, if you'll excuse me, I have a man to catch."

As she pushed her way through the crowd, she heard one whisper to another, "She's trying to catch a man using a giant peanut as bait? That woman really is a wacko."

"Cracked," the man next to him agreed.

"Mm-hm," confirmed another, as he gazed after her wistfully. "But a cuter nut I never did see."

With more hope and enthusiasm than he had felt in over a week, Cam gripped the steering wheel of his sport-utility truck and drove north as fast as he dared. It seemed fitting somehow to be heading off to Big Bear to sketch out his plans of how to win Lucy back, considering it was her favorite vacation spot. One month after he first met the woman of his dreams, every word of their original conversation remained etched in his heart.

He grinned. It felt good to have Gabby on his side in this. It was so generous of her to offer to help him—even allowing him to take up some of her weekend, which she had planned to spend with her family. It was just the shot in the arm he needed right now. Ever since Lucy had broken up with him, he had forced himself to quietly wait. So she thought he was out to use her, just to get his money? Well, he had figured, he would just show her! Now that his birthday was past, there wouldn't be any reason to doubt him, would there?

He'd intended to convince her all on his own. But when Gabby called him that morning—complete with an explanation of how the whole misunderstanding had begun—several pieces of the puzzle fell into place. After talking with Alex, Gabby put two and two together and explained the situation to him. Cam subsequently placed a call and dragged a confession out of his sister. As he suspected, she hadn't intended to scare Lucy off; quite the contrary, she hoped that the two would get married before Cam's birthday and was certain they were secretly planning to do so—even though Cam had been denying it all along and had suggested to her that bringing the subject up to Lucy would be unwise.

It was clear that Alex's comments had been misunderstood by Lucy, who had trouble trusting men anyway. Cam's heart ached. He hurt for her. He hadn't realized how being left at the altar had affected Lucy—she was like a skittish colt, ready to bolt at the first sign of trouble. He hoped Lucy wasn't suffering too much—although he did hope that she was missing him at least half as desperately as he was missing her.

He set his lips in a thin, determined line. If he had anything to say about it, she wouldn't have to miss him much longer.

Lucy crammed the nut costume in the backseat of her Honda, jumped in behind the wheel, and drove as fast as the law allowed—and perhaps even a bit faster at times—until she reached her office.

Down in the lobby, with the clothes she'd worn to work that morning tucked under her arm, she hit the elevator button fourteen or fifteen times in quick succession before giving up in frustration and impatiently heading for the stairs. By the time she reached her office on the fourth floor, she was thoroughly winded.

The door was locked. Not a good sign. Lucy inserted her key and turned it hard.

"Gab-by?" she puffed, pushing her way through the front doors. A quick glance around the room confirmed that her assistant wasn't there. "Gabrielle?" Just to be sure, she poked her head in the inner office, which proved equally vacant.

Disappointed, even though it was exactly what she had

expected, Lucy stopped just long enough to drag a comb through her hair and change back into her work clothes. Though the almond V-neck was a bit rumpled, the navy stretch pants were none the worse for the wear, and the stylish black boots helped to restore a shred of her shaken confidence.

Lucy took one last minute to reapply her red spice lipstick; after all, if she was, as Gabby so delicately put it, "going in for the kill," she might as well look her best. Then she headed back out the door.

She didn't have to think twice about where she might find them. There was only one possibility. The cabin owned by Gabby's family, the same one where Lucy and her siblings had spent so many happy vacations, the one in the photo of her sisters that Lucy had shown Cam on the very first day they met. The irony stung almost as much as the betrayal.

As she headed out State Route 18 toward Lake Arrowhead and Big Bear Lake, Lucy struggled to make sense of her emotions. She knew that Gabby would never deliberately hurt her—at least, she thought she knew that. Most likely this was a simple misunderstanding. Once Gabby understood how Lucy really felt—that she really loved Cam—she'd back away and let the two of them work things out.

That was, of course, if Cam even wanted to be with Lucy anymore. Which was a question that remained unanswered. The men in the psych lab seemed to think he was pretty excited about spending the weekend with Gabby.

Lucy's stomach lurched. How could they be spending the weekend together? Gabby liked men and dated a lot of them, but she didn't generally stay overnight with them. And Cam...well, Lucy had been certain that he wasn't the sleepover type. Even during the brief time they had been dating, he had always been careful to respect and maintain their physical boundaries, for both moral and spiritual reasons.

What on earth could have induced him to change his behavior now? And did she even want him anymore if that was the choice he'd been willing to make?

Now, now. Don't jump to conclusions, Lucy, she tried to tell herself. *Haven't you done that enough by now? Just because he's coming up to the cabin, that doesn't mean he plans to stay overnight.* She started to breathe more naturally again. *And even if he does plan on staying the night, that doesn't mean he plans to let anything happen physically.* Her stomach clenched at the very thought. *Although it would be foolish and stupid for them to think they could stay together and not let anything happen.* Lucy often warned her clients of the dangers of getting too involved physically and encouraged them as strongly as she could *not* to become sexually active with each other until after marriage. It was too horrible to think that maybe Cam and Gabby had decided to cross that line.

No, no, she reminded herself. *You don't know that's the case. Remember, you've decided to stick this out, to hear what Cam has to say. Don't condemn the man before he's even had a chance to explain. That's what got you into this mess in the first place.*

But, she admitted fiercely, *he'd better have a good explanation.*

The winding hundred-plus-mile route to the resort was a peaceful one. As she drove, Lucy began to calm down and was soon drinking in the breathtaking vistas and austere landscapes along the way. She cherished the time to think, and by the time she spotted the green-gray chaparral shrubs of the San Bernardino Mountains, Lucy had her thoughts fairly in order. Soon the smaller trees gave way to full-grown forests, and she knew she was almost there.

A man-made lake born as a result of a single-arch dam built in 1883 to irrigate the orange groves in Redlands, Big Bear Lake was now the site of one of Southern California's most popular summer and winter resorts. A favorite of fishermen, boaters, horseback riders, skiers, skaters, tobogganers, campers, and picnickers alike, Big Bear was not only beautiful but tranquil. Though considering the cauldron of feelings boiling within her, Lucy guessed it might not seem so peaceful to Cam and Gabby once she got there today.

She'd driven it so many times Lucy hadn't bothered to take a map, and at first she missed the turnoff. But quickly realizing her mistake, she turned the car around, pointed herself back in the right direction, and managed to find the correct side road.

Carefully Lucy studied the houses as she passed. She didn't remember the house number but knew she'd know it when she saw it. Sure enough, her pulse quickened as the familiar cabin came into view—with Cam's RAV 4 and Gabrielle's Volkswagen Rabbit both parked out front.

Lucy sucked in a quick breath. Until she saw the two together, it hadn't fully seemed real. Her palms turned clammy as she approached the house...and kept right on going.

The move surprised her. Why hadn't she stopped? Lucy kept going past two or three more houses before pulling off the road and parking. Somehow she felt she needed the element of surprise. There was no sense in announcing her arrival by slamming the car door in the driveway. She'd hike back down the road and knock on the door...after looking in the window perhaps. If she didn't do a little investigating, they might just deny the whole thing. But they certainly couldn't do that after she had seen them with her own eyes in their little love nest.

Lucy gave her fashionable boots a look of disgust. Chic wasn't any help to her now. Where were those cross trainers when she really needed them?

She had no choice but to wear the offending footwear, however, so she clomp-clomped her way down the gravel roadway all the way to the cabin.

Lucy glanced to the left. She glanced to the right.

She glanced behind her, then to the left again.

Feeling like a refugee from a James Bond movie, she tiptoed up onto the porch. On the door she spied a note that read "Cam, the door's open. Let yourself in. I went to town for groceries—be right back. Gabby."

Well. Wasn't that just sweet? Lucy sneered.

She eased her way along the porch floor and attempted to peek in through the living-room window. To her dismay, however, her view was completely blocked by a wide yellow gingham curtain that some overachieving guest or owner had made. Lucy grumbled under her breath. The thing had never been there before. Now she'd have to try another window or simply go up to the front door and knock. That, of course, would be the civilized, socially acceptable, responsible thing to do.

Not feeling particularly civilized, social, or responsible, she picked her way back down the creaky porch stairs and stumbled on the last one.

"Ai-ee-mmph." Stifling a cry, Lucy fell to the ground, twisting her ankle and skinning her left knee on the gravel sidewalk.

She blinked back tears as the stinging began, then took a moment to catch her breath. Not daring to sit there in full view for any longer than a few seconds, however, she wiped the worst of the soil and bits of leaves off her bloodied knee and crept along the dirt surrounding the house until she reached the north side.

"Ouch," she said quietly under her breath, allowing herself to indulge in at least a moment of pain. As if things weren't bad enough! Now she'd have to confront Cam while her knee bled. How was she supposed to explain that?

She looked up at the window. The cabin was built on a hill with the side landscaping sloping downhill, making it impossible for her to just walk up and peek into the window. She'd have to pull herself up by the arms.

Well, this just keeps getting better and better.

Trying to remember the last time she'd been to a gym, Lucy wedged her fingers onto the window sill, pulled as hard as she could...and moved only a fraction of an inch. *Mm. What a jock I am.* She pulled harder, until her fingers were pressed even more tightly to the window frame. As she pulled, her fingers started to slip. Lucy scooted them a bit to the right, hoping to get a better grip.

"Ouch!" She cried again as a splinter dug its way into her index finger.

She instantly regretted it. Hearing footsteps above her, Lucy pressed her body up against the side of the house and waited. The sound of wood scraping against wood sounded in her ears as someone—Cam, she could only suppose—opened the window and looked around.

Oh, please don't look down. Please, please, puh-leeeeze.

Apparently satisfied, the person inside shut the window once more. Lucy listened as the footsteps padded away, then breathed a sigh of relief.

Not yet ready to give in, she glanced around desperately, hoping to find something that might give her a boost up to window level. Quickly she spied an overturned bright green bucket, approximately twenty feet away in the neighbor's side yard.

Lucy hobbled over to it as fast as her twisted ankle and bloody knee would allow. Within seconds, she had it positioned just below the window of Gabby's house and was climbing up on it, carefully keeping the bulk of her weight on her one good foot. Using the pads of her fingers to help her, Lucy pulled herself upward until her eyes were level with the window sill. She leaned forward, the bucket wobbling dangerously beneath her, getting closer and closer until...

"Aaiiii-eeee!" She didn't even bother to muffle her voice this time. As two laughing gray eyes appeared on the other side of the glass, Lucy stumbled backward against the bucket, lost her footing, and fell awkwardly to the forest floor.

"Lucy!" she heard Cam's voice, muffled through the glass.

"Ow." Lucy lifted her head off the dirt and pressed one hand to her forehead, which had gotten scraped against a tree root. It, too, was now bleeding. At least her face and knee matched.

"Are you all right?" Lucy stared at Cam, wondrously, as he approached her, open-armed. Even there in the woods, dressed in a gray heather sweater, jeans, and moccasins, he looked like a million bucks. His face was a mixture of concern and surprise as he approached her, arms outstretched. He didn't even have the decency to appear embarrassed or guilty at being caught at Gabby's vacation house, Lucy thought bitterly.

"I'm fine," she sniffed and pulled herself to her feet, shaking off Cam's offer of assistance.

He took a step back and looked at her curiously. "What are you doing here?" She couldn't read the expression on his face.

"I might ask you the same thing." Lucy heard a touch of self-righteousness creep into her tone. *Stop it,* she told herself. This was not why she'd come to confront Cam. She wanted to win him back, not drive him away. But as the words slipped past her lips, she couldn't seem to control the hurt and anger that went with them.

"I suppose you're going to point out that I'm spying on you again—which, of course, I am," she admitted. Might as well air out the really dirty laundry right away. "And I'm not proud of it," she said. "But *you!* You, Cam! How could you—?" She bit her lip until it bled too. "Ow. I mean…why would you—?" She looked around at the forest, wishing she could run into the trees and disappear. Why was this so hard?

"What?" Cam shrugged helplessly. "Why would I what?"

Lucy licked the dust from her lips. "Why would you come here with Gabby?" It came out more like a wounded cry than the detached inquiry she had intended.

"With…what?" Cam's face grew pale. He looked at her soberly. "Are you saying—?" Then, unbelievably, his face cracked into a grin, and he started laughing uncontrollably.

Lucy stared at him. She hated it when he did that.

"You know, this isn't funny!" She planted her hands on her hips, as if that might somehow subdue him. "Stop it!" she commanded furiously. "I'm glad you've enjoyed yourself today because I certainly haven't! Can you imagine how I felt when they told me at your department that you had come up to Big Bear with my assistant of all people? My friend?" Cam stopped smiling. He wasn't laughing anymore. "I've heard of some low blows in my time," Lucy told him, "but this takes the cake. And there I was, dressed up like a nut, singing my little song— and it was all for nothing!" She paced as she spoke, not even looking at him now.

"A nut? Singing? What? Lucy—" Cam broke in, but she kept on talking, right over him.

"I don't want to hear excuses," she said flatly, throwing out one arm in a stop gesture. "Believe me, I've been thinking about it all the way up here, and there isn't one reason you could come up with that I haven't already hashed over again and again in my mind." She tried to look and sound understanding. "Of course, you and Gabby have every right in the world to go out with each other. And if that's what you two really want to do, I won't stand in your way," she said unselfishly. "But—" She faltered then, searching for the right words. She didn't feel terribly magnanimous. She felt jealous and hurt and angry…and scared.

"But what?" Cam stepped up to her then and looked deeply into her eyes. Lucy shuddered. How could he look so calm when everything was such a mess? Why didn't he look as though he hated her? He simply looked calm and inquisitive and maybe even a little hopeful. The possibility seemed to fortify her own heart.

"Look, I don't know what's going on here," she said diplomatically, "and I really don't have the right to ask, I suppose. But—" Lucy took another deep breath. She might as well come out and say it. What did she have to lose? "But I want to ask! I want to know if you really care about Gabby because if you do, it's going to tear me apart. It's not that I want to mess things up for you and Gabby." Lucy felt as though her heart might break. If Cam and Gabrielle really wanted to be together, how could she begrudge them that? They were two of her favorite people in the world, and they deserved happiness.

But then, didn't she?

"If you've made up your mind, I imagine I'll find some way to deal with it somehow, though I'll be sorry for the rest of my life for letting you go." Lucy drew in a deep, bracing breath. "But, Cam, if you're not sure about Gabby, and she's not sure about you, well, then maybe there's still a chance that—"

"Lucy." His voice was low and gravelly now, as he put his arms on her elbows and pulled her close.

Lucy's heart leaped, though she didn't know exactly what his gesture meant. She wanted desperately to lay her head on his shoulder, to lose herself in the circle of his arms and drink in the comfort of his embrace. But she couldn't. Not yet. Not until she had told him everything that she had come to say. Not until she knew how he really felt.

She put one hand to his strong chest and stepped back so that she could see his face better. "Cam," she said softly, "I realized over the past week that I made a terrible mistake. I wasn't fair to you, and I wasn't fair to me. I wasn't willing to hang in there, to give things a real chance. To find out what your true intentions were. I wanted to enjoy the good times, but I wasn't at all prepared for the pain."

His eyes warm and kind, Cam reached out with his fingertips and gently touched the tender skin around the cut on her forehead. "Looks like you got even more pain than you bargained for," he said softly.

Lucy ventured the tiniest of smiles. "If that was the worst of the pain, I wouldn't be here," she said honestly. "But it's been torture not being with you this week. Cam, I'm so sorry." She had never meant the words more. "I wouldn't blame you if you never forgave me, if you don't want to give me a second chance," she said. "But I hope you do."

Cam raised one hand to her cheek, and Lucy raised her own to meet it.

"I just need to know, once and for all, if you really don't love me anymore," she said, her voice catching in her throat. Her cheeks burned. It was the first time she'd said the *L* word to Cam, in any context, and she felt like a nervous schoolgirl. "Because…because—"

"Because what, Lucy?" Cam's gaze was searching, questioning.

"Because I've realized that…that…" *Lucy, spit it out.* "…that I love you too." Cam's face broke into a great grin at that, but Lucy didn't stop long enough to acknowledge it. "I was afraid, Cam," she confessed breathlessly. "And I'm still afraid. But the only thing I'm more scared of than the possibility of losing you later is the reality of losing you now."

"Silly woman," he said smiling down at her tenderly.

"What?" Lucy felt torn by conflicting emotions. "How can you say that?" It should have made her angry, but Cam somehow made the word sound like an endearment.

"Thinking that you'd lost me after one little breakup. Now that's silly. As far as I'm concerned, you're still my girl."

"But, Cam," Lucy protested. "How can you say that? We haven't talked for a week. And now you're here with Gabby," she said sadly.

A voice from behind them broke in. "Who's here with Gabby?"

Lucy spun around at the sound. "Gabby!" She looked frantically at Cam, but he didn't appear in the least distressed at being found with his arms around her and in fact even tightened his grip on her waist, as if anticipating that she might pull away.

Gabrielle looked equally unruffled. "Who's here with me?" She looked from Cam's amused grin to Lucy's stricken face. "Who...Cam?" She snorted derisively and dug into the personal-size bag of potato chips she carried in one hand. "Like, as my date? For the weekend? Oh yeah. Mom would love that."

At the reference to Gabrielle's mother, Lucy glanced over her assistant's shoulder, where she spied not only Gabby's mom, but her sister and two brothers, all climbing out of a decidedly worse-for-wear station wagon. "Uh...hi, Mrs. Palermo," Lucy said contritely. "Anna...Tony...Al." Of course! Why hadn't she noticed? If Gabby had gone to the store, as her note to Cam indicated, why would her car have been parked in front of the house? Someone else would have driven her to town, meaning that Gabby and Cam couldn't have been staying at the cabin alone.

"Oh!" Mrs. Palermo eased her plump body over to where Lucy and Cam stood. "So this is your young man, Lucy! We've heard all about him. How wonderful that the two of you finally made up." Giving them a benevolent smile, she turned and headed for the cabin door. "We'll just leave you two alone. Kids?"

Lucy stood speechless as Gabby's three siblings filled their arms with brown paper grocery bags and followed their mother into the house. Gabby stayed behind and, when the door had closed behind her sister, looked directly at Lucy. "Did you really think I came up here with Cam?" she asked pointedly.

"Uh…" Lucy searched for some way out. "I didn't really blame you," she said half-truthfully. "I knew if you did, you had a very good reason. I told you it was too late for me and Cam…"

"You'd better believe I had a good reason," Gabby cut in. She jutted her chin at the man in question. "Did you tell her?" she asked.

Cam shook his head. "She hasn't given me a chance."

Gabby nodded. "Yeah, she's like that."

"Hey!" Lucy pouted. "Don't talk about me like I'm not here."

"Oh, you're here all right," Gabby observed. "But what I want to know is what happened to you on the way here," she said, taking in Lucy's cut forehead and bloody knee.

"Oh." Lucy shrugged. "This is nothing. You should have seen the giant nut."

"Again with the nut!" Cam shook his head helplessly. "I have absolutely no idea what's going on here. All I know is, I finally have the woman I love back in my arms, where she belongs."

Bolstered by that little comment, Lucy tightened her own hold around his shoulders and ventured a tiny smile. "The woman you love, huh?"

"Well, duh," Gabby said, rolling her eyes. "As if the man hasn't made it perfectly obvious already. I don't suppose he told you that the reason he's here is to get help in figuring out how to get you back? Or that there never was any secret birthday wedding planned to get his inheritance."

"Oh?" Lucy was having a hard time catching her breath. "Is that true, Cam?"

"Yes, it's true." Happily, he pulled her closer to him. "But I have to admit, things worked even better and faster than I could have hoped. Look at us now," he said, smiling down into her eyes.

"Ugh. Again with the mushy stuff. Do you mind? I'm eating," Gabby said, popping another chip in her mouth. But she didn't look like she was truly bothered. "After you left, I picked Alex's brain a bit, then called Cam to fill him in," she said to Lucy. "I told him I was coming up to my family's cabin this weekend, but if he wanted to come up for the afternoon I'd do a little brainstorming with him and help him come up with a battle plan." She studied Lucy for another moment. "You really did think I was up here with him, didn't you?" she said incredulously. It was clear what she meant.

"I'm sorry, Gabby," Lucy said. It did seem ridiculous, now that she knew the truth. It felt so good to be in Cam's arms again. But she could hardly bring herself to relax and enjoy it, for fear she had ruined her friendship with Gabby. "I don't know what to say."

Gabby considered this for a moment, then put two fingers into the cellophane bag and pulled out another greasy chip. "Well...don't say anything," she said at last. "I'm gonna chalk it up to temporary insanity, you being out of your mind with loooove and all." She smirked.

"Gabs!" Lucy untangled herself from Cam's arms and gave her friend a big hug. "You are the greatest."

"Yes. Yes, I am," Gabrielle agreed. "Would you mind telling my boss? I've been wanting a raise."

"Ahem." Lucy cleared her throat. "Not that great. If I recall, you were supposed to be at the office all day, taking calls. Not out taking a vacation day with your family."

"Oops. Okay. Point well taken." Gabby shrugged and looked back over her shoulder at the porch. "I suppose I should take Mom's cue and leave you two little loooovebirds alone." As she made her way up the stairs, Lucy gratefully made a mental note to forgive Gabby in the future for all acts of social ineptness and general insensitivity. This act of kindness had to exceed them all.

"Watch that last step," Lucy called after her.

"It's a doozy, eh?" Gabby looked at Lucy's bruises and laughed.

"You have no idea."

Finally, Gabrielle was gone, and Lucy and Cam were alone again.

"I thought she'd never leave," he said gruffly, clasping her by the hand and pulling her to him.

"Be nice," Lucy warned, a smile playing about her lips. "Gabby was very gracious. She could have really rubbed my nose in this whole mess, you know."

"I know." She felt the rough skin of Cam's hand as he gently cupped her cheek and gazed at her in wonder. "I was afraid I'd never hold you like this again," he said gruffly.

"Me too," Lucy whispered. She leaned into him and laid her cheek against the comforting strength of his chest. "You know, you could have rubbed my nose in this too," she said quietly.

Cam said nothing.

"Why didn't you?" She fingered the buttons on his shirt and waited.

"Don't you know?" Cam sounded surprised.

"Should I?" She lifted her face and gazed up into his eyes, half-expecting to find judgment but saw nothing but love there.

"Lucy," he said warmly, pressing his lips tenderly against her hair. "My love. Don't you know by now? I don't ever want to hurt you. I love you. I don't want you to feel bad; I want you to feel cherished. Adored. Because you are."

Lucy drew a shaky breath. "I don't deserve you," she said, gratefully wrapping both her arms around him again.

"No more than I deserve you," he said simply. "But we have each other. So there you have it. We're two undeserving people, with all the love in the world."

"But...what about the money?" She hated to bring it up, but she had to know. "We didn't even get to celebrate your birthday together."

"Hunh," Cam snorted. "I never cared about the money. I have you. That's all I care about. I have a perfectly good job; I'll pay Alex back in time. I can always get more money, but I can never get another *you*. And as for my birthday, I'm celebrating right now. Now that I have the best birthday gift ever."

Lucy liked the sound of that. She snuggled up against him. "And you're not mad?" She still needed to be sure.

"Sweetheart," Cam said confidently, "at this moment I'm so full of love and gratitude because God brought you back to me, there isn't room for anything else." He reached out with both hands and held her fingers so they just lightly rested in his. "We're in this together for the long haul. Am I right?"

She sighed happily, convinced at last. "You're right."

Cam smiled. "Are you my little nut bar?"

Lucy laughed heartily, remembering the morning's fiasco, which she had yet to share with him. "Never nuttier."

"Well then," Cam said, sounding pleased. He pulled Lucy into him arms one last time and grinned as she raised her lips to his. "Come here then. Because I think it's time you and I made up for lost time, my love."

And so they did.